Wyoming Wedding
by Sara Orwig

"You know common sense tells me to say no to you," Brianna replied.

"I don't see that. You stand to gain a lot and lose very little unless you can't stand to be with me."

"You know full well there's no danger of any woman not being able to stand you," she said.

"Until this moment I was beginning to wonder. This is the coolest reception I've ever got."

He placed his hand on the car door, blocking her from opening it. Leaning closer, he lowered his voice. "I've asked you to be my wife tonight and we've never even kissed. That's a giant unknown when there's a marriage proposal between us."

Her pulse had raced all night, but now her heart thudded and she looked at his mouth. "I can remedy that one," she said, tingling at the thought of kissing him.

She moved in closer, stood on tiptoe and placed her lips on his.

His kiss might be her undoing.

Available in August 2010
from Mills & Boon® Desire™

CLAIMING KING'S BABY

BY
MAUREEN CHILD

WYOMING WEDDING

BY
SARA ORWIG

⊕ MILLS & BOON®

First published in Great Britain 2010
Harlequin Mills & Boon Limited,
Eton House, 18-24 Paradise Road, Richmond, Surrey TW9 1SR

The publisher acknowledges the copyright holders of the individual works as follows:

Claiming King's Baby © Maureen Child 2009
Wyoming Wedding © Sara Orwig 2009

ISBN: 978 0 263 88175 2

51-0810

Harlequin Mills & Boon policy is to use papers that are natural, renewable and recyclable products and made from wood grown in sustainable forests. The logging and manufacturing processes conform to the legal environmental regulations of the country of origin.

Printed and bound in Spain
by Litografia Rosés S.A., Barcelona

CLAIMING KING'S BABY

BY
MAUREEN CHILD

Dear Reader,

I can't tell you how much I enjoy writing about the King family! And I'm delighted that so many of you are enjoying them as much as I do.

Writing about this extended family is always an adventure, because no matter what, the King men always manage to surprise me.

Take Justice King for example: a typical rancher on the surface, but underneath, Justice is a man haunted by the past and tormented by the fact that he allowed the woman he loved to walk out on him.

Maggie Ryan King is the perfect match for Justice. She's loyal and stubborn and determined to make her soon-to-be-ex-husband pay for letting what they'd had together slip away.

As a physical therapist, Maggie's temporarily back at King Ranch, helping Justice recover from a riding accident. But while his body heals, his heart is being steamrolled. By the one woman he can never forget.

These two have a lot of things to work through – and secrets to reveal – and I really hope you enjoy their story!

Happy reading,

Maureen

Maureen Child is a California native who loves to travel. Every chance they get, she and her husband are taking off on another research trip. The author of more than sixty books, Maureen loves a happy ending and still swears that she has the best job in the world. She lives in Southern California with her husband, two children and a golden retriever with delusions of grandeur. Visit Maureen's website at www.maureenchild.com.

To the Estrada Family:
Steve, Rose, Alicia, Lettie, Patti and Amanda.
Good friends. Great neighbours.
We love you guys.

One

Justice King opened the front door and faced his past.

She stood there staring at him out of pale blue eyes he'd tried desperately to forget. Her long, light red hair whipped around her head in a cold, fierce wind, and her delectable mouth curved into a cynical half smile.

"Hello, Justice," said a voice that haunted his dreams. "Been a while."

Eight months and twenty-five days, he thought but didn't say. His gaze moved over her in a quick but thorough inspection. She was tall, with the same stubborn tilt to her chin that he remembered and the same pale sprinkle of freckles across her nose. Her full breasts rose and fell quickly with each of her rapid breaths, and that more than anything else told him she was nervous.

Well, then, she shouldn't have come.

His gaze locked back on hers. "What're you doing here, Maggie?"

"Aren't you going to invite me in?"

"Nope," he said flatly. One thing he didn't need was to have her close enough to touch again.

"Is that any way to talk to your wife?" she asked and walked past him into the ranch house.

His wife.

Automatically, his left thumb moved to play with the gold wedding band he'd stopped wearing the day he had allowed her to walk away. Memories crashed into his mind, and he closed his eyes against the onslaught.

But nothing could stop the images crowding his brain. Maggie, naked, stretched out on his bed, welcoming him. Maggie, shouting at him through her tears. Maggie, leaving without a backward glance. And last, Justice saw himself, closing the door behind her and just as firmly shuttering away his heart.

Nothing had changed.

They were still the same people they'd been when they married and when they split.

So he pulled himself together, and closed the front door behind them. Then he turned to face her.

Watery winter sunlight poured from the skylight onto the gleaming wood floors and glanced off the mirror hanging on the closest wall. A pedestal table held an empty cobalt vase—there'd been no flowers in this hall since Maggie left—and the silence in the house slammed down on top of them both.

Seconds ticked past, marked only by the tapping of Maggie's shoe against the floor. Justice waited her out, knowing that she wouldn't be able to be quiet for long. She never had been comfortable with silence. Maggie was the most talkative woman he'd ever known. Damned if he hadn't missed that.

Three feet of empty space separated them and still, Justice felt the pull of her. His body was heavy and aching and everything in him clawed at him to reach out for her. To ease the pain of doing without her for far too long.

Yet he called on his own reserves of strength to keep from taking what he'd missed so badly.

"Where's Mrs. Carey?" Maggie asked suddenly, her voice shattering the quiet.

"She's on vacation." Justice cursed inwardly, wishing to hell his housekeeper had picked some other time to take a cruise to Jamaica.

"Good for her," Maggie said, then tipped her head to one side. "Glad to see me?"

Glad wasn't the word he'd use. *Stunned* would be about right. When Maggie had left, she'd sworn that he would never see her again. And he hadn't, not counting the nights she appeared in his dreams just to torment him.

"What are you doing here, Maggie?"

"Well, now, that's the question, isn't it?"

She turned away and walked slowly down the hall, bypassing the more formal living room before stepping into the great room. Justice followed, watching as she looked around the room as if reacquainting herself with the place.

She looked from the floor-to-ceiling bookshelves on two walls to the river stone hearth, tall and wide enough for a man to stand in it upright. The log walls, with the white chinking between them that looked like horizontal striping. The plush chairs and sofas she'd bought for the room, gathered together into conversation areas, and the wide bank of windows that displayed an unimpeded view of the ranch's expansive front yard. Ancient trees spread shade across most of the lawn, flowers in the neatly tended beds dipped and swayed with the ocean wind and from a distance came the muffled roar of the ranch tractor moving across the feed grain fields.

"You haven't changed anything," she whispered.

"Haven't had time," he lied.

"Of course." Maggie spun around to face him and her eyes were flashing.

Justice felt a surge of desire shoot through him with the force of a lightning strike. Her temper had always had that effect on him. They'd been like oil and water, sliding against each other but never really blending into a cohesive whole. And maybe that was part of the attraction, he mused.

Maggie wasn't the kind of woman to change for a man. She was who she was, take her or leave her. He'd always wanted to take her. And God help him, if she came too close to him right now, he'd take her again.

"Look," she said, those blue eyes of hers still snapping with sparks of irritation, "I didn't come here to fight."

"Why are you here?"

"To bring you this."

She reached into her oversize, black leather bag and pulled out a legal-size manila envelope. Her fingers traced the silver clasp briefly as if she were hesitating about handing it over. Then a second later, she did.

Justice took it, glanced at it and asked, "What is it?"

"The divorce papers." She folded her arms across her chest. "You didn't sign the copy the lawyers sent you, so I thought I'd bring a set in person. Harder to ignore me if I'm standing right in front of you, don't you think?"

Justice tossed the envelope onto the nearest chair, stuffed his hands into the back pockets of his jeans and stared her down. "I wasn't ignoring you."

"Ah," she said with a sharp nod, "so you were just what? Playing games? Trying to make me furious?"

He couldn't help the half smile that curved his mouth. "If I was, looks like I managed it."

"Damn right you did." She walked toward him and stopped just out of arm's reach. As if she knew if she came any closer, the heat between them would erupt into an inferno neither of them would survive.

He'd always said she was smart.

"Justice, you told me months ago that our marriage was over. So sign the damn papers already."

"What's your hurry?" The question popped out before he could call it back. Gritting his teeth, he just went with it and asked the question he really wanted the answer to. "Got some other guy lined up?"

She jerked her head back as if he'd slapped her.

"This is *not* about getting another man into my life," she told him. "This is about getting a man *out* of my life. You, Justice. We're not together. We're not going to be together. You made that plain enough."

"You leaving wasn't my idea," he countered.

"No, it was just your fault," she snapped.

"You're the one who packed, Maggie."

"You gave me no choice." Her voice broke and Justice hissed in a breath in response.

Shaking her head, she held up one hand as if for peace and whispered, "Let's just finish this, okay?"

"You think a signed paper will finish it?" He moved in, dragging his hands from his pockets so that he could grab her shoulders before she could skitter away. God, the feel of her under his hands again fed the cold, empty places inside him. Damn, he'd missed her.

"You finished it yourself, remember?"

"You're the one who walked out," Justice reminded her again.

"And you're the one who let me," she snapped, her gaze locked on his as she stiffened in his grasp.

"What was I supposed to do?" he demanded. "Tie you to a chair?"

She laughed without humor. "No, you wouldn't do that, would you, Justice? You wouldn't try to make me stay. You wouldn't come after me."

Her words jabbed at him but he didn't say anything. Hell, no, he hadn't chased after her. He'd had his pride, hadn't he? What was he supposed to do, beg her to stay? She'd made it clear that as far as she was concerned, their marriage was over. So he should have done what exactly?

She flipped her hair back out of her face and gave him a glare that should have set him on fire. "So here we are again on the carousel of pain. I blame you. You blame me. I yell, you get all stoic and stone-faced and nothing changes."

He scowled at her. "I don't get stone-faced."

"Oh, please, Justice. You're doing it right now." She

choked out a laugh and tried to squirm free of his grip. It didn't work. She tipped her head back, and her angry eyes focused on his and the mouth he wanted to taste more than anything flattened into a grim slash. "Our fights were always one-sided. I shout and you close up."

"Shouting's supposed to be a good thing?"

"At least I would have known you cared enough to fight!"

His fingers on her shoulders tightened, and he met that furious glare with one of his own. "You knew damn well I cared. You still left."

"Because you had to have it all your way. A marriage is *two* people. Not just one really pushy person." She sucked in a breath, fought his grip for another second or two, then sighed. "Let me go, Justice."

"I already did," he told her. "You're the one who came back."

"I didn't come back for this." She pushed at his chest.

"Bullshit, Maggie." His voice dropped to a whisper, a rough scrape of sound as the words clawed their way out of his throat. "You could have sent your lawyer. Hell, you could have mailed the papers again. But you didn't. You came here. To *me*."

"To look you in the eye and demand that you sign them."

"Really?" He dipped his head, inhaled the soft, flowery scent of her and held it inside as long as he could. "Is that really why you're here, Maggie? The papers?"

"Yes," she said, closing her eyes, sliding her hands up his chest. "I want it over, Justice. If we're done, I need all of this to be finally over."

The feel of her touching Justice sparked the banked fires within and set them free to engulf his body. It had always been like this between them. Chemistry, pure and simple. Combustion. Whenever they touched, their bodies lit up like the neon streets of Vegas.

That, at least, hadn't changed.

"We'll never be done, Maggie." His gaze moved over her. He loved the flush in her cheeks and the way her mouth was parted on the sigh that slipped from between her lips. "What's between us will never be over."

"I used to believe that." Her eyes opened; she stared up at him and shook her head. "But it has to be over, Justice. If I stay, we'll only hurt each other again."

Undoubtedly. He couldn't give her the one thing she wanted, so he had to let her go. For her sake. Still, she was here, now. In his arms. And the past several months had been so long without her.

He'd tried to bury her memory with other women, but he hadn't been able to. Hadn't been able to want any woman as he wanted her. Only her.

His body was hard and tight and aching so badly it was all he could do not to groan with the pain of needing her. The past didn't matter anymore. The future was a hazy blur. But the present buzzed and burned with an intensity that shook him to his bones.

"If we're really done, then all we have is now, Maggie," he said, bending to touch the tip of his tongue to her parted lips. She hissed in a breath of air, and he knew she felt exactly as he did. "And if you leave now, you'll kill me."

She swayed into him even as she shook her head. Her

hands slid up over his shoulder, and she drove her fingers up, into his always-too-long dark brown hair. The touch of her was molten. The scent of her was dizzying. The taste of her was all he needed.

"God, I've missed you," she admitted, her mouth moving against his. "You bastard, you've still got my heart."

"You ripped mine out when you left, Maggie," he confessed. His gaze locked with hers, and in those pale blue depths he read passion and need and all the emotions that were charging through him. "But you're back now and damned if I'll let you leave again. Not now. Not yet."

His mouth came down hard on hers, and it was as if he was alive again. For months, he'd been a walking dead man. A hollowed-out excuse for a human being. Breathing. Eating. Working. But so empty there was nothing for him but routine. He'd lost himself in the ranch workings. Buried himself in the minutiae of business so that he had no time to think. No time to wonder what she was doing. Where she was.

Months of being without her fired the desire nearly choking him, and Justice gave himself up to it. He skimmed his hands up and down her spine, sliding them over the curve of her bottom, cupping her, pressing her into him until she could feel the hard proof of his need.

She groaned into his mouth and strained against him. Justice tore his mouth from hers and lowered his head to taste the long, elegant line of her throat. Her scent invaded him. Her heat swamped him. And he could think only of taking what he'd wanted for so long.

He nibbled at her soft, smooth skin, feeling her shivers of pleasure as she cocked her head to one side, allowing him greater access. She'd always liked it when he kissed her neck. When his teeth scraped her skin, when his tongue drew taut, damp circles just beneath her ear.

He slid one hand around, to the front of her. He cupped her center with the palm of his hand. Even through the fabric of her tailored slacks, he felt her heat, her need, pulsing at him.

"Justice…"

"Damn it, Maggie," he whispered, lifting his head to look down at her. "If you tell me to stop, I'll…"

She smiled. "You'll what?"

He sighed and let his forehead drop to hers. "I'll stop."

Maggie shifted her hold on him, moving to cup his face between her palms. She hadn't come here for this, though if she were to be completely honest, she'd have had to admit that she'd hoped he would hold her again. Love her again. She'd missed him so much that the pain of losing him was a constant ache in her heart. Now, having his hands and mouth on her again was like a surprise blessing from the suddenly benevolent fates.

When she'd first left him, she'd prayed that he'd follow her, take her home and make everything right. When he hadn't, it had broken her heart. But she'd tried to go on. To rebuild her life. She found a new job. Found an apartment. Made friends.

And still there was something missing.

A part of her she'd left here, at the ranch.

With him.

Looking up into the dark blue eyes that had captivated her from the first, she said, "Don't stop, Justice. Please don't stop."

He kissed her, hard and long and deep. His tongue pushed into her mouth, claiming her in a frenzy of passion so strong she felt the tide of it swamp her, threaten to drown her in an overload of sensation.

From the top of her head to the tips of her toes, Maggie felt a rush of heat that was incredible. As if she were literally on fire, she felt her skin burn, her blood boil and her heart thunder in her chest. While his mouth took hers, his clever fingers unzipped her slacks so that he could slide one hand down the front of her, beneath the fragile elastic of her panties to the swollen, hot flesh awaiting him.

She shivered as he stroked her intimately. She parted her legs for him, letting her slacks slide down to pool on the floor. She didn't care where they were. Didn't care about anything but feeling his hands on her again. Maggie nearly wept as he pushed first one finger and then two deep inside her.

Sucking in a gulp of air, she let her head fall back as she rode his hand, rocking her hips, seeking the release only he could give her. The passion she'd only ever found with him. She heard his own breath coming hard and fast as he continued to stroke her body inside and out. His thumb worked that so sensitive bud of flesh at the heart of her, and Maggie felt her brain sizzle as tension coiled inside her, tighter, tighter.

"Come for me, Maggie," he whispered. "Let me watch you shatter."

She couldn't have denied him even if she'd wanted

to. It had been too long. She'd missed him too much.
Maggie held on to his shoulders, fingers curling into the
soft fabric of the long-sleeved shirt he wore, digging into
his hard muscles.

Her mind spun, splintering with thoughts, images,
while her body burned and spiraled even closer to its
reward. She'd never felt anything like this with any man
before him. And after Justice…she'd had no interest in
other men. He was the one. She'd known it the moment
she'd met him three years before. One look across a
crowded dance floor at a charity event and she'd known.
Instantly. It was as if everything in the world had held
utterly still for one breathless moment.

Just like now.

There was nothing in the world but him and his
hands. His touch. His scent. "Justice—I need…"

"I know, baby. I know just what you need. Take it. Take
me." He touched her deeper, pushing his fingers inside
her, stroking her until her breath strangled in her throat.

Until she could only groan and hold on to him. Until
her body trembled and the incredible tension within
shattered under an onslaught of pleasure so deep, so
overwhelming, all she could do was shout his name as
wave after wave of completion rolled over her, through
her, leaving her dazed and breathless.

And when the tremors finally died away, Maggie
stared up into Justice's lake-blue eyes and watched him
smile. She was standing in the living room, with her
pants down, trembling with the force of her reaction to
him. She should have been…embarrassed. After all,
anyone could have walked into the ranch house.

Instead, all Maggie felt was passion stirring inside again. His hands were talented, heaven knew. But she wanted more. She wanted the slide of Justice's body into hers.

Licking her lips, she blew out a breath and said, "That was…"

"…just the beginning," he finished for her.

Two

Sounded good to Maggie.

Yet… She glanced around the empty room before looking back at him. "Mrs. Carey's not here, but—"

"Nobody's here," he said quickly. "No one's coming. No one is going to interrupt us."

Maggie sighed in relief. She didn't want any interruptions. Justice was right about one thing—their past was gone. The future was gray and hazy. All she had was today. This minute. This one small slice of time, and she was going to relish every second of it.

Her fingers speared through his thick, soft hair, her nails dragging along his scalp. He always kept it too long, she thought idly, loving the way the dark brown mass lay across his collar. He had a day's worth of dark stubble on his jaws, and he looked so damned sexy he made her quiver.

Her breasts ached for his touch and as if he'd heard that stray thought, he pulled back from her slightly, just far enough so that his fingers could work the buttons on her pale pink silk blouse. Quickly, they fell free and then he was sliding the fabric off her shoulders to drop to the floor. She stepped out of her slacks, kicked off her half boots and slipped her lacy panties off.

Then he undid her bra, tossing it aside, and her breasts were free, his hands cupping her. His thumbs moved over her peaked nipples until she whimpered with the pleasure and the desire pumping fresh and new through her system. As if that climax hadn't even happened, her body was hot and trembling again.

Need crashed down on her, and at her core she ached and burned for him.

"You're beautiful," he whispered, drawing his mouth from hers, glancing down at her breasts, cupped in his palms. "So damn beautiful."

"I want you, Justice. Now. Please, now."

One corner of his mouth tipped into a wicked smile. His eyes flashed and in an instant he'd swept her up into his arms, stalked across the room and dropped her onto one of the wide sofas. She stared up at him as he tugged his shirt up and over his head. And her mouth watered. His skin, so tanned, so strong, so sculpted. God, she remembered all the nights she'd lain in his arms, held against that broad, warm chest. And she trembled at the rise of passion inside her.

She scooted back on the sofa until her head was

resting on a pillow. Maggie held her arms out toward him. "What're you waiting for, cowboy?"

His eyes gleamed, his jaw went tight and hard. He finished undressing in a split second but still Maggie thought he was taking too long. She didn't want to wait. She was hot and wet and so ready for him that she thought she'd explode and die if he didn't take her soon.

He came to her and Maggie's gaze dipped to his erection, long and thick and hard. Her breath caught on a gasp of anticipation as Justice leaned down, tore the back cushions off the sofa and tossed them to the floor to make more room for them on the overstuffed couch. The dark green chenille fabric was soft and cool against her skin, but Maggie hardly noticed that slight chill. There was far too much heat simmering inside her, and when Justice covered her body with his, she could have sworn she felt actual flames sweeping over them.

"I've missed you, babe," he told her, bracing himself on his hands, lowering his mouth to hers, tasting, nibbling.

"Oh, Justice, I've missed you, too." She lifted her hips for him, parting her thighs, welcoming him home. He pushed his body into hers with one hard stroke. She groaned, loving the long, deep slide of his flesh claiming hers. He filled her and she lifted her legs higher, hooking them around his waist, opening herself so that she could take him even deeper.

And still it wasn't enough. Wasn't nearly enough. She groaned, twisting and writhing beneath him as he moved in and out of her depths in plunging strokes that fanned the flames engulfing her.

It had been too long, she thought wildly. She didn't

want soft and romantic. She wanted hard and fast and frantic. She wanted to know that he felt the same crushing need she did. She wanted to feel the strength of his passion.

"Harder, Justice," she whispered. "Take me harder."

He looked down at her and his eyes flashed. "I'm holding back, Maggie. It's been too long. I don't want to hurt you."

She cupped his face in her palms, fought to steady her breath and finally shook her head and smiled. "The only thing that hurts is when you hold back. Justice, I *need* you. All of you."

His jaw clenched tight, he swept one arm around her back, holding her to him even as he pushed off the couch. With their bodies locked together, her legs wrapped around his waist, he eased her onto the oriental carpet covering the hardwood floors. With her flat on her back, he levered himself over her, hands at either side of her head. Grinning down at her, he muttered, "Told you when you bought 'em those damn couches were too soft."

She grinned right back at him. "For sitting, they're perfect. For this…yeah. Too soft."

She lifted her hips then, taking him deeper inside. When he withdrew a moment later, she nearly groaned, but then he was back, driving himself into her, pistoning his hips against hers and she felt all of him. Took all of him. His need joined hers.

He lifted her legs, hooking them over his shoulders, tipping her hips higher so that he could delve even deeper, and Maggie groaned in appreciation. She slapped her hands onto the carpet and hung on as he moved faster and faster, driving them both to a shuddering climax that hovered just out of reach.

"Yes, Justice," she said, her voice nothing more than a strained hush of sound. "Just like that."

Again and again, his body claimed hers, pushing into her soft, hot folds, taking everything she offered and giving all that she could have wanted. She looked up into his eyes, saw the flash of something delicious wink in their depths and knew in that one blindingly clear instant that she would never be whole without him.

Without him.

That one random thought hovered at the edges of her mind and filled her eyes with tears even as her body began to sing and hum with the building tensions that rippled through her senses.

He touched her at their joining. Rubbing his thumb over that one spot that held so many incredible sensations. And as he touched her, Maggie hurtled eagerly toward the enormous climax waiting for her. As her body exploded with the force of completion, she screamed his name, and still she heard the quiet voice in the back of her mind whispering, *Is this our last time together?*

Then Justice gave himself over to his own release, her name an agonized groan sliding from his throat. When he collapsed atop her, Maggie held him close as the last of the tremors rippled through their joined bodies and eased them into oblivion.

And if her heart broke just a little, she wouldn't let him know it.

* * *

The rest of the weekend passed in a blurry haze of passion. But for a few necessary trips to the kitchen, Justice and Maggie never left the master bedroom.

After that first time in the living room, Justice made a call to his ranch manager, Phil, and told him to handle the ranch problems himself for the next few days. It hadn't exactly been a promise of forever, but Maggie had been happy for it.

All the same, she was crazy and she knew it. Setting herself up for another fall. As long as Justice King was the man she loved, she wasn't going to find any peace. Because they couldn't be together without causing each other pain and being apart was killing her.

How was that fair?

She sighed a little, her gaze still fixed on him. The only light in the room came from the river stone hearth, where a dying fire sputtered and flickered. Outside, a winter storm battered at the log mansion, tiny fists of rain tapping at the glass. And within Maggie, a different sort of storm raged.

What was she supposed to do? She'd tried living without him and had spent the most miserable nine months of her life. She'd tried to lose herself in her work, but it was an empty way to live. The sad truth was she wanted Justice. And without him, she'd never be really happy.

He was the most amazing lover she'd ever known. Every touch burned, every breath caressed, every whispered word was a promise of seduction that kept her hovering on the brink of a new climax no matter how many times he pushed her over the edge. Her skin hummed long after he stopped touching her. She closed her eyes and felt him inside her. Felt their hearts pounding in rhythm and couldn't help wondering, as she always had, how two people could be so close and so far apart at the same time.

Now she watched him get out of bed and walk naked across the bedroom. His body was long and lean and tanned from all the years of working in the sun. His dark brown hair hung past his shoulders. She'd always found that hair of his to be sexy as hell and what made it even sexier was that he was oblivious to just how good he looked. How dangerous. Her heartbeat quickened as her gaze moved over his back, and down over his butt. He moved with a stealthy grace that was completely innate. Everything about him was, she had to admit, fabulous. He was enough to make any woman toss her panties in the air and shout hallelujah. And she was no different.

He went into a crouch in front of the hearth. The fire was dying and he set a fresh log on the fading flames. Instantly the fire blazed into life, licking at the new wood, hissing and snapping.

Maggie watched Justice. His legs were muscled and toned from hours spent in a saddle. His back and shoulders were broad and sculpted from the hard work he never spared himself. As a King, he could have hired men to do the hard work around the ranch. But she knew it had always been a matter of pride to him that *he* be out there with those who worked for him.

Justice King was a man out of time, she thought, sweeping one arm across the empty space in the bed where he'd been lying only moments ago. He would have been completely at home in medieval times. He would have been a Highlander, she mused, her imagination dressing him in a war-torn plaid and placing a claymore in his fist.

As if he knew she was watching him, Justice turned his face to her, and the flickering light of the fire threw dancing shadows across his features. He looked hard and strong and suddenly so unapproachable that Maggie's heart gave a lurch.

She was setting herself up for pain and she knew it. He was her husband, but the bonds holding them together were frayed and tattered. In bed they were combustible and so damn good it made her heart hurt. It was when they were *out* of bed that things got complicated. They wanted different things. They each held so tightly to their own bottom line that compromise was unthinkable.

But it was Sunday night. The end of the weekend. She'd have to return to her world soon, and knowing that this time with him was nearly over was already bringing agonizing pain.

The storm blowing in off the coast howled outside the window. Rain hammered at the glass, wind whistled under the eaves and, Justice noticed, Maggie had started thinking.

Never had been a good thing, Justice told himself as he watched his wife study him. Whenever Maggie got that look on her face—an expression that said she had something to say he wasn't going to like—Justice knew trouble was coming.

But then, he'd been halfway prepared for that since this "lost" weekend had begun. Nothing had changed.

He and Maggie, despite the obvious chemistry they shared, were still miles apart in the things that mattered, and great sex wasn't going to alter that any.

Her red-gold hair spilled across her pillow like hot silk. She held the dark blue sheet to her breasts even as she slid one creamy white leg free of the covers. She made a picture that engraved itself in Justice's mind, and he knew that no matter how long he lived, he would always see her as she was right at this moment.

He also knew that this last image of her would torment him forever.

"Justice," she said, "we have to talk."

"Why?" He stood up, crossed to the chair where he'd tossed his jeans and tugged them on. A man needed his pants on when he had a conversation with Maggie King.

"Don't."

He glanced at her. "Don't what?"

"Don't shut me out. Not this time. Not now."

"I'm not doing anything, Maggie."

"That's my point." She sat up, the mattress beneath her shifting a little with her movements.

Justice turned his head to look at her, and everything in him roared at him to stalk to her side, grab her and hold her so damn tight she wouldn't have the breath to start another argument neither of them could win.

Her hair tumbled around her shoulders, and she lifted one hand to impatiently push the mass behind her shoulders. "You're not going to ask me to stay, are you?"

He shouldn't have to, Justice told himself. She was his damn wife. Why should he have to ask her to be with him? She was the one who'd left.

He didn't say any of that, though, just shook his head and buttoned the fly of his jeans. He didn't speak again until his bare feet were braced wide apart. A man could lose his balance all too easily when talking to Maggie. "What good would it do to ask you to stay? Eventually, you'd leave again."

"I wouldn't have to if you'd bend a little."

"I won't bend on this," he assured her, though it cost him as he noted the flash of pain in her eyes that was there and then gone in a blink.

"Why not?" She pushed out of the bed, dropping the sheet and facing him, naked and proud.

His body hardened instantly, despite just how many times they'd made love over the past few hours. Seemed his dick was always ready when it came to Maggie.

"We are who we are," he told her, folding his arms across his chest. "You want kids. I don't. End of story."

Her mouth worked and he knew she was struggling not to shout and rail at him. But then, Maggie's hot Irish temper was one of the things that had first drawn him to her. She blazed like a sun during an argument— standing her ground no matter who stood against her. He admired that trait even though it made him a little crazy sometimes.

"Damn it, Justice!" She stalked to the chair where she'd left her clothes and grabbed her bra and panties. Slipping them on, she shook her head and kept talking. "You're willing to give up what we have because you don't want a child?"

Irritation raced through him; he couldn't stop it. But he wasn't going to get into this argument again.

"I told you how I felt before we got married, Maggie," he reminded her, in a calm, patient tone he knew would drive her to distraction.

As expected, she whipped her hair back out of her eyes, glared at him fiercely, then picked up her pale pink blouse and put it on. While her fingers did up the buttons, she snapped, "Yes, but I just thought you didn't want kids that instant. I never thought you meant *ever.*"

"Your mistake," he said softly.

"But one you didn't bother to clear up," she countered.

"Maggie," he said tightly, "do we really have to do this again?"

"Why the hell not?" she demanded. Then pointing to the bed, she snapped, "We just spent an incredible weekend together, Justice. And you're telling me you feel *nothing?*"

He'd be a liar if he tried. But admitting what he was feeling still wouldn't change a thing. "I didn't say that."

"You didn't have to," she told him. "The very fact that you're willing to let me walk…*again*…tells me every-thing I need to know."

His back teeth ground together until he wouldn't have been surprised to find them nothing more than gritty powder in his mouth. She thought she knew him, thought she knew what he was doing and why, but she didn't have a clue. And never would, he reminded himself.

"Hell, Justice, you wouldn't back down even if you did change your mind, would you? Oh, no. Not Justice King. His pride motivates his every action—"

He inhaled deeply and folded his arms across his bare chest. "Maggie…"

She held up one hand to cut off whatever else he might say, and though he felt a kick to his own temper, he shut up and let her have her say.

"You know what? I'm sick to death of your pride, Justice. The great Justice King. Master of his Universe." She slapped both hands to her hips and lifted her chin. "You're so busy arranging the world to your specifications that there is absolutely no compromise in you."

"Why the hell should there be?" Justice took a half step toward her and stopped. Only because he knew if he got close enough to inhale her scent, he'd be lost again. He'd toss her back into the bed, bury himself inside her—and what would that solve? Not a thing. Sooner or later, they'd end up right here. Back at the fight that had finally finished their marriage.

"Because there were *two* of us in our marriage, Justice. Not just you."

"Right," he said with a brief, hard nod. He didn't like arguments. Didn't think they solved anything. If two people were far enough apart on an issue, then shouting at each other over it wasn't going to help any. But there was only just so much he was willing to take. "You want compromise? We each give a little? So how would you manage that here, Maggie? Have *half* a child?"

"Not funny at all, Justice." Maggie huffed out a breath. "You knew what family meant to me. What it still means to me."

"And you knew how I felt, too." Keeping his gaze steady and cool on hers, he said, "There's no compromise here, Maggie, and you know it. I can't give you what you want, and you can't be happy without it."

As if all the air had left her body, she slumped, the flash of temper gone only to be replaced by a well of defeat that glimmered in her eyes. And that tore at him. He hated seeing Maggie's spirit shattered. Hated even more that he was the one who'd caused it. But that couldn't be helped. Not now. Not ever.

"Fine," she said softly. "That's it, then. We end it. Again."

She picked up her slacks and put them on. Shaking her head, she zipped them up, tucked the tail of her shirt into the waistband and then stepped into her boots. Lifting her arms, she gathered up the tangle of her hair and deftly wound it into a knot at the back of her head, capturing that wild mass and hiding it away.

When she was finished, she stared at him for a long moment, and even from across the room Justice would have spared her this rehashing of the argument that had finally torn them apart. But this weekend had proven to him as nothing else ever would, that the best thing he could do for her was to step back. Let her hate him if she had to. Better for her to move the hell on with her life.

Even if the thought of her moving on to another man was enough to carve his heart right out of his chest.

Maggie picked up her purse, slung it over her shoulder and stared at him. "So, I guess the only thing left to say is thanks for the weekend."

"Maggie…"

Shaking her head again, she started walking toward the door. When she came close to him, she stopped and looked up at him. "Sign the damn divorce papers, Justice."

She took another step and he stopped her with one hand on her arm. "It's pouring down rain out there. Why don't you stay put for a while and wait out the storm before you go."

Maggie pulled her arm free of his grasp and started walking again. "I can't stay here. Not another minute. Besides, we're not a couple, Justice. You don't have the right to worry about me anymore."

A few seconds later, he heard the front door slam. Justice walked to the windows and looked down on the yard. The wind tore her hair free of its tidy knot and sent long strands of red flying about her face. She was drenched by the rain almost instantly. She climbed into the car and fired up the engine. Justice saw the head-lights come on, saw the rain slash in front of those twin beams and stood there in silence as she steered the car down the drive and off the ranch.

Chest tight, he watched until her taillights disap-peared into the darkness. Then he punched his fist against the window and relished the pain.

Three

Justice threw his cane across the room and listened to it hit the far wall with a satisfying clatter. He hated needing the damn thing. Hated the fact that he was less than he used to be. Hated knowing that he needed help, and he sure as hell hated having his brother here to tell him so.

He glared at Jefferson, his eldest brother, then pushed up and out of the chair he was sitting in. Justice gathered up his pride and dignity and used every ounce of his will to make sure he hobbled only a little as he lurched from the chair to the window overlooking the front yard. Sunlight splashed through the glass into the room, bathing everything in a brilliant wash of light.

Justice narrowed his eyes at his brother, and when he was no more than a foot away from him, he stopped and said, "I told you I can walk. I don't need another damn therapist."

Jefferson shook his head and stuffed both hands into the pockets of what was probably a five-thousand-dollar suit. "You are the most stubborn jackass I've ever known. And being a member of this family, that's saying something."

"Very amusing," Justice told him and oh-so-casually shot out one hand to brace himself against the log wall. His knuckles were white with the effort to support himself and take the pressure off his bad leg. But he'd be damned if he'd show that weakness to Jefferson. "Now, get out."

"That's the attitude that ended up bringing me here."

"How's that?"

"You've chased off three physical therapists in the past month, Justice."

"I didn't bring 'em here," he pointed out.

Jefferson scowled at him, then sighed. "Dude, you broke your leg in three places. You've had surgery. The bones are healed but the muscles are weak. You need a physical therapist and you damn well know it."

"Don't call me 'dude,' and I'm getting along fine."

"Yeah, I can see that." Jefferson shot a quick glance to Justice's white-knuckled grip on the wall.

"Don't you have some inane movie to make somewhere?" Justice countered. As head of King Studios, Jefferson was the man in charge of the film division of the King empire. The man loved Hollywood. Loved traveling around the world, making deals, looking for talent, scouting locations himself. He was as footloose as Justice was rooted to this ranch.

"First I'm taking care of my idiot brother."

Justice leaned a little harder against the log wall. If Jefferson didn't leave soon, Justice was going to fall on his ass. Whether he wanted to admit it aloud or not, his healing leg was still too weak to be much good. And that irritated the hell out of him.

A stupid accident had caused all of this. His horse had stumbled into a gopher hole one fine morning a few months back. Justice had been thrown clear, but then the horse rolled across his leg, shattering it but good. The horse had recovered nicely. Justice, though, was having a tougher time. After surgery, he now carried enough metal in his bones to make getting through airport security a nightmare, and his muscles were now so flabby and weak it was all he could do to force himself to move.

"It's your own damn fault you're in this fix anyway," Jefferson said, as if reading Justice's mind. "If you'd been riding in a ranch jeep instead of sitting on top of your horse, this wouldn't have happened."

"Spoken like a man who's forgotten what it was like to ride herd."

"Damn right," Jefferson told him. "I put a lot of effort into forgetting about predawn rides to round up cattle. Or having to go and find a cow so dumb it got lost on its own home ranch."

This is why Jeff was the Hollywood mogul and Justice was the man on the ranch. His brothers had all bolted from the home ranch as soon as they were old enough, each of them chasing his own dream. But Justice's dreams were all here on this ranch. Here is where he felt most alive. Here, where the clear air and the open land could let a man breathe. He didn't mind the hard work. Hell, he relished it. And his brother knew why he'd been astride a horse.

"You grew up here, Jeff," he said. "You know damn well a horse is better for getting down into the canyons. And they don't have engines that scare the cattle and cause stress that will shut down milk production for the calves, not to mention running the jeeps on the grass-lands only tears them up and—"

"Save it," Jeff interrupted, holding up both hands to stave off a lecture. "I heard it all from Dad, thanks."

"Fine, then. No more ranch talk. Just answer this." Justice reached down and idly rubbed at his aching leg. "Who asked you to butt into my life and start hiring physical therapists I don't even want?"

"Actually," Jefferson answered with a grin, "Jesse and Jericho asked me to. Mrs. Carey kept us posted on the situation with the therapists, and we all want you back on your feet."

He snorted. "Yeah? Why're you the only one here, then?"

Jefferson shrugged. "You know Jesse won't leave Bella alone right now. You'd think she was the only woman in the world to ever get pregnant."

Justice nodded, distracted from the argument at the moment by thoughts of their youngest brother. "True. You know he even sent me a book? *How to Be a Great Uncle*."

"He sent the same one to me and Jericho. Weird how he did this turnaround from wandering surfer to home-and-hearth expectant father."

Justice swallowed hard. He was glad for his brother, but he didn't want to think about Jesse's imminent fatherhood. Changing the subject, he asked, "So where's Jericho?"

"On leave," Jefferson told him. "If you'd open your e-mails once in a while, you'd know that. He's shipping out again soon, and he had some leave coming to him so he took it. He's soaking up some sun at cousin Rico's hotel in Mexico."

Jericho was a career marine. He loved the life and he was good at his job, but Justice hated that his brother was about to head back into harm's way. Why hadn't he been opening his e-mails? Truth? Because he'd been in a piss-poor mood since the accident. He should have known, though, that his brothers wouldn't just leave him alone in his misery.

"That's why you're here, then," Justice said. "You got the short straw."

"Pretty much."

"I should have been an only child," Justice muttered.

"Maybe in your next life," Jefferson told him, then pulled one hand free of his slacks pocket to check the time on his gold watch.

"If I'm keeping you," Justice answered with a bared teeth grin, "feel free to get the hell out."

"I've got time," his brother assured him. "I'm not leaving until the new therapist arrives and I can make sure you don't scare her off."

Wounded pride took a bite out of Justice and he practically snarled at his brother. "Why don't you all just leave me the hell alone? I didn't ask for your help and I don't want it. Just like I don't want these damn therapists moving in here like some kind of invasion." He winced as his leg pained him, then finished by saying, "I'm not even gonna let this one in, Jeff. So you might as well head her off."

"Oh," Jefferson told him with a satisfied smile, "I think you'll let this one stay."

"You're wrong."

The doorbell rang just then and Justice heard his housekeeper's footsteps as she hustled along the hall toward the door. Something way too close to panic for Justice's own comfort rose up inside him. He shot Jefferson a quick look and said, "Just get rid of her, all right? I don't want help. I'll get back on my feet my own way."

"You've been doing it your own way for long enough, Justice," Jefferson told him. "You can hardly stand without sweat popping out on your forehead."

From a distance, Justice heard Mrs. Carey's voice, welcoming whoever had just arrived. He made another try at convincing his brother to take his latest attempt at help and leave.

"I want to do this on my own."

"That's how you do everything, you stubborn bastard. But everybody needs help sometimes, Justice," his brother said. "Even you."

"Damn it, Jefferson—"

The sound of two women's voices rippled through the house like music, rising and falling and finally dropping into hushed whispers. That couldn't be a good sign. Already his housekeeper was siding with the new therapist. Wasn't anyone loyal anymore? Justice scraped his free hand through his hair, then scrubbed his palm across his face.

He hated feeling out of control. And ever since his accident, that sensation had only been mounting. He'd had to trust in daily reports from his ranch manager rather than going out to ride his own land. He'd had to count on his housekeeper to take care of the tasks that needed doing around here. He wanted his damn life back, and he wasn't going to get it by depending on some stranger to come in and work on his leg.

He'd regain control only if he managed to come back from his injuries on his own. If that didn't make sense to anyone but him, well, he didn't care. This was *his* life, his ranch and, by God, he was going to do things the way he always had.

His way.

He heard someone coming and shot a sidelong glance at the open doorway, preparing himself to fire whoever it was the minute she walked in. His brothers could just butt the hell out of his life.

Footsteps sounded quick and light on the wood floor, and something inside Justice tightened. He had a weird feeling. There was no explanation for it, but for some reason his gut twisted into knots. Glancing at his brother, he muttered, "Just who the hell did you hire?"

Then a too-familiar voice announced from the doorway, "Me, Justice. He hired me."

Maggie.

His gaze shot to her, taking her in all at once as a man dying of thirst would near drown himself with his first taste of water. She was wearing blue jeans, black boots and a long-sleeved, green T-shirt. She looked curvier than he remembered, more lush somehow. Her hair was a tumble of wild curls around her shoulders and framing her face with fiery, silken strands. Her blue eyes were fixed on him and her mouth was curved into a half smile.

"Surprise," she said softly.

That about covered it, he thought. Surprise. Shock. Stunned stupid.

He was going to kill Jefferson first chance he got.

But for now he had to manage to stay on his feet long enough to convince Maggie that he didn't need her help. Damn it, she was the absolute last person in the world he wanted feeling sorry for him. Lifting his chin, he narrowed his gaze on her and said, "There's been a mistake, Maggie. I don't need you here, so you can go."

She flinched—actually flinched—and Justice felt like the bastard Jefferson had called him just a moment or two ago. But it was best for her to leave right away. He didn't want her here.

"Justice," his brother said in a long-suffering sigh.

"It's okay, Jeff," Maggie said, walking into the room, head held high, pale blue eyes glinting with the light of battle. "I'm more than used to your brother's crabby attitude."

"I'm not crabby."

"No," she said with a tight smile, "you're the very soul of congenial hospitality. I just feel all warm and fuzzy inside." Then she took a hard look at him. "Why are you standing?"

"What?"

Beside him, Jeff muffled a laugh and tried to disguise it with a cough. It didn't work.

"You heard me," Maggie said, rushing across the

room. When Justice didn't move, she grumbled something unintelligible, then dragged a chair over to him.
She pushed him down onto it, and it was all Justice
could do to hide the relief that getting off his feet gave
him. "Honestly, Justice, don't you have any sense at
all? You can't put all your weight on your bad leg or
you'll be flat on your back again. Why aren't you using
a cane at least?"

"Don't have one," he muttered.

"He threw it across the room," Jeff provided.

"Of course he did," Maggie said. She spotted the
cane, then walked to retrieve it. When she came back to
his side, she thrust it at him and ordered, "If you're
going to stand, you're going to use the cane."

"I don't take orders from you, Maggie," he said.

"You do now."

"In case you didn't notice the lack of welcome, I'm
firing you."

"You can't fire me," she told him, leaning down to
stare him dead in the eye. "Jefferson hired me. He's
paying me to get you back on your feet."

"He had no right to." Justice sent his brother a hard
glare, but Jefferson was rocking back and forth on his
heels, clearly enjoying himself.

Maggie straightened up, fisted her hands at her hips
and stared down at him with the stern look of a general
about to order troops into battle. "He did hire me, though,
Justice. Oh, and by the way, I've heard about the other
three therapists who've come and gone from here—"

Justice looked past her to glare at his brother but
looked back to Maggie again when she continued.

"—and you're not going to scare me off by throwing your cane. Or by being rude and nasty. So no need to try."

"I don't want you here."

"Yes," she said and a flicker of something sharp and sad shot through her eyes. "You've made that plain a number of times. But you can just suck it up. Because I'm here. And I'm staying. Until you can stand up without brackets of pain lining the sides of your mouth or gritting your teeth to keep from moaning. So you know what? Your best plan of action is to do exactly what I tell you to do."

"Why's that?"

"Because, Justice," she said, bracing her hands on the arms of his chair and leaning in until their faces were just a breath apart, "if you listen to me, you'll heal. And the sooner that happens, the sooner you'll get rid of me."

"Can't argue with her there," Jeff pointed out.

Justice didn't even glance at his brother. His gaze was locked with Maggie's. Her scent wafted to him like the scent of wildflowers on a summer wind. Her eyes shone with a silent challenge. Now that he was over the initial shock of seeing her walk into his life again, he could only hope to God she walked back out really soon.

Just being this close to her was torture. His body was pressing against the thick denim fabric of his jeans. Good thing she'd pushed him into a chair so damn fast or she and his brother would have been all too aware of the kind of effect she had on him.

Maggie stared into Justice's eyes and felt her heart hammer in her chest. Seeing him again was like balm to an open wound. But seeing him hurt tore at her. So she was both relieved and miserable to be here.

Yet how could she have turned down Jefferson's request that she come to the ranch and help out? Justice was still her husband. Though he probably didn't realize that. No doubt he'd never even noticed that though he had signed the divorce papers and mailed them to her, she had never filed them with the courts. Naturally, even if he had noticed, Justice would have been too stubborn to call her and find out what was going on.

And as for Maggie? Well, she had had her own reasons for keeping quiet.

Strange. The last time she'd left this ranch, she'd been determined to sever the bond between her and Justice once and for all. But that plan had died soon enough when things had changed. Her life had taken a turn she hadn't expected. Hadn't planned for. A rush of something sweet and fulfilling swept through her and Maggie almost smiled. Nothing Justice did or said could make her regret what her life was now.

In fact, that was one of the reasons she'd come to help him, she told herself. Of course she would have come anyway, because she couldn't bear the thought of Justice being in pain and needing help he didn't have. But there was more. Maggie had leaped at Jefferson's request to come to the ranch, because she'd wanted the chance to show her husband what he was missing. To maybe open his stubborn eyes to the possibilities stretched out in front of him.

Now, though, as she stood right in front of him and actually *watched* a shutter come down over his eyes, effectively blocking her out, she wondered if coming here had been the right thing to do after all.

Still, she *was* here. And since she was, she would at least get Justice back on his feet.

"So, what's it going to be, Justice?" she asked. "Going to play the tough, stoic cowboy? Or are you going to cooperate with me?"

"I didn't ask you to come," he told her, ignoring his brother standing just a foot or so away.

"Of course you didn't," Maggie retorted. "Everyone knows the great Justice King doesn't need anyone or anything. You're getting along fine, right?" She straightened up and took a step back. "So why don't you just get up out of that chair and walk me to the door."

His features tightened and his eyes flashed dangerously, and just for a second or two Maggie was half afraid he'd try to do just that and end up falling on his face. But the moment passed and he only glared at her. "Fine. You can stay."

"Wow." She placed one hand on her chest as if she were sighing in gratitude. "Thank you."

Justice glowered at her.

Jefferson cleared his throat and drew both of their gazes to him. "Well, then, looks like my work here is done. Justice, try not to be too big of an ass. Maggie," he said, moving to plant a quick kiss on her forehead, "best of luck."

Then he left and they were alone.

"Jefferson shouldn't have called you," Justice said quietly.

"Who else would he call?" Maggie looked at his white-knuckled grip on the cane he held in his right fist. He was angry, she knew. But more than that, he was

frustrated. Her husband wasn't the kind of man to
accept limitations in himself. Having to use a cane to
support a weakened leg would gnaw at him. No wonder
he was as charming as a mountain lion with its foot
caught in a trap.

He blew out a breath. "I could get Mrs. Carey to
throw you out."

Maggie laughed shortly. "She wouldn't do it. She
likes me. Besides, you need me."

"I don't need your help or your pity. I can do this
on my own."

A flare of indignation burst into life inside her. "That
is so typical, Justice. You go through your life self-
sufficient and expecting everyone else to do the same.
Do it yourself or don't do it. That's your style."

"Nothing wrong with that," he argued. "A man's got
to stand on his own."

"Why?" She threw both hands high and let them fall.
"Why does it always have to be your way? Why can't you
see that everyone needs someone else at *some* point?"

"I don't," he told her.

"Oh, no, not you. Not Justice King. You never ask for
help. Never admit to needing anyone or anything. Heck,
you've never even said the word *please*."

"Why the hell should I?" he demanded.

"You're a hard man," Maggie said.

"Best you remember that."

"Fine. I'll remember." She stepped up close to him,
helped him up from the chair despite his resistance
and when he was standing, looked him dead in the eye
and said, "As long as *you* remember that if you want

to get your life back, you're going to have to take orders from me for a change."

Late that night Justice lay alone in the bed he used to share with his wife. He was exhausted, in pain and furious. He didn't want Maggie looking at him and seeing a patient. Yet, all afternoon she'd been with him, taking notes on his progress, telling him what he'd been doing wrong and then massaging his leg muscles with an impersonal competence that tore at him.

Every time she'd touched him, his body had reacted. He hadn't been able to hide his erection, but she'd ignored it—which infuriated him. It was as if he meant nothing to her. As if this were just a job.

Which it probably was.

Hell, what did he expect? They were divorced.

Grabbing the phone off the nightstand, he stabbed in a number from memory and waited impatiently while it rang. When his brother answered, Justice snapped, "Get her out of my house."

"No."

"Damn it, Jefferson," Justice raged quietly with a quick look at the closed door of his bedroom. For all he knew Maggie or Mrs. Carey was out wandering the hall, and he didn't want to be overheard. Which was the only thing that kept his voice low. "I don't want her here. I made my peace with her leaving, and having her here again only makes everything harder."

"Too bad," Jefferson shot back. "Justice, you need help whether you want to admit it or not. Maggie's a great therapist and you know it. She can get you back

on your feet if you'll just swallow your damn pride and
do what she tells you."

Justice hung up on his brother, but that didn't make
him feel any better. *Swallow his pride?* Hell, his pride
was all he had. It had gotten him through some tough
times—watching Maggie walk out of his life, for
instance—and damned if he was going to let it go now,
when he needed it the most.

He scooted off the edge of the bed, too filled with
frustration to try to sleep anyway. He could watch the
flat-screen television he'd had installed a year ago, but
he was too keyed up to sit still for a movie and too
pissed off already to watch the news.

Disgusted by the need for it, Justice reached for his
cane and pried himself off the mattress, using the thickly
carved oak stick for balance. His injured leg ached like
a bad tooth, and that only served to feed the irritation
already clawing at his insides. Shaking his head, he
hobbled toward the window but stopped dead when he
heard…something.

Frowning, he turned toward the doorway and the hall
beyond. He waited for that noise to come again, and
when it did, his scowl deepened. What the hell?

He made his way to the door, flung it open and
stood on the threshold, glancing up and down the
hallway. The wall sconces were lit, throwing golden
light over the narrow, dark red-and-green carpet, which
lay like a path down the polished oak floors. The
hallway was empty, and yet…

There it was again.

Sounded like a cat mewling. Justice moved toward

the sound with slow, uncertain steps. Just one more reason to hate his damn cane and his own leg for betraying him. A few months ago he'd have stalked down this hallway with long strides. Now he was reduced to an ungainly stagger.

He followed the sound to the last door at the end of the hallway. The room Maggie was to stay in while she was on the ranch. At least he'd been able to order *that* much. He'd wanted her as far from his bedroom as possible to avoid the inevitable temptation.

Outside her door he cocked his head and listened. The house made its usual groaning noises as night settled in and the temperature dropped. Seconds ticked past and then he heard it again. That soft, wailing sound that he couldn't quite place. Was she crying? Missing him? Regretting coming to the ranch?

He should knock, he told himself. But if he did and she told him to go away, he'd have to. So instead, Justice turned the knob, threw open the door and felt the world fall out from beneath his feet.

Maggie.

Holding a baby.

She looked up at him and smiled. "Hello, Justice. I'd like you to meet Jonas. My son."

Four

"What? Who? How? What?" Justice jolted back a step, hit the doorjamb and simply stared at the woman and baby on the wide, king-size bed.

Maggie's gaze locked on his as she answered his questions in order. "My son. Jonas. The usual way. And again, my son."

Pain like Justice had never known before shot through him with a swiftness that stole his breath and nearly knocked him off his feet.

Maggie had a son.

Which meant she had a lover.

She was with someone else.

Everything in him went cold and hard. Amazing, really, how big the pain was. He'd told himself he was over her. Assured himself that their marriage was done and that it was for the best. For both of them. Yet now, when he was slapped with the proof that what they'd shared was over, the sharp stab of regret was hard enough to steal his breath. The thought of Maggie lying in another man's arms almost killed him. But then, what had he expected? That they'd get a divorce and she'd join a convent? Not his Maggie. She had too much fire.

Clearly, it hadn't taken her too long to move on. Her son looked to be several months old, which meant that she'd rolled out of his bed into someone else's real damn fast. Which made him wonder whether she'd been involved with someone else already when they'd had that last weekend together. That thought chewed on Justice, too. All the time they'd been rolling around in his bed, she'd had another guy waiting for her? What the hell was up with that?

He wanted to shout. To rage. But he didn't. He locked up everything inside him and refused to let her see that he was affected at all. Damned if he'd give her the satisfaction of knowing that she still had the power to cut him.

He had his pride, after all.

"Not going to say anything else?" she asked, swinging her legs off the bed and lifting the baby to sit at her hip.

He wiped one hand across his whiskered jaw and fought for indifference. "What do you want me to say? Congratulations? Fine. I said it." His gaze stayed locked on hers. He wouldn't look at the chubby-cheeked infant making insensible noises and gurgles.

"Don't you want to know who his father is?" she asked, moving closer with small, deliberate steps.

Why the hell was she doing this? Did she really enjoy

rubbing the fact of her new relationship in his face? He hoped she was enjoying the show because, yeah, he did want to know. Then he wanted to find the guy and beat the crap out of him. But that wasn't going to happen. "None of my business, is it?"

"Actually, yes," she said, turning her head to plant a kiss on the baby's brow before looking back at Justice. "It sort of is. Especially since *you're* his father."

Another jolt went through Justice, and he wondered idly how many lightning strikes a man could survive in one night. Whatever game she was trying to run wouldn't work. She didn't have any way of knowing it, of course, but there was no possible way he was that baby's father.

So why the hell would she lie? Was the real father not interested in his kid? Is that why Maggie sought to convince Justice that he was the father instead? Or was it about money? Maybe she was trying to get some child support out of this. That would be stupid, though. All it would take was a paternity test and they'd all know the truth.

Maggie wasn't a fool. Which brought him right back to the question at hand.

What was she up to?

And why?

He stared at her, reading a challenge in her eyes. He still couldn't bring himself to look at the child. It was there, though, in his peripheral vision. A babbling, chortling statement on Justice's failure as a husband and Maggie's desire for family, provided by some other guy.

Pain grabbed at him again, making the constant ache

in his leg seem like nothing more substantial than a stubbed toe.

"Nice try," he said, fixing his gaze on her with a cold distance he hoped was easily read.

"What's that mean?"

"It means, Maggie, I'm *not* his father, so don't bother trying to pawn him off on me."

"Pawn him—" She stopped speaking, gulped in air and tightened her hold on the baby, who was slapping tiny fists against her shoulder. "That's not what I'm trying to do."

"Really?" Justice swallowed past the knot in his throat and managed to give her a tight smile that was more of a baring of his teeth than anything else. "Then why is he here?"

"Because I am, you dolt!" Maggie took another step closer to him, and Justice forced himself to hold his ground. With the weakness in his leg, if he tried to step back, he might just go down on his ass, and wouldn't that be a fine end to an already spectacular day?

"I'm his mother," Maggie told him. "He goes where I go. And I thought maybe his daddy would like a look at him."

One more twist of the knife into his gut. He hadn't been able to give her the one thing she'd really wanted from him. Now seeing her with the child she used to dream of was torture. Especially since she was looking into his eyes and lying.

"I'm not buying it, Maggie, so just drop it, all right? I'm not that kid's father. I'm not anybody's father. So why the song and dance?"

"How can you know you're not?" she argued, clearly willing to stick to whatever game plan she'd had in mind when she got here. "Look at Jonas. Look at him! He has your eyes, Justice. He has your hair. Heck, he's even as stubborn as you are."

As if to prove her point, the baby gave up slapping at her shoulder for attention, reached out and grabbed hold of Maggie's gold, dangling earring. He gave it a tug, squealing in a high-pitched tone that made Justice wince. Gently, Maggie pried that tiny fist off her earring and gave her son a bright smile.

"Don't pull, sweetie," she murmured, and her son cooed at her in delight.

That softness in her voice, the love shining in her eyes, got to him as nothing else could have. Justice swallowed hard and finally forced himself to look at the child. Bright red cheeks, sparkling dark blue eyes and a thatch of black hair. He wore a diaper and a black T-shirt that read Cowboy in Training and was waving and kicking his chubby arms and legs.

Something inside him shifted. If he and Maggie had been able to have children, this is just what he would have expected their child to look like. Maybe that's why she thought her ploy would work on him. The kid looked enough like Justice that she probably thought she could convince him he was the father and then talk him out of a paternity test.

Sure. Why would she think he'd insist on that anyway? They had been married. The timing for the child was about right. She'd have no reason to think that he wouldn't believe her claims. But that meant that whoever had fathered the boy had turned his back on them. Which, weirdly, pissed him off on Maggie's behalf. What the hell kind of man would do that to her? Or to the baby? Who wouldn't claim his own child?

He watched the boy bouncing up and down on Maggie's hip, laughing and drooling, and told himself that if there were even the slightest chance the boy was actually his, Justice would do everything in his power to take care of him. But he knew the truth, even if Maggie didn't.

"He's a good-looking boy."

Maggie melted. "Thank you."

"But he's not mine."

She wanted to argue. He could see it in her face. Hell, he knew her well enough to know that there was nothing Maggie liked more than a good argument. But this one she'd lose before she even started.

He couldn't be Jonas's father. Ten years before, Justice had been in a vicious car accident. His injuries were severe enough to keep him in a hospital for weeks. And during his stay and the interminable testing that was done, a doctor had told him that the accident had left him unlikely to ever father children.

The doctor had used all sorts of complicated medical terms to describe his condition, but the upshot was that Jonas couldn't be his. Maggie had no way of knowing that, of course, since Justice had never told anyone about the doctor's prognosis. Not even his brothers.

Before he and Maggie got married, when she started talking about having a family, he'd told her that he didn't want kids. Better to let her believe he chose to remain childless rather than have her think he was less than a man.

His spine stiffened as that thought scuttled through his brain. He hadn't told her the truth then and he wouldn't now. Damned if he'd see a flash of pity in her eyes for him. Bad enough that she was here to see him struggle to do something as simple as *walk*.

"So who were you with, Maggie?" he asked, his voice a low and dark hum. "Why didn't he want his kid?"

"I was with *you,* you big jerk," she said tightly. "I didn't tell you about the baby before because I assumed from everything you'd said that you wouldn't want to know."

"What's changed, then?" he asked.

"I'm here, Justice. I came here to help you. And I decided that no matter what, you had the right to know about Jonas."

If it were possible, Maggie would have said that Justice's features went even harder. But what was harder than stone? His eyes were flat and dark. His jaw was clenched. He was doing what he always had done. Shutting down. Shutting her out. But why?

Yes, she knew he'd said he didn't want children, but she'd been so sure that the moment he saw his son, he'd feel differently. That Jonas would melt away his father's reservations about having a family.

She'd even, in her wildest fantasies, imagined Justice admitting he was wrong for the first time in his life. In her little dream world, Justice had taken one look at his son, then begged Maggie's forgiveness and asked her to stay, to let them be a family. She should have known better. "Idiot."

"I'm not an idiot," he told her.

"I wasn't talking to you," she countered. He was so close to her and yet so very far away.

The house was quiet, tucked in for the night. Outside the windows was the moonlit darkness, the ever-present sea wind blowing, rattling the windowpanes and sending tree branches scratching against the roof.

Justice stood not a foot from her, close enough that she felt the heat of his body reaching out for her. Close enough that she wanted to lean into him and touch him as she'd wanted to during the therapeutic massage she'd given him earlier.

Instantly, warmth spiraled through her as she remembered his response to her hands moving on the weakened muscles in his leg. His erection hadn't been weak, though, and hadn't been easy to ignore, especially since being near him only made her want the big dummy more than ever.

"Look," Justice muttered, breaking the spell holding Maggie in place, "I'm willing to do the therapy routine. I don't like it, but I need to get back on my feet. If you can help with that, great. But if you staying here is gonna work, you're going to have to drop all of this crap about me being your baby's father. I don't want to hear it again."

"So you want me to lie," she said.

"I want you to stop lying."

"Fine. No lies. You are Jonas's father."

He gritted his teeth and muttered, "Damn it, Maggie!"

"Don't you swear in front of my son." She glanced at Jonas and though he was only six months old, she could see that he was confused and worried about what was happening. His big eyes looked watery, and his lower lip trembled as if he were getting ready to let a wail loose.

Justice barked out a harsh laugh. "You think he understood that?"

She glanced at the baby's big blue eyes, so much like his father's, and stroked a fingertip along his jaw soothingly. "I think he understands tone," she said quietly. "And I don't want you using that tone in front of him."

He blew out a breath, scowled ferociously for a second, then said, "Fine. I won't cuss in front of the kid. But you quit playing games."

"I'm not playing."

"You're doing something, Maggie, and I can tell you now, it's not going to work."

She stared up at him and shook her head. "I knew you were stubborn, Justice, but I never imagined you could be *this* thick-headed."

"And I never figured you for a cheat." He turned and started to painstakingly make his way out of the room into the hall.

Just for a second she watched him walk away and her heart ached at the difficulty he had. Seeing a man as strong and independent as Justice leaning on a cane tore at her. His injuries weren't permanent, but she knew what it was costing his pride to haltingly move away from her.

But though she felt for him, she wasn't about to let him get away with what he'd just said.

"*Cheat?* A cheat?" Maggie inhaled sharply, cast another guilty glance at her son and gave him a smile she didn't feel. She wouldn't upset her baby for the sake of a man who was so blind he couldn't see the truth when it was staring him in the face. "I am not a cheat or a liar, Justice King."

He didn't look back at her. He just kept moving awkwardly down the hall, his cane tapping against the floor runner. If his plan was to escape her, he'd have to be able to move a lot faster than that, Maggie told herself. Quickly, she walked down the hall, stepped out in front of him and forced him to stop.

"Get out of the way," he murmured, staring past her, down the hall at his open bedroom door.

"You can think whatever you like of me, but you will, by God, not ignore me," she told him, and the fact that he kept avoiding meeting her eyes only further infuriated her. This had so not gone the way she'd hoped and expected.

When Jefferson called her, asking her to come help Justice, she'd taken it as a sign. That this was the way they would come together again. That the time was finally right for Justice to meet the son he didn't know about. Apparently, she had been wrong.

"Are you too cowardly to even look at me?" she demanded, knowing that the charge of coward would get his attention.

Instantly, he turned his dark blue gaze on her and she saw carefully banked anger simmering up from their depths. Well, good. At least he was feeling *something*.

"Don't push me, Maggie. For both our sakes. If you want me to watch my tone around your son, then don't you push me."

He was furious—she could see that. But beyond the anger there was hurt. And that tore at her. He didn't have to be hurt, darn it. She was offering him their son, not the plague.

"Justice," she said softly, smoothing one hand up and down her baby's back, "you know me better than anyone. You know I wouldn't lie to you about this. You are my son's father."

He snorted.

Insulted and stung by his obvious distrust, she stepped back from him. How could he believe that she was lying? How could he have ever claimed to love her and *not* know that she was incapable of trying to trick him in this way? What the hell kind of a husband was he, anyway?

"I'm trying to be understanding," she said, but her temper simmered just beneath the words. "I know this is probably all a surprise."

"You could say that."

"But I'm not going to say it to you again. I won't argue. I won't force you to admit your responsibilities—"

"I always face my responsibilities, Maggie. You should know that."

"And you should know I'm not a liar."

He blew out a breath, cocked his head to one side and stared into her eyes. "So what? We call it a draw? A standoff? An armed truce?"

"Call it whatever you want, Justice," Maggie said, before he could say something else that would hurt her. "All I'm going to say is that if you don't believe me about Jonas, then it's your loss, Justice. We created a beautiful, healthy son together. And I love him enough for both of us."

"Maggie…"

She placed one hand on the back of her son's head, holding him to her tenderly. "And in case you were wondering why I waited until now to tell you about Jonas... It's because I was worried about how you'd react." She laughed shortly, sharply. "Imagine that. Wonder why?"

He muttered something under his breath, and judging by the expression on his face, she was just as happy she'd missed it.

"The sad truth is, Justice, I never wanted my son to know that his own father hadn't wanted him."

His eyes went colder, harder than before, and Maggie shivered a little under his direct gaze. A second passed, then two, and neither of them spoke. The hall light was soft and golden, throwing delicate shadows around the wide, empty passage. They were alone in the world, the three of them, with an invisible and apparently impenetrable wall separating Maggie and her son from the man who should have welcomed them with open arms.

At last, Justice turned his gaze to the boy who was watching him curiously. Maggie watched her husband's features soften briefly before freezing up into that hardened, take-no-prisoners expression she knew so well. After several long moments he lifted his gaze to hers, and when he spoke, his voice was so soft she had to hold her breath to hear him.

"You're wrong, Maggie. If I *was* his father, I would want him."

Then he brushed past her, the tip of his cane making a muffled thumping sound as he made his way to his room. He didn't look back.

And that nearly broke Maggie's heart.

Five

"Run the calves and their mamas to the seaward pasture," Justice told Phil, his ranch manager, three days later. "You can leave the young bulls in the canyons for now. Keep them away from the heifers as much as you can."

"I know, boss." Phil turned the brim of his hat between his hands as he stood opposite the massive desk in Justice's study.

Phil was in his early fifties, with a tall, lanky body that belied his strength. He was a no-BS kind of guy who knew his job and loved the ranch almost as much as his boss. Phil's face was tanned as hard and craggy as leather from years spent in the sun. His forehead, though, was a good two shades lighter than the rest of him, since his hat was usually on and pulled down low.

He shifted uneasily from foot to foot, as if eager to get outside and back on his horse.

"We've got most of the herd settled into their pastures now," he said. "There was a fence break in the north field, but two of the boys are out there now fixing it."

"Okay." Justice tapped a pen against the top of his desk and tried to focus the useless energy burning inside him. Sitting behind a desk was making him itchy. If things were as they should be, he'd be out on his own horse right now. Making sure things were getting done to his specifications. Justice wasn't a man to sit inside and order his people around. He preferred having his hand in everything that went on at King Ranch.

Phil Hawkins was a good manager, but he wasn't the boss.

Yet even as he thought it, Justice knew he was lying to himself. His itchy feeling had nothing to do with not trusting his crew. It was all about how he hated being trapped in the damn house. Now more than ever.

The past few days, he'd felt as if he was being stalked. Maggie was following him around, insisting on therapy sessions or swims in the heated pool or nagging at him to use the damn cane he'd come to hate. Hell, he'd had to sneak away just to get a few minutes alone in his office to go over ranch business with Phil.

Everywhere he went, it seemed, there was Maggie. Back in the day, they'd have been falling into each other's arms every other minute. But nothing was as it had once been. These days, she looked at him as if he were just another patient to her. Someone to feel bad for. To fix up. To take care of.

Well, he didn't need taking care of. Or if he did, he'd never admit it. He didn't want her being *paid* to be here. Didn't want to be her latest mission. Her cause. Didn't want her touching him with indifference.

That angry thought flashed through his mind at the same time a twinge of pain sliced at his leg. Damn thing was near useless. And three days of Maggie's torture hadn't brought him any closer to healing and getting on with his life. Instead, she seemed to be settling in. Making herself comfortable in the log house that used to be her home.

She was sliding into the rhythm of ranch life as if she'd never left it. She was up with the dawn every day and blast if it didn't seem she was deliberately close enough to him every morning so that Justice heard her talking to her son. Heard the baby's nonsensical prattle and cooing noises. Could listen in on what he wasn't a part of.

She was everywhere. Her or the baby. Or both. He heard her laughing with Mrs. Carey, smelled her perfume in every room of the house and caught her playing with her son on several occasions. She and the baby had completely taken over his house.

There were toys scattered everywhere, a walker with bells, whistles and electronic voices singing out an alphabet song. There was a squawking chicken, a squeaky dog and a teddy bear with a weird, tinny voice that sang songs about sharing and caring. Hell, coming down the stairs this morning, he'd almost killed himself when his cane had come down on a ball with a clown's face stamped on it. There were cloth books, cardboard books and diapers stashed everywhere just in case the kid needed a change. That boy had to go through a hundred of them a day. And what was with all the books? It was not as if the baby could read.

"Uh, boss?"

"What?" Justice shook his head, rubbed at his aching leg and shifted his gaze back to Phil. That woman was now sneaking into his thoughts so that he couldn't even *talk* about ranch business. "Sorry," he said. "My mind wandered. What?"

Phil's lips twitched as if he knew where his boss's mind had slipped off to. But he was smart enough not to say anything. "The new grasses in the east field are coming in fine, just like you said they would. Looks like a winner to me."

"That's good news," Justice said absentmindedly. They'd replanted one of the pastures with a hardier stock of field grass, and if it held up to its hype, then the herd would have something to look forward to in a few months.

Running an organic cattle ranch was more work, but Justice was convinced it was worth it in the long run. The cowboys he had working for him spent most of their time switching the cattle around to different pastures, keeping the grass fresh and the animals on the move. His cows didn't stand in dirty stalls to be force-fed grains. King cattle roamed open fields as they'd been meant to.

Cattle weren't born to eat corn, for God's sake. They were grazers. And keeping his herds moving across natural field grasses made the meat more tender and sweet and brought higher prices from the consumer. He had almost sixty thousand acres of prime grassland here on the coast and another forty thousand running along-side his cousin Adam's ranch in central California.

Justice had made the change over to natural grazing and organic ranching nearly ten years ago, as soon as he took over the day-to-day running of King Ranch. His father hadn't put much stock in it, but Justice had been determined to run the outfit his way. And in that time, he'd been able to expand and even open his own online beef operation.

He only wished his father had lived to see what he'd made of the place. But his parents had died in the same accident that had claimed Justice's chances of ever making his own family. So he had to content himself with knowing that he'd made a success of the family spread and that his father would have been proud.

"Oh, and we got another offer on Caleb," Phil was saying, and Justice focused on the man.

"What was it?"

"Thirty-five thousand."

"No," Justice told him. "Caleb's too valuable a stud to let him go for that. If the would-be buyer wants to pay for calves out of Caleb, we'll do that. But we're not selling our top breeding bull."

Phil grinned. "That's what I told him."

Some of Justice's competitors were more convinced it was his breeding stock that made his cattle so much better than others, and they were continually trying to buy bulls. They were either too stupid or too lazy to realize that fresh calves weren't going to change anything. To get the results Justice had, they were going to have to redo their operations completely.

The door to the study swung open after a perfunctory knock, and both men turned to look. Maggie stood in the open doorway. Faded jeans clung to her legs and the King Cattle T-shirt she wore in bright blue made her eyes shine like sapphires. She gave Phil a big smile. "You guys finished?"

"Yes, ma'am," Phil said.

"No," Justice said.

His ranch manager winced a little as he realized that he'd blown things for his boss.

Maggie looked at her husband. "Which is it? Yes or no?"

Frowning, Justice scowled at his foreman, silently calling him *traitor*. Phil just shrugged, though, as if to say it was too late now.

"We're finished for the time being," Justice reluctantly admitted.

"Good. Time for your exercises," Maggie told him, walking into the room and heading for his desk.

"Then I'll just go—" Phil waved his hat in the direction of the door "—back to work." He nodded at her. "Maggie, good to see you."

"You, too," she said, giving the other man the kind of brilliant smile that Justice hadn't seen directed at him in far too long.

"He hasn't changed at all," Maggie mused.

"You haven't been gone that long."

"Funny," she said, "feels like a lifetime to me."

"I guess it would." Justice didn't want her in here.

This was his office. His retreat. The one room in the whole place that hadn't been colored by her scent. By her presence. But it was too late now.

As she wandered the room, running her fingertips across the leather spines of the books in the shelves, he told himself that from now on, he'd see her here. He'd feel her here. He'd be able to close his eyes and imagine her with him, the sound of her voice, the sway of her hips, the way the sunlight through the window made her hair shine like a fire at midnight.

Squirming uncomfortably in his chair now, Justice said, "You know, if you don't mind, I've got some paperwork to catch up on. Things pile up if you don't stay on top of them. Think I'll skip the exercises this morning."

She gave him the sort of smile she would have given a little boy trying to get away with cutting school. "I don't think so. But if you want, we can change things up a little. Instead of a half hour on the treadmill, we could walk around the ranch yard."

Sounded like a plan to him. He hated that damn treadmill with a raging passion. What the hell good was it, when a man had the whole world to walk in? Who would choose to walk on a conveyor belt? And if she didn't have him on that treadmill, she had him doing lunges and squats, with his back up against the wall. He felt like a lab rat, moving from one maze to the next. Always inside. Always moving and getting exactly nowhere.

The thought of getting outside was a blessing. Outside. Into the air, where her perfume would get lost in the wind rather than clinging to every breath he took. "Fine."

He pushed up from his black leather chair, and as he

stepped around the edge of the desk, Maggie approached and held out his cane. He took it, his fingers brushing against hers just enough to kindle a brand-new fire in his gut. He pulled back, tightened his grip on the head of the blasted cane and started for the door.

"You're walking easier," she noted.

Irritation spiked inside him. He remembered a time when she had watched his ass for a different reason. "Yeah," he admitted. "It still hurts like a bitch, but maybe it's a little better."

"Wow. Quite the compliment to my skills."

He stopped and turned to look at her. "Maybe I'm doing well enough to just cut the therapy short."

"Ooh, good effort," she said and walked past him toward the front door.

Now it was his turn to watch her ass, and he for damn sure wasn't doing it to check out her ability to walk. Then something struck him: the fact that she didn't have her son on her hip. "Uh, don't you have to watch…"

"Jonas?" she provided.

"Yeah."

"Mrs. Carey has him. She loves watching him," Maggie said, striding down the hall to the front door. Her boots, which clacked against the wood floor, sounded like a quickening heartbeat. "Says he reminds her so much of you it's almost eerie."

Justice scowled at her back. She managed to get one or two of those pointed digs in every day. Trying to make him see something that wasn't there. A connection between her son and him.

He should just tell her, he thought, snatching his

battered gray felt hat off the hook by the door. Tell her that he was sterile and be done with it. Then she could stop playing whatever game she was playing and he wouldn't have to put up with any of this anymore.

But if he did that, she'd know. Know everything. Why he'd let her go. Why he'd lied. Why he felt less than a man because he hadn't been able to give her the one thing she'd wanted. And, damn it, once he told her the truth, she'd feel sorry for him—and he couldn't stand that. Better for him if she thought him a bastard.

Maggie listened to the uncertain steps of her husband coming up behind her and stopped on the porch to wait for him. She took that moment to admire the sweep of land stretching out in front of her. She'd missed this place almost as much as she'd missed Justice. The wide yard was neatly tended, the flower beds were spilling over with bright, colorful blossoms and from somewhere close by, the lowing of a cow sounded almost like a song.

Just for a second or two, all of Maggie's thoughts and worries drifted away, just drained out of her system as if they'd never been there. She took a deep breath of the sweet air and smiled at two herd dogs, a mutt and a Lab, chasing each other across the front yard. Then she sensed Justice coming up behind her, and in an instant tension coiled deep in the pit of her stomach.

She would always sense him. Always be aware of him on a deep, cellular level. He touched something inside her that no one else ever had. And when they were apart, she felt his absence keenly. But feeling connected to a man who clearly didn't share the sentiment was just a recipe for disaster.

"It's really beautiful," she whispered.

"It is."

His deep voice rumbled along her spine and tingled through her system. Why did it have to be *him* who did this to her? she wondered and glanced over her shoulder at him. He wasn't looking at the ranch; he was watching her, and her knees went a little wobbly. Maggie had to lock them just to keep upright. The man's eyes should be illegal. His smile was even more lethal—thank heaven she didn't see it often.

"You used to love it here," he said quietly, letting his gaze slide from her to where the dogs chased each other in dizzying circles.

"I did," she admitted and took a deep breath.

From the moment she had first seen this ranch, it had felt like home to her. As if it had only been waiting for her to arrive, the ranch had welcomed her. Maggie had always been amazed that she could stand on her porch and feel as though she were in the middle of the country, when in reality the city was just a short freeway ride away.

Here on the King Ranch it was as if time had not exactly stood still but at least had taken a break, slowed down. She'd always thought this would be a perfect place for her children to grow up. She'd imagined watching four or five King kids racing through the yard laughing, running to her and Justice for hugs and kisses and growing up learning to care for the ranch as much as their father did.

But those dreams had died the night she'd left Justice so many months ago.

Now she was nothing more than a barely tolerated visitor, and Jonas would never know what it was like to grow up among his father's memories.

Or to grow up with his father's love.

Justice was deliberately closing himself off from not only her but also the child they'd made together. That was something she couldn't forgive. Or understand. Justice had always been a hard man, but he was also a man devoted to family. To his brothers and the King heritage. So how could he turn his back on his own son?

In the past three days, Justice had done everything in his power to avoid so much as being in the same room with Jonas. Her heart twisted painfully in her chest, but she wouldn't *force* him to care, even if she could. Because then his love wouldn't mean a thing. To her or her son. So she would be professional and keep her emotions tightly leashed if it killed her.

"Loving this place didn't keep you here," he pointed out unnecessarily.

"No, it didn't," she said. "It couldn't."

He shook his head and frowned, squinting out from beneath the brim of his hat. "It could have. You chose to leave."

"I'm not going over that same old argument again, Justice."

"Me neither," he said with a shrug. "I'm just reminding you."

Maggie inhaled slowly, deeply. She told herself to bank her temper, to not let him get to her. It wasn't easy, especially since Justice had always known exactly which of her buttons to push to get a reaction. But as satisfying as it would be to shout and rage and give in to her frustration by telling him just what she was thinking, it wouldn't do a darn bit of good.

"We should walk." She spoke up fast, before her temper could override her more rational side. Then she turned to offer him her arm so she could assist him getting down the short flight of steps leading from the porch to the yard.

Instantly, he scowled at her and stepped around her, the tip of his cane slamming down onto the porch. "I'm not completely helpless, Maggie. I can get around without holding on to your arm. You're half my size."

"And trained to help ambulatory patients get around. I'm stronger than I look, Justice. You should remember that."

He shot her one hard, stony glare. "I'm not one of your patients, damn it."

"Well, yeah," she countered, feeling the first threads of her patience begin to unravel, "technically, you are."

"I don't want to be—don't you get that?"

She felt the cold of his stare slice right into her, but Maggie had practice in facing down his crab-ass attitude. "Yes, Justice. I get it. Despite the great trouble you've taken in trying to hide how you feel about me being here, I get it."

His mouth flattened into a grim line, and she glared right back at him.

"You still won't leave, though, will you?"

"No. I won't. Not until you're on the mend."

"I am mending."

"Not fast enough and you know it. So suck it up and let's get the job done, all right?"

"Stubbornest damn woman I've ever known," he muttered darkly and, using his cane to take most of his weight, took the steps to the drive. The minute his feet hit the drive, both ranch dogs stopped their playing, leaped up, ears perked, then with yips of delight, charged at him.

"Oh, for heaven's sake." Maggie jumped out in front of him to keep the too-exuberant dogs from crashing into Justice and bowling him right over, but it wasn't necessary.

"Angel. Spike." Justice's voice was like thunder, and when he snapped his fingers, both dogs instantly obeyed. As one, they skidded to a stop and dropped to the ground, their chins on their front paws as they looked up at him.

Maggie laughed in spite of herself. Going down on one knee, she petted each of the dogs in turn, then looked up at the man watching her. "I'd forgotten just how good you were at that. The dogs always did listen to you."

One corner of his mouth quirked briefly. "Too bad I could never get you to do the same."

Straightening up, Maggie met his gaze. "I never was the kind of woman to jump at the snap of your fingers, Justice. Not for you, not for anyone."

"Wouldn't have had you jump," he told her.

"Really. And what command would you have had me follow if you could?"

He shifted his gaze from hers, looked toward the barn and the pastures beyond and said softly, "Stay."

Six

A ping of regret echoed inside Maggie at his statement, sending out ripples of reaction like the energy released when a tuning fork was struck. Her entire body seemed to ache as she watched him walk away, keeping his gaze averted.

"You would have told me to stay?" she repeated, hearing the break in her own voice and hating it. "How can you say that to me now?"

He didn't answer her, just kept walking slowly, carefully. The only sign of his own emotions being engaged was how tightly he held on to his cane. Maggie's back teeth ground together. The man was just infuriating. She could tell that he was regretting what he had said, but that was just too bad for him.

The first time she'd walked away from him and their

marriage, it had nearly ripped her heart out of her chest. He hadn't said a word to her. He'd watched her go, and she'd felt then that he hadn't really cared. She'd told herself through her tears that clearly their marriage hadn't been everything she'd thought it was. That the dream of family she was giving up on had been based in her own fantasies, not reality.

She'd thought that Justice couldn't possibly have loved her as much as she loved him. Not if he could let her go without a word.

Then months later, they shared that last weekend together—and created Jonas—and still, he'd let her go. He'd stayed crouched behind his walls and locked away whatever he was thinking or feeling. He'd simply shot down her dreams again and dismissed her.

And even then she hadn't been able to file the signed divorce papers when he'd returned them to her. Instead, she'd tucked them away, gone through her pregnancy, delivered their son and waited. Hoping that Justice would come to her.

Naturally, he hadn't.

"How could you do it?" she whispered and thought she saw his shoulders flinch. "How could you let me leave when you wanted me to stay? Why, Justice? You didn't say a *word* to me when I left. Either time."

He stopped dead and even the cool wind sliding in off the ocean seemed to still. The dogs went quiet and it felt as if the world had taken a breath and held it.

"What was there to say?" His jaw tightened and he bit off each word as if it tasted bitter.

"You could have asked me to stay."

"No," he said, heading once more for the barn. "I couldn't."

Maggie sighed and walked after him, measuring her steps to match his more halting ones. Of course he couldn't ask her to stay, she thought.

"Oh, no, not you. Not Justice King," she grumbled and kicked at the dirt. "Don't want anyone to know you're actually capable of feeling something."

He stopped again and this time he turned his head to look at her. "I feel plenty, Maggie," he said. "You should know that better than anyone."

"How can I know that, Justice?" She threw her hands high, then let them fall to her sides again. "You won't tell me what you're thinking. You never did. We laughed, we made love but you never let me *inside,* Justice. Not once."

Something in his dark blue eyes flashed. "You got in. You just didn't stay long enough to notice."

Had she? She couldn't be sure. In the beginning of their marriage, it was all heat and fire. They hadn't been able to keep their hands off each other. They took long rides, they spent lazy rainy days in bed and Maggie would have told anyone who had asked that she and Justice were truly happy.

But, God knew, it hadn't taken much to shake the foundations of what they'd shared, so how real could any of it have been?

Her shoulders slumped as she watched him continue on to the barn. He held himself straighter, taller, as if knowing she'd be watching and not wanting to look anything but his usual, strong self. How typical was that, Maggie thought.

Justice King never admitted weakness. He'd always been a man unable to ask for anything—not even for help if he needed it—because he would never acknowledge needing assistance in the first place. He was always so self-reliant that it was nearly a religion to him. She'd known that from the beginning of their relationship, and still she wished things had been different.

But if wishes were horses, as the old saying went…

Maggie was shaken and not too proud to admit it, at least to herself. Pushing her turbulent thoughts to a back corner of her mind to be examined later, she took a deep breath, forced some lightheartedness into her voice and quickly changed the subject.

"So," she asked, glancing back at the two dogs trotting behind them, "why are Angel and Spike here instead of out with the herd?"

There was a pause before he answered, as if he were grateful for the reprieve.

"We're training two new dogs to help out," he said. "Phil thought it best to give these two a couple days off while the new pups are put through their paces."

She'd been a rancher's wife long enough to know the value of herd dogs. When the dogs worked the cattle, they could get into tight places a cowboy and his horse couldn't. The right dog could get a herd moving and keep it moving while never scaring the cattle into a stampede, which could cause injury both to cowboys and to herd. These dogs were well trained and were spoiled rotten by the cowboys, as she remembered. She'd teased Justice once that apparently sheepherders had been right about using dogs in their work and that finally ranchers had caught on.

She smiled, remembering how Justice had reacted—chasing her through the house and up the stairs, laughing, until he'd caught up to her in their bedroom. Then he'd spent the next several hours convincing her to take it back. No cattleman alive had ever taken advice from a sheepherder, he'd told her, least of all him.

Spike and Angel darted past Justice and Maggie, heading through the open doors of a barn that was two stories tall and built to match the main house's log construction. The shadows were deep, and the only sound coming from the barn was that deep, insistent lowing Maggie had heard earlier.

"Hey, you two, come away from there!" A sudden shout came from inside the barn, and almost instantly both dogs scuttled back outside and took off in a fast lope across the dirt. If they'd been children, Maggie was sure they would have been laughing.

"What's that about?" she asked, watching the dogs race each other to the water tank kept as a sort of swimming pool for herd dogs.

"Mike's got a cow and her calf in there. Probably didn't want the dogs getting too close," Justice told her, walking through the barn to the last stall on the right. There he leaned one arm on the top of the wood partition, clearly to take some weight off his leg, and watched as an older man expertly ran his hands up and down a nearly three-month-old calf's foreleg.

"How's he doing?"

"Better," Mike said, without looking up. "Swelling's down, so he and his mama can go back out to pasture tomorrow." Then he did lift his gaze and smiled when he spotted Maggie. "Well, now, you're a sight for sore eyes. Good to see you back home, Maggie."

"Thanks, Mike." She'd gotten more of a welcome from the cowboys and hired hands than she had from her own husband, she thought wryly. "So what happened to this little guy?"

Maggie wandered into the stall, keeping one wary eye on the calf's mother, then sank to one knee beside the smaller animal. He was, like most of Justice's herd, Black Angus. His black hide was the color of the shadows filling the barn, and his big brown eyes watched her with interest.

"Not sure, really," Mike said. "One of the boys saw the little guy limping out on the range, so he brought them in. But whatever was wrong, looks like it's all right now."

The calf wasn't small anymore. He was about six months old and wearing the King Ranch brand on his flank. He was well on his way to being the size of his father, which would put him, full grown, at about eleven hundred pounds. But the way he cuddled up to his mother, looking for food and comfort, made him seem like little more than an overlarge puppy.

The mingled aromas of hay and leather and cow mingled together in the vast barn and somehow made a soothing sort of scent. Maggie never would have believed she was capable of thinking that, since before meeting and marrying Justice, she had been a devout city girl. She'd once thought that there was nothing lovelier than a crowded shopping mall with a good-size latte stand. She had never liked the outdoors as a kid and had considered staying in a motel as close to camping as she ever wanted to get.

And yet being on the King Ranch had been so easy. Was it just because she'd loved Justice so much? Or was it because her heart had finally figured out where she belonged?

But then, she asked herself sadly, what did it matter now?

"See you later, Mike," she said, then tugged at Justice's arm. "Let's get you moving again. Gotta get your exercise in whether you want to or not."

"I never noticed that slave-driver mentality of yours before," Justice muttered as they left the barn and wandered around the side of the main house.

"You just didn't pay attention," she told him. "It was always there."

He was moving less easily, she noticed, and instinctively she slowed her pace. He fell into her rhythm and his steps evened out again. She knew how much he hated this. Knew that he detested having to depend on others to do things for him. And she knew he was in pain, though heaven knew he'd be roasted over live coals and still not admit to that. So she started talking, filling the silence so he would have to concentrate on something other than how hard it was to walk.

"Phil said you planted new grasses?" That was a brilliant stroke, Maggie thought. Get the man talking about the ranch and the prairie grass pastures and he'd get so involved, he wouldn't notice anything else. Not even pain.

"On the high pasture," he told her, easing around the corner of the log house to walk toward a rose garden that had originally been planted by his mother. "With the herd rotation, we'll keep the cattle off that grass until winter, and if it holds and we get some rain this fall, we'll have plenty of rich feed for the herd."

"Sounds good," she murmured, knowing her input wasn't needed.

"It was a risk, taking the cattle off that section early in the rotation, but we wanted to try out the new grasses and it had to have time to settle in and grow before winter, so…" He shrugged, looked down at her and unexpectedly smiled. "You're taking my mind off my leg, aren't you?"

"Well," she said, enjoying the full measure of a Justice King smile for as long as she could, "yeah. I am. Is it working?"

"It is," he said with a nod. "But I'm going to stop talking about it before you fall asleep while walking."

"It was interesting," she argued.

"Sure. That's why your eyes are glazed over."

Maggie sighed. "Okay, so the pastures aren't exactly thrilling conversational tidbits. But if you're talking about the ranch, you're not thinking about your leg."

He stopped, reached down and rubbed his thigh as if just the mention of it had fired up the aching muscles. He tipped his head back and looked up at the sky, a broad expanse of blue, dotted with thick white clouds. "I'm tired of thinking about my leg. Tired of the cane. Tired of being in the house when I should be on the ranch."

"Justice—"

"It's all right, Maggie," he said with a shake of his head. "I'm just impatient, that's all."

She nodded, understanding. She'd seen this before, usually in men, but some women had the same reaction. They felt as though their worlds would fall apart and crash if they weren't on top of everything at all times. Only they were capable of running their business, their homes, their children. It was a hard thing to accept help, especially since it meant also accepting that you could be replaced. However briefly.

"The garden looks good," she said abruptly.

He turned his head to look. "It does. Mom's roses are just starting to bloom."

Maggie led the way down the wide dirt path, lined on either side by pale, cream-colored bricks. The perfume of the roses was thicker the farther they went into the garden, and she inhaled deeply, dragging that scent into her lungs.

The rose garden spread out just behind the ranch house. A huge flagstone patio off the kitchen and great room led directly here, and Maggie had often had her morning coffee at the kitchen table, staring out at the garden Justice said his mother had loved.

The garden was laid out in circles, each round containing a different color and kind of rose. Justice's mother had turned this section of the ranch into a spring and summer wonder. Soon, Maggie knew, the garden would be bursting with color and scent.

She heard him behind her and turned to look at him. Behind him, the house sat, windows glistening in the sun. To her right was a stone bench, and she heard the splash of the water from the fountain that sat directly in the middle of the garden.

Justice was looking at her through narrowed eyes and, not for the first time, Maggie wondered what he was thinking about. What he saw when he looked at her. Did he have the same regrets she did? When he looked at the roses his mother had planted, did he see Maggie there, too? Was she imprinted on this house, his memories? Or had she become someone he didn't *want* to think about at all?

Well, that was depressing, she told herself and shook off the feeling deliberately. Instead, she cocked her head to one side, looked up at him and asked, "Do you remember that summer storm?"

After a second or two, he smiled and nodded. "Hard to forget that one." He glanced around at the neatly laid out flower beds, then kicked at one of the bricks at his feet. "It's the reason we laid these bricks, remember?"

A soft wind blew in and lifted her hair off her neck and Maggie grinned. "How could I forget? It rained so hard the roses were coming up out of the ground." She looked around and saw the place as it had been that long-ago night. "The ground couldn't hold any more water. And the roots of the bushes were pulling up just from the weight of the bushes themselves." She and Justice had raced outside, determined to save his mother's garden. "We were running around here for two hours, in the rain and the mud, propping up the rose bushes, trying to keep them all from being washed away."

"We did it, too," he mused, looking around now, as if reassuring himself that they'd been successful.

"Yeah, we did." She took a breath and asked, "Remember how we celebrated?"

His gaze fixed on hers, and she felt the heat of that stare slide right down into her bones. "You mean how we made love out here, covered in mud, laughing like loons?"

"Yes," she said, "that's what I mean." She took an instinctive step toward him. The past mingled with the present, memory tangling with fresh need. Her mouth went dry, her insides melted and something low and deep within her pulsed with desire. Passion. She remembered the feel of his hands on her. The taste of his mouth on hers. The heavy weight of him pressing her down, into cold, sodden earth. And she remembered she hadn't felt the cold. Hadn't noticed the rain. All she'd been aware of was Justice.

Some things didn't change.

The sun was blazing out of a spring sky. They were on opposite sides of a very large fence that snaked between them. Their marriage was supposedly over, and all that was keeping her here on the ranch was the fact that he needed her to help him be whole again.

And yet, none of that mattered.

She took another step toward him. He moved closer, too, his gaze locked on hers, heat sizzling in those dark blue depths until Maggie almost needed to fan herself. What he wanted was there on his face. As she was sure it was on hers. She needed him. Always had. Probably always would.

Standing here surrounded by memories was just stoking those needs, magnifying them with the images from the past. She didn't care. Maggie lifted one hand, cupped his cheek in her palm and felt the scratch of beard stubble against her skin. It felt good. Right. He closed his eyes at her touch, blew out a breath and moved even closer to her.

"Maggie…"

A baby's cry broke them apart.

Jolting, Maggie turned toward the sound and saw Mrs. Carey hurrying across the patio and down the steps, carrying a very fussy Jonas on her hip. The older woman had cropped gray hair and was wearing jeans and a long-sleeved T-shirt. Her tennis shoes didn't make a sound as she scurried toward them, an apologetic expression on her face.

Maggie walked to meet the woman, holding out her arms for her son. Jonas practically flung himself at his mother and wrapped his arms around her neck.

"I'm so sorry for interrupting," Mrs. Carey said, glancing from Maggie to Justice with a shrug. "But Jonas looked out the window, saw his mama and there was just no holding him back."

"It's okay, Mrs. Carey," Maggie told her, running one hand up and down her son's back in a soothing gesture that was already quieting the baby's cries and sniffles. The look on the housekeeper's face told Maggie she *really* regretted interrupting whatever had been going on. But maybe it was for the best, she thought. Maybe things would have gotten even more complicated if she and Justice had allowed themselves to be swept away by memories.

It only took another moment for Jonas to lift his head from Maggie's shoulder and give her a watery smile. "There now, no reason to cry, is there, little man?"

Jonas huffed out a tiny breath, grabbed hold of one

of Maggie's earrings, then turned his victorious smile on Justice and Mrs. Carey. As if he were saying, *See? I have my mommy. Just like I wanted.*

Justice moved off a little and sat down hard on the stone bench. "I'm done exercising, Maggie. Why don't you take your son into the house?"

Mrs. Carey, standing behind her boss, made a face at him that almost set Maggie laughing. But the truth was she was just too torn to smile about the situation. There her stubborn husband sat, with his son within arm's reach, and Justice had withdrawn from them. Sealed himself off behind that damn wall of his. Well, Maggie thought, maybe it was past time she tore some of that wall down. Whether he liked it or not.

Giving into the urge, Maggie jostled Jonas on her hip a bit, then asked, "Jonas, you want to go see your daddy?"

Justice's head snapped up and his eyes were wide and horrified briefly before they narrowed into dangerous slits. "I'm not his daddy."

"You are the most hardheaded, stubborn, foolish man I have ever known," Mrs. Carey muttered darkly. "Not enough sense to see the truth even when it's staring right at you with your own eyes."

"You might want to remember who you work for," Justice told her without looking at her, keeping his eyes fixed on Maggie and the boy.

"I believe I just described who I work for," Mrs. Carey told him. "Now I'm going back to the kitchen. Put a roast in for dinner."

When she was gone, Maggie stared at Justice for another minute, while the baby laughed and babbled to himself. But her mind was made up. She was going to force Justice to acknowledge their son. No more of this letting him avoid the baby, scuttling out of rooms just as she entered. No more walking a wide berth around the situation. It was time for him to be shaken up a bit. And there was no better way to do it than this.

"Here you go, sweetie. Go see your daddy." Maggie swung Jonas down and before Justice could get off the bench, she plopped the baby into his lap.

Both baby and man wore the same startled expression, and they looked so much alike that Maggie actually laughed.

Justice didn't hear her. He was holding his breath and watching the baby on his lap as if it were a live grenade. He expected the tiny boy to start shrieking in protest at being handed over to a stranger. But instead, Jonas looked up at him and a slow, cautious smile curved his tiny mouth.

He had two teeth, on the bottom, Justice noted, and a stream of drool sliding out of his mouth. His hair was black, his eyes a dark blue and his arms and legs were chubby pistons, moving at an incredible rate. Justice kept one hand on the boy's back and felt the rapid beat of the baby's heart beneath his hand.

For days he'd steered clear of the child, told himself the baby was none of his concern. He hadn't wanted to be touched by the child. Hadn't wanted to look at Jonas and know that Maggie had found what she needed with some other man. Staying away had been much easier.

Yet now, as he considered that, he realized that for the first time in his life, he'd behaved like a coward.

He'd run from the child and what he meant to save his own ass. To protect himself.

What did that say about him?

Jonas laughed and Justice turned his attention to Maggie, who was watching them both with tears in her eyes. His heart turned over in his chest, and just for an instant he let himself believe it was real. That he and Maggie were together again. That Jonas was his son.

Then the sound of a car engine out front shattered the quiet. A moment later that engine was shut off and the solid slam of a car door followed. Before he could wonder who had arrived, Mrs. Carey shouted from inside, "Jesse and Bella are here!"

Justice stared up at Maggie, the moment over. "Take the baby."

Seven

"I can't tell you how glad I'll be to finally have this baby," Bella said with a groan as she eased back into one of the comfy chairs in the great room. Her long, dark hair lay across her shoulder in a thick braid and silver hoops winked from her ears. A wry smile curved her mouth as she ran one hand over her belly. "It's not all about wanting to sleep on my stomach again, though. I'm just so anxious to meet whoever's in there."

"You didn't find out the baby's sex?" Mrs. Carey asked.

"No," Bella said. "We decided to be surprised."

Maggie grinned. She'd felt the same way. She hadn't wanted to know the sex of her baby before she saw him for the first time. And she remembered all too clearly what the last couple of weeks of pregnancy were like. No wonder Bella was fidgety. There was the discomfort, of course. But more than that, there was a sense of breathless expectation that clung to every moment.

"And," Bella was saying, "I don't think Jesse can take much more of this. The man's on a constant red alert. Every time I breathe too deeply, he bolts for the phone, ready to call 911. He's so nervous that he's awake every couple of hours during the night, waking me up to make sure I'm all right."

"That's just as it should be," Mrs. Carey said, from her seat on the couch, where she held Jonas in the crook of her arm and fed him his afternoon bottle. "A man should be wrapped up in the birth of his child." She sniffed. "Some men, at least, know what to do."

It was really nice having the King family housekeeper on her side, Maggie mused, but at the same time, she felt she owed Justice some sort of defense.

"To be fair," Maggie said, "Justice didn't know I was pregnant."

"Would have if he hadn't been too stubborn to go after you in the first place," she countered with a sharp nod that said, that's all there is to it. "If he had, then you would have been here, at home while you were carrying this little sweetheart. And I wouldn't have had to wait so long to meet him."

It would have been nice, Maggie thought, to have been here, surrounded by love and concern during her pregnancy. Instead, she'd lived alone, in her apartment a half hour away in Long Beach. Thank God she'd had her own family for support.

"I can't believe you went through your whole pregnancy on your own," Bella said softly, her hands still moving restlessly over the mound of her belly. "I don't know what I would have done without Jesse."

"It wasn't easy," Maggie admitted, pouring Bella another glass of lemonade before slumping back into her own chair. She shot a quick look at her baby, happily ensconced in Mrs. Carey's arms, and remembered those months of loneliness. She'd missed Justice so much then and had nearly called him dozens of times. But her own pride had discounted that notion every time it presented itself. "I had my family," she said, reminding herself that she'd never really been completely alone. Besides, she didn't want these women feeling sorry for her. She hadn't had Justice with her, but she hadn't been miserable the whole time, either.

"That's good," Bella said softly, as if she understood exactly what Maggie was trying to do.

"My parents live in Arizona, but they were on the phone all the time and were really supportive. Both of my sisters were fabulous." Maggie grinned suddenly with a memory. "My sister Mary Theresa was even in the delivery room with me. Matrice was great, really. Don't know what I would have done without her there."

"I'm glad you weren't alone," Mrs. Carey said quietly, "but a woman should have her man at her side when her children are born."

In a perfect world, Maggie thought but didn't say. Instead, she sighed and said, "I wanted to tell him. I really did. But at the same time, Justice had already told me that he didn't want children."

Mrs. Carey snorted. "Darn fool. Don't know why he'd say that raised in this family, one of four kids. Why wouldn't he want children? Especially," she added, bending to kiss Jonas's forehead, "this little darling."

Maggie gave her a smile, delighted that Jonas had an honorary grandmother to dote on him. "I didn't understand why, either, but he'd made himself clear. So I couldn't very well show up here pregnant knowing how he felt about it. And besides…"

"You wanted him to want you for *you*, not for the baby," Bella said for her.

"Exactly," Maggie said on another sigh. She may have just met Bella King, but she had a feeling the two of them could be very close friends. But that wasn't likely to happen either, since the minute Justice recovered, she'd be leaving again—and this time she knew it would be for good. There'd be no coming back here, not if Justice could turn his back on his son.

With a heavy heart, Maggie glanced around the room and idly noted the splash of sunshine lying across polished floors and gleaming tables. The scent of freshly cut flowers hung in the air, and the only sounds were those made by her hungry son as he devoted himself to his snack.

"I understand that completely," Bella told her. "If I'd been in your situation, I would have done the same thing. You know, Jesse told me how happy you and his brother were together. And I can tell you he was really surprised when you two split up."

Mrs. Carey huffed out a disgusted breath.

"He wasn't the only one." Maggie felt a quick sting of tears behind her eyes, and she blinked fiercely to keep them at bay. The time for tears was long past. "I

would never have believed that Justice and I wouldn't
be together forever. But he's just so darn…"

"Stubborn. Bullheaded," Mrs. Carey supplied.

"That about covers it," Maggie said with a laugh,
relieved to feel her emotions settle again.

"So is Jesse," Bella said, then went on to describe
life with a husband who rarely let her walk across the
room without an escort. She started in by telling them
how her office at King Beach had been outfitted with
a resting chaise and that Jesse made sure she took a nap
every afternoon.

While Maggie listened, she tried to hide the pain she
felt. The envy, wrapping itself around her heart, for
what Bella shared with her husband. Jesse had already
come into the room twice in the past hour, ordering his
wife to put her feet up, getting her a pillow for her
aching back.

It was easy to imagine that Bella's whole pregnancy had been like that. With her eager, loving
husband dancing attendance on her. And Maggie
couldn't help but remember what her own pregnancy
had been like. Sure, she'd had her parents and her
sisters, but she hadn't had Justice. She hadn't had the
luxury of lying in bed beside the father of her child
while they spun daydreams about their baby's future.
She hadn't been able to share the excitement of a new
ultrasound photo. Hadn't been able to hold Justice's
hand to her belly so that he could feel Jonas moving
around inside her.

They'd both missed so much. Maybe she should have
come to Justice immediately on finding out she was

pregnant. Maybe she should have given him the chance then to acknowledge their child, to let them both into his life. But she'd been so sure she wouldn't be welcome. And frankly, his actions over the past few days supported her decision.

But then she remembered the look in Justice's eyes just an hour or so ago when she'd dropped Jonas into his lap. There had been an unexpected tenderness on his face, underlying the surprise and wariness. Maybe, she thought wistfully, if she'd just stood her ground long ago, things might have been different. Now, though, she'd never know for sure.

"You all right, honey?"

Mrs. Carey's concerned voice brought Maggie out of her thoughts to focus on what was happening. She shot a look at Bella in time to see a quick flash of pain dart over her features. "Bella?"

"I'm okay," she said, taking a deep breath. "It's just that my back's been bothering me all day. Probably just spasms from carrying around all this extra weight."

"A backache?" Maggie asked.

"All day?" Mrs. Carey added.

Bella grimaced, then said, "I probably just need another cookie."

"Um," Maggie started, "just when exactly are you due, Bella?"

"Oh, not for two weeks yet." She groaned a little as she pushed herself forward to reach for the plate on the table in front of her.

Maggie and Mrs. Carey exchanged a long, knowing look.

* * *

"You're crazy, you know that, right?" Jesse took a long pull of his beer and stretched his legs out in front of him, crossing them at the ankle.

Justice shot a look at his younger brother in time to see him shaking his head in disgust. The sun was hot, the breeze was cool and the patio was empty except for him and Jesse.

Maggie, Bella and Mrs. Carey were all in the house cooing over Jonas and talking about Bella's due-any-minute baby. He scowled to himself and took a drink of his own beer. Justice and Maggie had already legally separated by the time Bella and Jesse got together, but you wouldn't have known it from the way Maggie and Bella had instantly bonded. They were like two old friends already, and their chatter had eventually chased Jesse and Justice out to the patio for some quiet.

At least, that had been the plan.

"Crazy? Me?" Justice laughed shortly. "I'm not the one hauling my extremely pregnant wife around when she should be at home."

"Bella gets antsy sitting around the house. Besides, we're only forty minutes from the hospital—and you're changing the subject."

"Damn straight. Take the hint."

Jesse grinned, completely unfazed by Justice's snarl. "Why should I?"

"Because it's none of your business."

"When's that ever stopped a King?"

True, Justice thought. Never had a King been born who knew enough to keep his nose out of his brother's business.

"Look," Jesse said, "Jeff called, told me he'd hired Maggie, so I thought I'd bring Bella over to meet her sister-in-law. Nobody told me you had a son."

"I don't."

Laughing shortly, Jesse said, "You're so busy being a tight ass you don't even see it, do you?"

"I'm not talking about this with you, Jesse."

"Fine. Then I'll talk. You listen."

A cloud scudded across the sun, tossing the patio into shadow and dropping the temperature suddenly. Justice frowned at his brother, but Jesse paid no attention. He sat up, braced his forearms on his thighs and held his beer bottle between his palms. "I thought your leg was hurt, not your eyes."

"What's that supposed to mean?"

"It means, you dumb jerk, that Jonas looks just like you and you'd have to be blind not to see it."

"Black hair and blue eyes doesn't make him mine."

"It's more than that and you know it. The shape of his face. His nose. His hands. Damn it, Justice, he's a carbon copy of you."

"He can't be."

"Why the hell not?" Jesse's voice dropped and his gaze narrowed. "Why can't he be your son?"

Irritated beyond measure, pushed beyond endurance, Justice awkwardly got out of his chair and grabbed for his hated cane. Then he walked a few uneasy steps away from Jesse, stared out at the rose garden and told his brother what he'd never told another living soul before.

"Because I can't have kids."

"Says who?"

Justice choked out a laugh. Figured Jesse wouldn't react with any kind of tact. Just accept what his brother said and let it go. "A doctor. Right after the accident that killed Mom and Dad and laid me up for weeks."

"You never said anything."

He laughed again, a sound that was harsh and miserable even to his own ears. "Would you have?"

"No," Jesse said, standing up to walk to his side. "I guess not. But, Justice, doctors make mistakes."

He took a drink of his beer, letting the frothy cold liquid coat his insides and put out the fires of humiliation and regret burning within. "Not about that."

"God, you're an idiot."

"I'm getting awful tired of people calling me names," Justice muttered.

"You deserve it. How do you know that doctor wasn't wrong?" Jesse stepped out in front of him, forcing Justice to meet his gaze. "Did you ever get a second opinion?"

"You think I *liked* getting that news? Why would I go to someone else to hear the same damn thing again?"

Shaking his head wildly as if he couldn't believe what he'd just heard, Jesse blinked at his brother and said, "I don't know, to make sure the guy was right? Justice, you get a second opinion from vets on your cattle! Why wouldn't you do that for yourself?"

Justice wiped one hand across his face, then took another long swallow of his beer. He didn't like defending himself and liked even less the vague notion that his younger brother might be right. What if that doctor *had* been wrong? What if it had all been a mistake?

His heartbeat thundered in his chest and his mouth

went dry. If that were true, then he'd let Maggie walk out of his life for no reason at all. And worse, he had a son he'd only just met.

"No, he wasn't wrong," Justice muttered, refusing to accept the possibility. "He couldn't have been."

"Why?" Jesse demanded. "Because if he was wrong, that means you've wasted time with Maggie, neglected your son and are the Grand Poobah of Idiots?"

Grinding his back teeth together, Justice barely managed to mutter, "Pretty much."

"Well, here's something else for you to think about, your majesty. Even if he was right at the time, things change. But you never bothered to find out, did you? Damn, Justice. You really are—"

"—an idiot. Yeah, I know. Thanks for not saying it again."

"Give me time," Jesse told him with a half grin. "I'll get around to it."

"I'm sure. Y'know, I just told Jeff that I should have been born an only child."

"Like you could have made it through life without us!" Jesse laughed and clapped Justice on the shoulder. "Now, you know what you've got to do, right?"

"I have a feeling you're about to tell me."

"As you like to say, damn straight. Get a paternity test, Justice. It's easy. It's fast. And it'll tell you flat out if the doctor was wrong or not."

Paternity test. It would be easier, he thought, than finding another doctor and going through testing again himself. And he'd have his answer. One way or the other. A thread of worry snaked its way through his system, reminding him that if the results came back as negative, then he'd have to acknowledge that Maggie had lied to him. And that she had another man in her life. He ignored that worry completely.

"Maybe you're right," he murmured.

Jesse laughed. "Hell, it was worth the drive to the ranch just to hear you say that."

"Funny. That's really funny."

"This isn't." Jesse's smile faded and his voice dropped a notch. "Get this straightened out, Justice. Because if you don't, you're going to lose Maggie, your son, everything. Then you'll be a miserable bastard for the rest of your life and speaking as one of the people who'd have to put up with it, we'd rather not see that."

"You made your point." Justice had had more advice from people in the past couple of weeks than he'd had in the past five years. And he was damn tired of it.

"Glad to hear it. Now, how about another beer?"

"What the hell—"

"Justice!"

Maggie's shout had him spinning around and nearly toppling over but for Jesse's hand on his arm steadying him. She stood in the open doorway leading to the kitchen, and the wind swept her fiery hair into a dancing tangle around her head. "What is it?"

"It's Bella," Maggie called back, her gaze sliding from Justice to Jesse, who was already sprinting for the house. "It's time."

"How much longer?"

Maggie looked up at Justice and smiled. They'd been at the hospital for nearly five hours already and it felt like days. Funny, but when she herself had been in labor, it had seemed that time was rushing by, breathlessly. Now that she was expected to do nothing but sit and wait, time was at a crawl.

"No way to tell," she told him, tossing aside a six-month-old magazine she hadn't been reading anyway. "First-time babies can take anywhere from a few hours to a couple of days to make their appearance."

Justice looked horrified and Maggie stifled a laugh. He'd been a nervous wreck since they first bundled Jesse and Bella into the ranch SUV and hit the freeway. Neither of them had trusted Jesse to drive. He'd been practically vibrating with nerves when he called Bella's doctor to tell her they were headed to the hospital. Leaving Jonas with Mrs. Carey, Maggie had ridden shotgun while Justice drove and Jesse hovered over Bella on the backseat.

As soon as they had arrived at the sprawling medical center in Irvine, Jesse and Bella had been taken off to Maternity. Justice and Maggie, meanwhile, had been directed to the waiting room, which boasted the most uncomfortable chairs in the world. Short backs, narrow seats and hardwood arms made getting comfy a nearly impossible feat.

But, she supposed, comfort wasn't a real issue, since mostly the people waiting for news from the delivery room were too nervous to sit anyway. Still, she kept giving it a shot. "Justice, sit down and give your leg a rest, why don't you?"

"My leg's fine," he said, but his tight-lipped expression told the real truth. She knew he was in pain, but the man would never admit it.

"Okay, then sit down because you're making me nervous," she said.

He looked at her for a long minute, then took a seat beside her. A television was tuned to a twenty-four-hour comedy channel, the canned laughter and muttered conversations becoming a sort of white noise in the background. The walls were a pale hospital green and the carpet was multicolored, probably in an attempt to keep it from showing wear over the years. The scent of burned coffee hung in the air, a nasty layer over the medicinal stench of antiseptic.

"I hate waiting," Justice muttered, throwing a glance at the door opening onto the hallway that led to Labor and Delivery.

"No kidding? You hide it well." Maggie patted his arm absentmindedly.

Two other people, an older couple, were waiting in that room with them, having arrived just a half hour ago. The woman leaned forward and excitedly confided, "My daughter's about to make me a grandmother. It's a boy. His name will be Charlie, after my husband."

"Congratulations," Maggie said. "We're waiting to become an aunt and uncle."

"Isn't it wonderful?" The woman was practically glowing as she reached out blindly and took her husband's hand. "So thrilling to be a part of a miracle. Even in a small way."

Beside her, Justice shifted in his chair, but Maggie ignored him. "You're right, it is."

"The waiting is difficult, though," the woman admitted. "I'd do much better if I only knew what was happening…."

Whatever the woman might have said next was lost forever when a nurse in surgical scrubs poked her head in the door, smiling and asked, "Mr. and Mrs. Baker?"

"Yes!" The expectant grandmother leaped up out of her chair and would have rushed blindly at the nurse if her husband hadn't dropped both hands onto her shoulders. "That's us. How is Alison? Our daughter?"

"She's doing great and said to tell you that Charlie is calling for you."

"Ohmygoodness!" The woman turned her face into her husband's chest and, after a quick hug, looked back at the nurse. "We can see them now?"

"Of course. Follow me."

"What about us?" Justice demanded.

The nurse turned a questioning look on him. "I'm sorry?"

"It's nothing," Maggie told her, taking Justice's hand and giving it a squeeze. "Never mind."

"Good luck to you, dear," the new grandma said as they hustled out of the room after the nurse.

"What do you mean it's nothing?" Justice asked when they were gone. "We were here long before them!"

Maggie laughed at her husband's impatience. "Not exactly how it works, Justice."

"Well, it damn well should." He pushed up and out of his chair again, marched to the door and looked out. Then he turned back to her and said, "I feel like the walls are closing in on me in here. I don't think I can stay in this little room another minute."

"I'm kind of with you on that," Maggie said. "Let's take a walk."

For the next several hours, Justice and Maggie prowled the hallways of the hospital, checking in occasionally with the maternity ward. They wandered down to the nursery to look at the new babies and once again ran into the Bakers, who proudly pointed out little Charlie. They checked in with the nurses' station to get updates on Bella, and Maggie called the ranch to be assured by Mrs. Carey that Jonas had had his supper and his bath and was now sleeping soundly. She was told not to worry and to be sure to call the minute the baby was born.

"How did you do it?" Justice asked quietly when they were once more in the dreaded waiting room.

"Hmm? Do what?"

"This," he said, waving a hand as if to encompass the hospital, the maternity ward and all they contained. "How did you do it alone?"

"I wasn't alone," she told him. "Matrice was with me."

"Your sister." He blew out a breath. "You should have told me. I would have been here."

Outside, night crouched at the windows. The lights in the waiting room were dim, and thankfully, they had shut off the television, since they were the only two people in the room. Now she almost wished for that background noise so that the silence between them wouldn't seem so overwhelming.

Looking into Justice's eyes now, she would have liked to believe he was right. That had she called him from the hospital, he would have rushed right over to be at her side. But she knew better. In her heart of hearts, she just knew.

"No, you wouldn't have, Justice," she said with a sigh. "You wouldn't have believed me then any more than you do now."

He pushed one hand through his long black hair, scrubbed the other across the back of his neck and admitted, "Maybe you're right. Maybe I wouldn't have believed you. But I would have come to you anyway, Maggie. I would have been with you through this."

Something inside her eased just a little. To know that—to believe that he would have come whether or not he thought he was her baby's father was a gift. Yet even as she admitted that, there was another voice inside her demanding to be heard.

"Do you really think I would have wanted you here if you thought I was lying to you?" Before he could answer, she added, "And do you really believe that I would have called you to watch me give birth to another man's child?"

He watched her as long silent moments ticked past. Finally, though, he said, "No. You wouldn't have. To both questions." He rubbed absentmindedly at his thigh. "You really threw me hard, Maggie. Showing up at the ranch the way you did. With a boy you claim to be mine."

God, she was tired of defending herself. Sighing, she said, "He is yours. I'm not just claiming it."

He studied Maggie, his gaze moving over her features until she shifted uneasily under his steady regard. Eventually, he spoke. "I have something to tell you."

"What?" Maggie held her breath as hope jumped up inside her and waved its arms and legs excitedly. Was he finally going to admit that he knew Jonas was his? That she wasn't lying? Was he going to ask her to stay with him? Be a family?

"Mr. and Mrs. King?"

Maggie groaned at the interruption and turned her head to look at the nurse stationed in the doorway. Hours ago, she would have welcomed the woman. Now? What terrible timing. But the nurse was smiling and Maggie was already standing up to join Justice when she said, "Yes, that's us. Are Bella and the baby all right?"

"Everyone's fine," the nurse assured them. "Even the happy father is coming around."

"Coming around?" Justice repeated. "What—"

"He got a little light-headed in the delivery room," the nurse hedged.

"You mean he *fainted?*" Justice asked her, grinning like a big brother who would now have something on his sibling for the rest of his life.

"Justice…" Maggie said.

"You've been invited in to meet the newest member of your family," the nurse told them. "If you'll follow me."

"What was it?" Maggie asked. "Girl or boy?"

"I'll let the new mom tell you that," she said, leading them through a set of double doors and down a brightly lit hallway.

Two immensely pregnant women were wandering the halls, shuffling with slow steps as they hung on to IV poles for support. Their husbands were right on their heels, murmuring encouragement. In one room a woman moaned, and from yet another a new baby's indignant wail rose up like a discordant symphony.

Maggie felt Justice's hand on the small of her back and relished that small intimacy. Here at least, they were together. A team. Two people who had survived hours of expectation and were now about to be rewarded.

In Bella's room the new mom lay back, exhausted and gorgeous against her pillows, a tightly wrapped bundle cradled in her arms. Jesse stood beside her, still looking a little pale and glassy-eyed but happier than they'd ever seen him.

Maggie hurried forward, held on to the bedrail, stared down into a red, wrinkly face and declared it, "Beautiful. Just beautiful, Bella. So…boy or girl?"

"Boy," Jesse said proudly. "And we're keeping the J-name thing going, too. Uncle Justice, Aunt Maggie, I want you to meet Joshua."

Justice moved in closer, leaning over Maggie to get a good look at the newest King. She felt his breath on her cheek as he reached over, pulled the tightly wrapped white blanket down a bit so he could get a better view of the baby. She felt his indrawn breath as he studied his brother's son and heard the soft sigh escape him as he looked at Bella.

"He's a beauty, Bella. Good thing he looks like you."

"Hey!" Jesse grinned.

"Don't you think you'd better sit down?" Justice asked, a teasing note in his voice. "I hear the delivery was a little rough on you."

Jesse scowled and cast a disgusted glance at the open door even as Bella laughed delightedly. "Big-mouth nurse," he muttered before turning a look back on Justice. He jerked his head to one side, silently telling his brother he wanted to talk in private.

When they were far enough from the two women in the room, Jesse said, "I'm a father now, too, Justice. And I'm telling you, Jonas is your son. Don't lose this. Don't blow everything for your pride."

Justice, though, turned to look at Bella and Maggie, illuminated by the overhead light, both women looking down on that tiny boy with delirious smiles. "Now's not the time, Jesse."

"There's no better time, Justice," his brother told him. "Don't waste another minute."

Jesse moved back to his wife then, and Maggie soon joined Justice to go back to the ranch, leaving the new family to settle in together. As they stepped out of the hospital into the cold, clear night, Justice stopped, took a deep breath and thought about what Jesse had said to him, both here and at the ranch. What if he was right about all of it? What if Justice had been clinging to bad information for ten years?

"Wasn't he beautiful," Maggie asked, hunching deeper into the sweater she'd brought along with her. "So tiny. So perfect. So…" She stopped talking then, looked up at Justice and asked, "What is it? Is something wrong?"

He met her gaze and knew what he had to do. For all their sakes, it was time for the truth to come out.

"I want a paternity test run on Jonas."

Eight

A few days later, Justice was still feeling the effects of Maggie's fury. After an hour of lunges, wall squats and some fast walking on a treadmill, Maggie still wasn't finished with him.

She'd set up a massage table in the pool house behind the main house and had him stretched out atop it like a prisoner on a rack. Sunlight drifted in through heavily tinted windows that allowed the people inside to enjoy the view but kept anyone outside from peering in. The bubbling of the hot tub at one end of the pool sounded overly loud in the strained quiet, and quiet purr of the air conditioner sounded like a continuous sigh.

Justice paid no attention to his surroundings, though. Instead, he kept a wary eye on Maggie. Her hands were sure, her professional demeanor was firmly in place but her eyes were flashing with suppressed rage. He winced as she took hold of his foot and, lifting it, pushed his leg toward his chest. Muscles he'd been working hard stretched and pulled, and he ground his teeth together to keep any moans from sliding out of his throat.

He curled his hands around the edges of the table and held on while she forced him to push against her hands. Resistance training, she called it. Torture was more like it, Justice thought.

"You're enjoying this," he muttered.

"No, I'm not."

"Bullshit. You're pissed off and you're getting a charge out of making me pay."

"Justice," she said on a rush of breath, "I'm a professional physical therapist. I would never, under any circumstances, harm a patient under my care. Now push against me."

He did and still managed to say, "You're not trying to hurt me—I get that. But if it's a by-product, it won't bother you much, I'm thinking."

"I'm doing what's best for your rehabilitation," she said, "and resisting torturing you, despite how tempting the idea might be."

He pushed into her grip, focusing his strength, and he had to admit that since she'd been manhandling him, his leg was stronger and getting better every day. It still ached, but it was manageable and he rarely needed the cane anymore.

"I didn't ask for the test specifically to piss you off," he muttered, unwilling to leave it alone. Wanting her to see his side.

She inhaled sharply, set his leg down on the table and fisted her hands at her hips. "What do you want me to say, Justice? That I'm fine with you arranging for our son to be poked with a needle because you don't trust me? Not gonna happen."

She'd argued with him, of course, that night at the hospital. Her temper had flared and shone like a beacon as she faced him down and told him just what she thought of a man who would put an infant through an unnecessary test. But Justice hadn't been swayed.

The day he'd found out he couldn't father children, the news had almost killed him. Not only had he lost his parents—his past—in that accident, he'd lost his future as well. He was no different than any other man. He'd dreamed of family, of passing on King Ranch to another generation who would love and care for it as he had. And to have those dreams shattered in an instant had been devastating.

Yet now that Jesse had planted all of those thoughts in his mind, he had to wonder: had the doctor been wrong? He had to know the truth. Had to know if Jonas was his. If he really did have a son. And nothing Maggie said had changed his mind.

They'd arranged for the paternity test the next morning, taking the baby to one of the King laboratories. Sometimes, he told himself, it paid to be a member of a huge, successful family. The Kings had their fingers in just about every pie worth having in California. No matter what one of them might need, there was generally a cousin who could provide it.

They'd put a rush on the paternity test, and even with

that it would be another few days before they had the results. Justice had never been good at waiting, and this time it was even harder. There was so much riding on the outcome of this test. Not just his pride, he told himself, but the direction of his very future.

She poured some liquid into her hands, scrubbed her palms together, then began what she called "deep tissue mobilization." In other words, a hard massage, he thought and sighed as her fingers and palms worked magic on his leg. His surgical scar was white and fresh-looking despite being completely healed. Her hands on his leg felt like a blessing. Her touch was sure, firm and, just as she said, professional. He wanted more. He wanted her hands on other parts of him, too. But he wasn't going to get that, not when she was this furious.

"How does this feel?" she asked, working from the sole of his foot, up his calf to his thigh and back down again.

If she glanced at the erection pushing at the fly of his shorts, she'd know just how it felt, he thought and grimly tried to bring his body under control. "Good," he said bluntly. "It's all good."

"You're improving, Justice. I'm glad to see it."

"Are you?"

"Of course I am. That's why I'm here, remember? And the sooner you're back on your own feet, the sooner I can take Jonas and leave."

He reached out, grabbed one of her hands and held on. "You're not going anywhere until those test results come back in, Maggie."

She pulled her hand free of his grip. "I'm not going

anywhere until my job is done," she corrected. "When it is, you won't be able to stop me from leaving."

He ran one hand over his face. "Damn it, Maggie, don't you see why I had to do this?"

"No. I don't see." She grabbed up a towel, dried her hands and continued, "You had my word, Justice. You could have believed me."

"I don't just want your word. I want proof." He pushed up onto his elbows and stared at Maggie.

Her hair was in a thick ponytail at the back of her neck. She wasn't wearing makeup, but then, she didn't really need any. Her eyes were hot and filled with fury, and her delectable mouth kept working as if she were biting back hundreds of words she wanted to fling at him.

The day was warm and she wore jeans shorts and a sleeveless T-shirt for their exercise session. Her skin was smooth and pale, and Justice wanted nothing more than to grab her, pull her down on top of him and bury himself inside her. With that mental image firmly planted in his mind, he could almost *feel* her damp heat surrounding him. Feel her body moving on his. See her as she leaned over him, brushing his chest with her bare breasts.

Damn it.

He swung his legs off the table in a hurry, hoping she hadn't seen his erection, hard and all too eager for her. Around Maggie, he seemed to be little better than a teenager. Always hard. Always ready.

"Come on," she said, stepping around the table to wrap one arm around his waist. "You need to sit in the hot tub awhile. Ease your muscles."

He thought about refusing her offer to help him walk

to the far end of the pool. Then he told himself he'd be a fool for not taking the opportunity to touch her. Her scent rose up to greet him, and the soft fall of her hair against his skin felt like silk. He draped one arm across her shoulders and, with her aid, walked barefoot across the cool, sky-blue tiles lining the edge of the pool.

"Here you go," she said as they reached the partitioned-off area of the pool. There was a bench along the half circle of the hot tub, and Justice lowered himself onto it, hissing a little as the warm, bubbling water caressed his body.

"I turned the heat down a bit," Maggie was saying. "I don't want you parboiled, just warm and relaxed."

He doubted he'd ever be fully relaxed when she was around, but he didn't bother telling her that. Instead, he just looked up at her, standing on the tiles, watching him with her "professional mien" in place. Where was *his* Maggie? The one with fire in her eye. The one who turned him inside out with a single touch.

"Why don't you join me?" he asked. She started to refuse but he kept talking. "You look like you need to relax as much as I do, Maggie."

She bit her lip, blew out a breath and said, "I'm too mad at you, Justice. There wouldn't be any relaxing. For either of us."

"Fine, then," he said, slapping the frothing water with the flat of his hand. "Sit down and yell at me. You always did feel better after a good rant."

Her lips twitched and he knew he'd won.

"I don't have a bathing suit."

"I won't tell if you don't," he coaxed, mouth dry,

wanting—no, *needing* to see her strip down to nothing to join him in the warm, bubbling water.

She took a deep breath and blew it out again. "Okay. But just for a few minutes. Then I should go in and take care of Jonas."

"He's fine with Mrs. Carey."

"I know that," she countered, stepping out of her jean shorts to reveal pale pink silk panties, "but he's *my* son and my responsibility."

Justice just nodded. He didn't trust himself to speak anyway. She lifted the hem of her shirt and tugged it up and over her head, giving him his first look at a wisp of a pale pink bra that exactly matched her panties. Maggie always had loved good lingerie. And he'd always considered himself a lucky bastard.

When she stepped into the water, though, he stopped her. "Aren't you going to take those off?"

She glanced down at herself, then at him. Laughing, she told him, "I don't think so. It's not safe to be naked around you, Justice."

Since his erection was now pushing against the button fly of his own shorts, demanding to be set free, he had to silently agree with her.

She eased down onto the bench opposite him and with a sigh, tipped her head back onto the rim of the pool. "God, you were right. This feels amazing."

Her lean, toned legs half floated in the water, directly in front of one of the jets, and Justice's mouth watered as he watched her. He reached down and readjusted himself, hoping to ease his discomfort. It didn't help. But he knew what would. Deftly, he undid the buttons on his shorts and pushed them off, shoving them to the floor of the pool. Instantly, his aching groin was eased, free of the constricting shorts. But he needed more.

He needed *Maggie*.

He moved closer to her while her eyes were closed. His gaze locked on her breasts, bobbing just above the water's edge, her dark, rosy nipples perfectly defined by the wet silk. She might have thought she was protecting herself by staying semiclothed, but all she'd managed to do was tempt even more thoroughly. Wet silk clung to her skin, displaying far more than it hid.

When he was close enough, he reached out to slide one hand up her calf. Instantly, her eyes flew open and she floundered a bit, until she was again seated on the bench, gaze fixed on him. "What're you doing?"

Justice moved closer still. "Helping us both relax."

"I don't think so," she said, shaking her head and scooting farther from him.

"Don't be so skittish, Maggie," he soothed. "It's not like we're strangers."

She held up one finger, holding him at bay. "No, we're not strangers, Justice. That's why we shouldn't do this. It'll only confuse things even more than they already are."

"Impossible," he countered, coming closer. The warm water felt great on his skin, the slide of his hand along her wet leg, once he took hold of her again, felt even better.

"Okay, maybe you have a point," she said, nodding. "But I'm still mad at you."

He grinned briefly. "Some of our best sex happened when you were mad at me."

"Okay," she admitted with a quick nod, "that's true, too. But that doesn't mean I want you now."

"Liar." He took hold of her foot and pulled her toward him, sliding his hands up her legs as she floated to him in the frothing water.

She hissed in a breath. "You're cheating."

"Damn straight."

"Justice, this won't solve anything."

"Maybe it doesn't have to," he told her, his hands now gripping her bottom. "Maybe it just has to happen."

She looked at him and squirmed in his grip, as if she were trying to get comfortable. "Maybe," she acknowledged. "But maybe we shouldn't let it."

"Too late," he whispered and moved off the bench so that he could turn her in his grasp, holding her floating body in front of the pulsing jets of water streaming into the tub.

"Cheating again!" she accused on a sigh as her legs parted and the thrum of the warm, pulsing water caressed her center.

While the hot tub worked its magic, Justice worked some of his own. Supporting her head with one arm, he used his free hand to undo the front clasp of her bra, freeing her breasts, her hard nipples. He dipped his head and took first one, then the other, into his mouth, rolling his tongue across their sensitive tips, feeling Maggie shudder beneath him as tumultuous sensations gathered within her.

He couldn't seem to taste her enough. How had he lived these long months without her in his arms? He suckled her, and she whimpered, both from his attentions and the steady beat of the water on her tender flesh. He knew what she was feeling because he felt it, too.

The hunger. The need. The raw urgency racing through his bloodstream. He had to have her. Reaching down, he tore her panties down and off her legs and then held her thighs apart so that the warm water could caress her even more intimately.

She grabbed at his shoulders and groaned from deep in her throat as she lifted her hips into the water jet, aching, needing. He watched her face as her eyes swam with desire and her breath caught in her throat. Then she turned her gaze on him and whispered, "I want you inside me, Justice."

That was all he needed to hear. He pulled her toward him, locked his mouth onto hers and eased them both down onto the bench. She straddled him, her knees at either side of his hips, and then lowered herself down onto him, inch by slow, incredible inch. She took him inside, into the heat. Into the heart of her, and Justice couldn't look away from her amazing eyes while he filled her, pushing himself deeply into her body.

Their gazes fixed on each other, they moved as one, racing toward the inevitable finish that they both so desperately needed. Justice felt whole. Felt complete. Felt as if nothing else in the world mattered but this moment. This woman. She was all. She was everything. And when her lips parted and she cried out his name as her body trembled and shook with the force of her release, he knew he'd never seen anything more lovely.

Only moments later, he gave himself up to the

wildness calling him and willingly followed her into a dazzling world that only lovers knew.

"It didn't change anything," Maggie muttered while she dressed Jonas in his pajamas that night. Her son smiled and laughed, a rolling, full-throated sound that never failed to tear at her heart.

She had him lying on her bed, since the two of them were still sharing a room. Thank heaven it was at the opposite end of the hall from the master bedroom. After what had happened between them that afternoon, she didn't think it would be a wise idea to be too close to him.

"You think it's funny, do you?" she asked her son, smiling at him as she bent to plant a kiss on his belly. "You think Mommy is making a fool of herself? You're right, she probably is. And you know what? She's still not sorry."

The baby pulled at her hair, and Maggie gently untangled his fingers. She put first one chubby foot then the next into his footed blue sleeper, then swiftly did up the zipper, snapping the jammies closed at the neck. Jonas kicked and squirmed on Maggie's bed until she scooped him up and cuddled him close.

Nothing in the world smelled better than a baby fresh from his bath. His skin was soft and warm and the heavy, solid weight of her son in her arms eased the ache in her heart substantially.

She didn't regret making love with Justice that afternoon, but at the same time she could admit that it had probably been a mistake. Nothing was settled between them. She was still furious with him for insisting on a paternity test when any fool could look at Jonas and know without a doubt he was Justice's son. And she was frustrated by the fact that no matter how hard she tried to get past the barriers Justice had erected around his own heart, they still stood tall and strong against her.

"But you know what really gets to me, sweetie?" she crooned, keeping her voice light and soothing as she bounced her son on her knee. "Your daddy wants a paternity test yet he's still avoiding you. Why's that, hmm? Do you know? Can you tell Mommy?"

Jonas laughed and cooed and waved his arms as if he were trying to fly, and Maggie smiled at the tiny boy who had so filled her heart. She couldn't imagine her life without Jonas now. He was a part of her. Yet, the man who was his father was still a stranger to him.

"Well, little man," she said, making her decision in an instant, "it's time we changed all that, don't you think? It's time your daddy discovered just what he's been missing. I want him to know you. To know what we could all have had together."

Jonas burbled something that Maggie took to be agreement. Pushing off the bed, she carried the baby out of the room, along the hall and down the stairs, following the sound of the evening news on a television.

She spotted Justice the moment she walked into the great room. He was sprawled in one of the comfortable chairs positioned around the room, his gaze fixed on a flat-screen TV on the opposite wall. While a news anchor rambled on about the top stories of the day, Maggie crossed the room with determined steps.

When she got close, he looked up, directly into her eyes. She felt a quick thrilling rush through her system as heat pooled in the pit of her stomach and then slipped lower. Oh, he was dangerous, she told herself, with his dark eyes, long black hair and stern features. Then his gaze shifted to the baby and a wariness shone in his eyes briefly. Which told Maggie she was doing exactly the right thing. So she took a breath, steadied herself and forced a smile.

"I brought your son to say good-night."

He sat up straighter, narrowed his gaze on her and said, "Not necessary."

"Oh, it is, Justice," she told him, and in a sure, swift movement set the baby onto Justice's lap. The two of them blinked at each other, and Maggie would have been hard-pressed to say which of them looked more surprised by her actions.

"Maggie, the test isn't in yet, so—"

"He's your son, Justice. The test will prove that, even to you, very soon. So you might as well start getting to know him."

"I don't think—"

"You should know him, Justice," she said, not letting him finish. "And there's no time like now. So, you two be good and I'll go get his bottle."

Justice's eyes widened in horror. "You're leaving me alone with him?"

Maggie laughed. "Welcome to fatherhood."

She left the room after that but stayed in the hall, peeking into the room so she could watch the two men in her life interact. Justice looked as though he were holding a ticking time bomb and Jonas looked uncertain about the whole situation.

When the baby's lower lip began to tremble, Maggie almost went back inside. Then she heard Justice say, "Now don't cry, Jonas. Everything's going to be all right."

And in the hall, Maggie had to wonder if he'd just lied to his son for the first time.

As the days passed, Justice felt the strength in his leg continue to grow. But as his body healed, his heart was being torn open. Being with Maggie and yet separate from her was harder than he would ever have thought possible. Those few stolen moments in the hot tub hadn't been repeated, and now that time with her seemed almost like a dream. A dream that continued to haunt him no matter where he was or what he was doing.

He stood at the paddock in the bright sunshine and leaned his forearms atop the uppermost rail in the fence. With his hat pulled low over his eyes, Justice stared out at the horses being saddle-trained and told himself that he'd do well to simply concentrate on work.

Now that he was getting around better, he'd begun to take up more of the reins of the operation again, and it was good to feel more himself. Though he wasn't up yet for taking his own horse out onto the range, he would be soon. Until then, he spent as little time as possible inside the house—though he was seeing more of the baby these days. It seemed as though both Maggie and Mrs. Carey were bound and determined to see him connect with the child.

And to be honest, Justice was enjoying himself. That little boy had a way of tugging at a man's heart. Father or not, he was being drawn deeper into the web of feeling, caring. Only that morning, Jonas had curled his little fist around Justice's finger and that tiny, fierce grip had taken hold of him more deeply than he would have thought possible.

The exercise-and-massage sessions Maggie had devised were getting less tiring as he healed, and he both hated that fact and was relieved by it. One-on-one time with Maggie was dangerous because he wanted her now more than ever. He hated missing those moments, but he also needed the space to do some serious thinking. Once the paternity test results came in, he would know if Maggie had been lying to him all this time. He would know if the baby boy he was becoming more fond of every day was his son.

And he would know what he had to do.

If Maggie was lying, then he'd have to let her go again. No matter how much he still loved her, no matter how much he'd come to care for the boy, he wouldn't be used. By anyone. But even as he thought it, a voice in his head shouted at him that it wasn't in Maggie's nature to lie. She was as forthright and honest a person as he'd ever known.

Which meant that as far as she knew, she was telling the absolute truth. Jonas was his son. If the tests proved it out, then Justice was going to be a part of the boy's life, whether or not Maggie was happy about that.

However the chips fell, he and Maggie had some tough choices headed their way. So why clutter everything up further with sex?

"Hey, boss!"

Justice turned toward the voice and spotted Mike leading one of the young horses around the perimeter of the ring. "What?"

Mike pointed toward the house. "Looks like your boy there is a born ranch hand!"

Justice swiveled his head to look and saw Maggie and Jonas on the flagstone patio. She was kneeling beside Jonas, who sat astride a rocking horse that had been in the King family for decades. Mrs. Carey must have hauled it down from the attic, Justice mused, a smile on his face as he watched Jonas hold on to the reins and rock unsteadily, his mother's arm wrapped firmly around him.

Even from a distance, he heard the baby's delighted laugh and Maggie's soft chuckle, and the mingled sounds went straight to his heart. If she was lying, how the hell was Justice going to stand losing her and the baby?

Nine

Maggie was putting her laundry away when she noticed the corner of a brown envelope peeking out from beneath a stack of T-shirts.

The signed divorce papers.

She set the laundry down, reached into the drawer for the large manila envelope and carefully opened the metal tabs. Pulling the papers free, she let her gaze drift over the legalese that would have, if she'd only filed the damn things with the court, ended her marriage.

But then, that was the problem. Despite going to the trouble of getting the papers, of having Justice sign them, Maggie never really had wanted the marriage to be over. So now, she simply kept the signed documents with her. As a sort of talisman, she supposed. As long as she had them, she was still connected to

Justice. Jonas still had a father. And she had a chance at getting back what she and Justice had lost. Was she just fooling herself, though? Torturing herself with thoughts of reconciliation?

Sex between them was still off-the-charts great. But was that it? Was that all they shared now?

Sadly, she slid the papers back into the envelope, then dropped the package back into her drawer. Turning from the dresser, she walked to the open window over-looking the front of the house and stared out at the storm blowing in off the ocean.

The white sheers at the window billowed in the wind gusting in under the sash like ghosts fighting to be free of earth. Tree limbs clattered and seagulls wheeled and danced in the sky, taking refuge inland from the ap-proaching storm. She closed the window against the cold wind and told herself firmly that when she got back to her own apartment, she had to file those divorce papers. But even as she thought it, she knew she wouldn't do it.

"You're crazy, Maggie," she whispered.

"I always liked that about you."

She spun around quickly, hand splayed across her chest as if to keep her heart in place. "Nothing like a jolt of adrenaline to get the morning off to a great start."

"Didn't mean to startle you," Justice said as he walked into her room with slow, but even steps. "Thought you would have heard me coming down the hall."

She watched him as he moved without hesitating, or limping. He was nearly back to normal and hadn't used his cane in a couple of days. Soon, he wouldn't need her at all. Well, wasn't that a cheery thought?

"No, without the tapping of the cane giving you away, you're pretty stealthy."

He nodded, reached down to rub his thigh and said, "It's good to be rid of it."

"I'm sure it is." She moved back to the dresser and tucked her laundry into the proper drawers, then straightened, gave him a bright smile and said, "Well, I really should go down and get Jonas. Mrs. Carey's had him most of the morning."

"It can wait another minute." He moved to stand between her and the door and Maggie knew the only way she'd get past him was to brush up against him. And she didn't think that was a good idea. Not since her body remembered their time in the hot tub all too well and was just itching for more.

So instead she stopped, hitched one hip higher than the other and folded her arms over her chest. "Okay. What do you need, Justice?"

His gaze locked on hers, he said, "I think it's time you and I had a talk about what's going to happen when the test results come in."

"What do you mean?" Wariness crept into her voice, but she really couldn't help it.

"I mean, in a few days we'll know the truth. And if it turns out that Jonas really is my son…"

She bristled. God, she hated that he didn't trust her and instead needed substantiating proof from a laboratory.

"—then I'm going to want him raised here," Justice was saying and Maggie listened up. "On the ranch."

A sinking sensation opened up in the pit of her

stomach and her heart dropped into it. She shook her head. "No way."

"What?"

"You can't just take my son."

"If he's my son, too," Justice argued, "I can take my share of him."

She laughed shortly, a harsh scrape against her throat. "What do you plan to do? Cut him in half?"

He scowled and walked past her to sit on the edge of the bed. Rubbing his leg, he said, "Nothing so dramatic. If Jonas is mine, I want him raised here. I want him growing up where I did. This ranch is his heritage, and he should get to know it and love it like I do."

"All of a sudden you're worried about his *heritage?*" Maggie stalked across the floor toward him and stopped just before she got within strangling range. Because the way she was feeling at the moment, she really didn't trust herself. "Up until last week you wouldn't even admit to the possibility of his being your son. Now he has a heritage and you want to take him from me? I don't think so."

"Don't fight me on this, Maggie," Justice said, wincing a little as if his leg was paining him. "You'll lose."

For the first time since she'd arrived at the ranch, she wasn't concerned with Justice's pain. With the discomfort of his injury. In fact, she hoped his leg ached like a bitch. Why should she be the only one in pain here? All she knew was that he was going to take her baby from her. Well, it would have to be over her dead body.

She took a deep breath, held on to her heartache like a shield and said, "Oh, no, I won't lose. He's mine,

Justice. He's nearly six months old and up until little more than a week ago, you'd never seen him!"

"Because you didn't bother to tell me of his existence."

"You didn't believe me when I *did* tell you."

"Not the point." He waved that argument aside with a flick of his hand.

"It's exactly the point, Justice, and you know it."

Outside, clouds rolled in, the wind kicked up into a fierce dance and rain suddenly pounded on the windowpanes with a vicious rhythm.

Feeling as ragged and frenetic as the storm, Maggie stepped back from him and said firmly, "Jonas is going to be raised in the city. By me. My apartment is lovely. There's a park close by and good schools and—"

"A park?" Justice pushed off the bed and grimaced a little but kept coming, walking toward Maggie until she backed up just to keep a distance between them. "You want to give him a park when I've got thousands of acres here? The city's no place for a boy to grow up. He couldn't even have a *dog* in your apartment."

"Of course he can," she argued, temper spiking, desperation growing. "Pets are allowed in my building. We'll get a little dog as soon as he's old enough. A poodle, maybe."

He barked out a sharp laugh. "A *poodle?* What the hell kind of dog is that for a growing boy?"

"What do you want him to have, a pit bull?"

"The herd dogs. They're well-trained—he'll love 'em. We've got a new litter due in a few weeks, too. He'll have a puppy to grow up with and he'll love that, too."

He probably would, but that wasn't the point either,

Maggie thought, surrendering to the fires inside her, letting her temper boil until she wouldn't have been surprised to feel steam coming out of her own ears.

"That's not your decision to make."

"Damn straight it is. If Jonas is my son, I won't be separated from him."

"You never even *wanted* children, remember?" She was shouting now and didn't give a damn who heard her. The rain hammered the windows, the wind rattled the glass and Maggie felt as if she were in the center of the storm. This was a fight she was determined to win. She wouldn't give ground.

"Of course I did!" Justice's shout was even louder than hers. "I lied to you because I thought I couldn't have kids."

Dumbfounded, Maggie just stared at him for a second or two. A heartbeat passed, then another, as her brain clicked through information and presented her with a really infuriating picture. Eventually that temper kicked back in and all hell was cut loose.

"You lied to me?" she demanded. "Deliberately let me believe you just didn't want kids when you knew you couldn't have them at all? Why would you do that?"

She rushed him and pushed at his chest with both hands, so furious she could hardly breathe, let alone shout, yet somehow she managed. "You let me walk away from you rather than tell me the truth? What were you thinking?"

"I didn't want you to know," he said, capturing both of her wrists and holding them tightly. His gaze pierced into hers, and Maggie saw shame and anger and regret all tangled up together in his eyes. "I didn't want anyone to know. You think I wanted to tell you I was less than a man?"

Maggie just blinked at him. She couldn't believe this. Couldn't get her mind around it at all. "Are you a Neanderthal? Being able to father a child is not a measure of your manhood, you big dolt!"

"To me it is."

She saw the truth of that statement on his face, and it didn't calm her down any. Yanking her hands free of his grip, she wheeled around and started pacing the circumference of the room in fast, furious steps.

"All this time, we've been apart because you thought you were sterile?" She sent him a quick look and saw her words hit home.

His mouth tightened, his jaw clenched and every muscle in his body looked to be rigid, unforgiving. He didn't accept weakness, and of course that's how he would have seen himself. She knew that about him if nothing else. So, yes, she could understand that he would have thought it better to get a divorce than to confess to his wife that he was less than he thought he should be.

That's what she got for marrying a man whose pride was his major motivator. How typical of Justice. Then she stopped dead, studied her husband and hit him with what she'd just realized.

"It's your damn pride, isn't it?" she murmured, never taking her eyes off him. "That's what's at the bottom of all this. Why you didn't fight for me. Why you let me go. For the sake of your damn pride."

"Nothing wrong with pride, Maggie," he told her in

a voice that just barely carried over the sound of the storm raging outside.

"Unless you hold that pride more precious than anything else. Because that's what you did, Justice. Rather than admit to me you couldn't have children, you let our marriage end." The slap of that truth hurt her deeply. He'd chosen his own image of himself over their marriage. Over their love. "*That* was easier for you than losing your pride."

"You're the one who walked."

"So you keep reminding me," she said, moving back toward him now with slow, sure steps. "But you could have kept me, Justice. You could have stopped me with two words. *Please stay.* That's all you had to say and you know it. Hell, you admitted to me just the other day that you would have liked to say it. But you couldn't do it."

She shook her head as she stared up into dark blue eyes that suddenly looked as cold and deep as a storm-tossed ocean. "I loved you enough that I would have stayed with you if I thought you wanted me to. Instead you pulled away and closed yourself off and I had nothing. No children. No husband. So why the hell would I stay?"

He flinched and looked uncomfortable, but that was fleeting. In a heartbeat, he was back to being his stone-faced, in-control self.

"This is useless, Maggie." He pushed one hand through his hair, cast a quick look at the window and the storm beyond, then shifted his gaze back to her. "What's past is past. We can't change it. But know this. If Jonas is my son, I'm not going to give him up. If that boy is a King, he's going to be raised by Kings."

He left her then, walking quietly away without a backward glance, and when he was gone, Maggie felt cold right down to the bone. That icy pit in the bottom of her stomach was still there and now tangled with knots of nerves.

Everything Justice had just said had also been motivated by his pride, his pride in his child, and while she might ordinarily cheer for that, right now all it meant to her was that Justice would be a fierce opponent.

As that thought flew through her mind, Maggie realized that with his money and his family's power behind him, he might very well roll right over her and win custody if it ever went to court. Then what would she do?

She couldn't lose her son.

Everything in her went cold and still. Fear rocketed through her system, successfully dousing the fires of her temper.

This was so much more dangerous than she'd ever thought.

"I'll run away. I swear I will," Maggie said into the phone a half hour later. "I'll take Jonas and disappear."

"Calm down, sweetie," Matrice urged her. "Now just tell me what happened without the hysterics, okay?"

Sitting on her bed, watching her son stare out the window at the play of the storm outside, Maggie went over her whole fight with Justice. She told her elder sister everything, sparing neither of them, and by the time she was finished talking, she had to admit she felt better already, just for the spewing factor.

"I can't believe he'd be that dumb," Matrice said. "If

he'd just told you the truth before, none of this would have happened."

"I already covered that, believe me," Maggie told her and smiled when Jonas kicked his little legs as if he were desperately trying to get up and run.

"I know, but, oh, hold on—" She half covered the mouthpiece so that her voice was muffled as she said, "Danny, don't pour oatmeal on the cat, honey. That's a bad choice. Sorry," she told Maggie when she was back. "We're getting a late start on breakfast and Danny apparently wants to share."

Maggie smiled, thinking of her almost two-year-old nephew. The little boy attacked each day as if determined to get as much out of it as he could. Maggie could hardly wait to watch Jonas at that age. She looked down at her son, trying to grab hold of his own toes, and smiled. There was so much to look forward to. So much she could lose if Justice meant what he said and actually tried to take her son.

Fear galloped along her spine and Maggie took a deep breath, trying to rein it in.

"Mags? You there?" Matrice's voice brought Maggie back to earth and grounded her in the present.

Her older sister was matter-of-fact and down-to-earth, and she had enough common sense to talk Maggie off the proverbial ledge when she had to. Today, that talent was essential.

"I'm here, Matrice. Worried and a little nauseous, but I'm here."

"You don't have to worry."

"Easy for you to say."

Matrice laughed. "Honey, I'd be worried, too, if I actually believed that Justice would take you to court over your son."

"What makes you think he won't?"

"Because I'm brilliant and insightful. That's why you called me, remember?"

True. But still, Matrice hadn't seen Justice's face. His stern, determined expression.

"It's not going to go to court, I promise you, so relax a little, okay?"

"You don't know that," Maggie assured her, reaching out to smooth her hand across her son's inky black hair and skim her fingertips along his cheek. Instantly, Jonas made a grab for her finger and held on, as if he'd caught a prize. He couldn't possibly realize that he also had a grip on his mother's heart. "Justice is single-minded if nothing else, remember? And now that he's focused on Jonas and being a part of his life, there's nothing that will stop him. He'll do whatever he has to, to ensure he wins."

"But he can't win if he alienates you, and he knows it."

"Maybe. But he's so focused on Jonas."

Matrice chuckled. "That's not a bad thing, honey. You *wanted* him in Jonas's life, remember? That was one of the reasons you took the job when Jeff offered it. You wanted Justice to get to know his son. To want to be in his life."

"Yeah…" Okay, yes, that had been the plan. "But I didn't mean for him to take my son from me."

"He's not going to."

"You can't be sure of that."

"Yes, I can."

"How?" Maggie asked, really wanting to be convinced.

Her sister sighed into the phone. "Justice loves you, Mags. He always has. He wouldn't hurt you like that, and if you think about it, you'll see that's true."

"Yes, but…"

"And please, he's going to take the baby from you? Can you see him raising a baby on his own? It would be pitiful. Why, my own Tom hardly knows which end of the diaper goes under Danny's behind!"

"True," Maggie said, smiling now as her nerves began to unwind a little. She remembered the still-awkward way Justice held his son and knew that he'd be lost if he had to take care of the baby on his own. Then something occurred to her. "But he has Mrs. Carey and she's crazy about Jonas!"

"She's crazy about you, too," Matrice insisted. "No way would that woman help Justice take your son from you."

"Maybe not," she said with a sigh, lifting her gaze from the grinning baby to the stormy skies beyond the window. "But, Matrice, I can't help thinking this is going to get uglier before it gets any better."

"My money's on you, kid," her sister said.

A few hours later Justice studied the ranch report spread out on his desk, but he couldn't keep his mind from wandering. He'd put a call into King Labs and was unable to get an answer from them yet. What the hell was taking so long? Why couldn't they just finish the damn test and end the waiting?

He leaned back in his chair then, willing to admit at

least to himself that his mind wasn't on the ranch. Instead, it was tangled up with thoughts of Maggie and the boy who might be his son. And if he wasn't? he asked himself. What then? Then, he thought, Maggie would leave, taking Jonas with her, and life at the ranch would once again be quiet as the grave.

Was he really willing to go back to living like that?

Justice scrubbed both hands over his face. No, he wasn't. He hated the idea of once more being alone in this house but for Mrs. Carey. He didn't like the idea of not seeing toys everywhere. Of not hearing the baby cry or Maggie's laughter ringing through the halls.

But did he have a choice? Had there been too many lies to patch up a marriage that had once been so shining and right? Great sex wasn't enough. Not when there had been so many harsh words between a couple. Not when distrust roared up at every corner. And, as he'd told himself before, great sex only complicated things. Remembering the look on her face when he'd finally confessed the truth to her, Justice had to acknowledge that maybe what they'd once shared was too shattered to put back together. And if their marriage was really over, what was left?

A small boy who would need both of them.

He accepted that if Jonas wasn't his, then Maggie was lying to him. But hadn't he lied to her, too? Hadn't he done just what she'd accused him of doing—chosen his pride over their marriage? Was her lie so much more terrible than his? Would it be so bad to accept another man's child as his own?

People adopted every day. Why couldn't he?

Warming to his thoughts, Justice stood up and walked to the wide windows overlooking the ranch yard. The storm was still raging, matching the way he was feeling exactly. He laid one hand on the cold glass and felt the tiny slaps of the rain as the drops bounced against his palm.

All he had to do was accept Jonas and he would have an heir. He'd have a boy he could raise and teach. Did it really matter who had created him as long as Justice raised him?

A small voice in his mind whispered *yes, it matters*. And his pride stirred and did battle with his desires. He couldn't ask her to be his wife again. That was done. Maggie and he might be finished, but they could have something different, he thought now. Something less than a marriage, less than lovers and more than friendship. It could work.

He could have Maggie *and* a son if he was willing to bend.

The question was, could he?

When the study door opened behind him, Justice didn't even have to turn around to know she was there. Watching him. He felt the power of her gaze and waited for her to approach. Her steps were muffled against the thick rugs spread across the wood floor, but he heard her anyway. That sure, confident step was purely Maggie.

She stopped directly behind him, and he could have sworn he felt the heat of her body reaching out for his.

"I won't lose my son, Justice," she said, and though her voice was quiet, there was a ring of steel in her tone.

He admired that. Hell, he'd always admired Maggie.

Justice turned around to face her, and his gaze swept her up and down, noting the faded jeans, the cream-colored sweater and the wild tangle of her fiery hair. Her blue eyes were calm and fixed on him, but her chin was lifted into fighting mode and he knew she was ready to draw a line in the sand.

So he cut her off before she could.

"You don't have to," he said and saw the brief flash of confusion on her face. "I've been thinking about this since this morning, and an idea just came to me."

She tipped her head to one side to watch him warily. "What kind of idea?"

He leaned back against the window jamb, folded his arms across his chest and said, "I want you to move back to the ranch. You and Jonas."

"You mean once the test results are in."

"No," he said. "I mean now."

She shook her head as if she didn't quite understand what he was saying. And hell, who could blame her.

"But you don't even believe that Jonas is yours yet."

"Doesn't matter," he said and actually felt the ring of truth in that statement resonate in his soul. He'd made up his mind. Jonas would be his. Biologically or legally. "I can adopt him legally. Either way, he'll still be my son."

"I see," she said, though he was guessing she really didn't, since her features were carefully blank. "So, you want me to move back in as your wife?"

Step carefully, King, he told himself.

"No," he said quietly, "we're divorced and that's probably best. Maggie, we were always too combustible for our own good. I know our marriage is over. But there's no reason you can't move in here anyway. We can raise Jonas together and have a platonic relationship."

Her jaw dropped.

He smiled. It wasn't easy to surprise Maggie King.

"Platonic?" She repeated the word as if she couldn't quite believe he'd actually said it. "Whatever we have together, Justice, it's never been platonic."

"Doesn't mean it can't be," he countered. God knew, he wouldn't enjoy it much, but if that's what it took to have her and the baby in his world, then that's what he'd do. "We could have a good life, Maggie. We'd be close…friends."

"We'll never be just friends, Justice," she told him. "Don't you get that? There's too much between us. Too much passion to be stoppered up in a jar and set on a shelf somewhere to make things easier for you."

"You're taking this all the wrong way, Maggie. That's not what I'm trying to do."

"Isn't it?" She pushed both hands through her hair and growled briefly under her breath as if she were trying to get hold of her temper. "You've decided Jonas will be your son whether he is or not. You've decided that I can be your friend and live here at the ranch. But you're not saying anything about trying for something more, because Justice King doesn't make mistakes."

"What the hell are you talking about?"

"Don't you think I know what you're doing?" She laughed then, hard and fast. "God, I know you even better than you know yourself. You won't ask me to live with you as your wife again because that would mean you made a mistake when you let me leave you. And you don't make mistakes, do you, Justice?"

He just stared at her. How was a man supposed to unravel the wild logic women came up with? "How the hell did you twist this around like that?"

"Because I know you." She laughed shortly and shook her head while she waved one finger at him. "You don't want platonic, Justice, any more than I do. You just figure that's the easiest way to get me to agree. Then, once I'm living here at the ranch, you can change things. You've probably got it all planned out in your mind. I can just see it," she continued, wiggling her fingers in wide circles that got smaller and smaller. "You'll work it around to the arrangement that will suit you best. And what suits you, Justice, is me in your bed. You want *me*. You want our bodies tangled together. You want hot breath and soul-stealing kisses."

He took a long, slow breath and then swallowed hard. Figured Maggie would make this more difficult than it had to be. Figured she would see right through his "platonic" offer, too. The woman always had been way too smart. "Of course I want you—that's obvious enough—but it doesn't mean we can't live as friends."

"Oh, of course it does. It would be impossible. You and I, Justice, were never meant for platonic." Then she went up on her toes, wrapped her arms around his neck and pulled him in for a long, deep kiss that held as much fury as passion.

Justice would have sworn he felt heat swamp him from the top of his head to the bottoms of his feet. She was fire and light and heat and seduction. His arms snaked around her middle, held on tight and pressed her to him, aligning her body to his. He was tight and hard for her in an instant and knew she was making her point all too well.

Then the kiss was over and she was looking up into his eyes. "Deny that, if you can. We're not friends. We're lovers." Her arms dropped from around his neck. "Or we were. Now, I'm not sure what we are anymore. The only thing I'm sure of is, I won't lose my son."

She turned her back on him and stomped out of the room without once looking back. But why should she? She'd made her point.

His arms felt empty without her in them. His body was on fire and slowly cooling now that Maggie was gone. Damn it, he hated the cold. He wanted the heat. He wanted *her*. And he always would. She was right. They couldn't live together as friends. So what did that leave them?

They had a past.

They might have a future.

All it would cost him was his pride.

Ten

"You're as stubborn as he is, I swear." Mrs. Carey gave her soup pot a stir, then fisted her hands at her hips. "That poor baby is going to have a head like a rock thanks to his parents."

Maggie sat at the kitchen table, drinking tea she didn't want and staring through the window at Justice as he carried Jonas around the ranch yard. Spring sunshine fell out of a perfect sky. Angel and Spike were racing in circles, making Jonas laugh with delight, and the wide grin on Justice's face stole her breath away.

Yet here she sat in the kitchen. It was a bright, cheery room, with dozens of cabinets, miles of countertop and the comforting scent of homemade soup bubbling on the stove. But Maggie didn't feel comforted. More like... disconnected.

At the end of a very long week, she felt as though she were walking a tightwire fifty feet off the ground with no net beneath her. Days crawled past and she and Justice might as well have been living in separate homes. She hadn't touched him in days, though she'd dreamed about him every night. Thought about him every waking moment.

And still there didn't seem to be an answer.

"What am I supposed to do?" Maggie asked with a shake of her head. "He wants us to be *friends.*"

Mrs. Carey snorted. "Anyone can see you two weren't destined for friendship."

Smiling wryly, Maggie said, "I agree, but what if that's all that's left to us?"

Mrs. Carey walked to the table, sat down opposite her and folded her hands neatly on top of a brick-red placemat. Staring Maggie in the eyes, she asked bluntly, "If all that's left is friendship, why does the air sizzle when the two of you are together?"

Maggie laughed. "Excuse me?"

"Do I look like I'm a hundred and fifty years old?" Mrs. Carey snorted again and clucked her tongue. "Because I'm not. And anyone with half an eye could have seen the way you two were around each other the past couple of weeks. I nearly caught fire myself, just watching the two of you look at each other."

No point in denying the truth, Maggie thought. So she didn't try. "Not lately, though."

"No," Mrs. Carey allowed. "What I've got to wonder is why? What changed?"

"What hasn't?" Reaching for a cookie from the plate

in the center of the table, Maggie took a bite, chewed, then swallowed. "He wants Jonas, but he hasn't said he wants *me*."

"Pfft." The older woman waved away that statement with one dismissive hand. "You know he does."

"What I know and what I need to hear are two different things," Maggie said, letting her gaze slide once again to the two most important men in her life. She looked out the window just in time to see Justice plant a kiss on Jonas's forehead.

Her heart melted. She'd wished for this for so long, that Justice would know and love his son, and now it was happening. The only problem was that she should have been more specific in her wishes. She should have hoped that the *three* of them would find one another.

"Maggie, you more than anybody know that Justice doesn't always say what he's feeling," Mrs. Carey said softly, drawing her gaze away from the window. "You love him. I can see it in you."

"Yeah, I love him," she admitted. "But that doesn't change anything."

The other woman laughed. "Oh, honey. It changes everything. With love, anything's possible. You just can't give up."

"I'm not the one giving up," she retorted, defending herself. "Justice is the one who won't budge."

"Hmm…"

"What's that mean?"

"Nothing at all," Mrs. Carey said with a sigh. "Just seems to me that people as stubborn as you and Justice have an obligation to the world to stick together. Spare two other people from having to put up with either of you."

She had to laugh. One thing about Justice's housekeeper, you never had to wonder what she was thinking.

"Now, why don't you go outside and join your men?"

She wanted to. She really did. But things were so strained between Justice and her at the moment that she wasn't at all sure she'd be welcomed. Besides, now that Justice was almost back to full strength, she'd be leaving soon and taking Jonas with her, no matter what the baby's father thought about it. So why not let the two of them have some time together while they could?

But, oh, the thought of leaving the ranch again, leaving *Justice* again, was killing her. And the fear that he might make good on his promise and try to take her son was chilling. Pain was gathering on the near horizon, and she knew that when it finally caught up to her, it was going to be soul crushing.

"No," Maggie said, standing up slowly. It was time she started getting used to the fact that she wasn't going to be with Justice. Brace for the coming pain as best she could. "I think I'll go upstairs, take a long bath and start getting ready for tonight."

Mrs. Carey nodded. "It's good that you're going with him."

Maybe it was, Maggie thought, but maybe it would turn out to be an exercise in torture for both of them. She'd agreed days ago to attend the Feed the Hungry charity dance with Justice.

Feed the Hungry was a local foundation the King Ranch donated hundreds of thousands of dollars every year to in order to stock local food banks. Maggie had even helped plan the event when she and Justice were still together. So attending with him had seemed like a good idea when he'd first broached the subject.

But now…she wasn't so sure. Looking down at the woman still seated at the table, she asked, "Are you certain you don't mind babysitting while we go? Because if you do, I can stay home and—"

"It's a joy to watch that baby, and you well know it," Mrs. Carey told her with a smile. "So if you're thinking of chickening out at the last minute, you can't use me as an excuse."

Maggie's lips twitched. "Some friend you are."

"Honey, I am your friend. And as your friend, I'm telling you to go upstairs. Take a bath. Do your hair and makeup and wear that gorgeous dress you bought yesterday." She stood up, came around the table and gave Maggie a brief, hard hug. "Then you go out with your husband. Dance. Talk. And maybe remember just what it is you two have together before it's too late."

Justice hated getting dressed up.

He felt uncomfortable in the tailored tux and wished to hell he was wearing jeans and his boots. He even had a headache from gathering up his hair and tying it into a neat ponytail at the back of his neck. He didn't get why it mattered what he wore to this damn thing. Why couldn't he just write a check and be done with it?

Scowling, he glanced around the hallway and noted that the cobalt blue vase held a huge bouquet of roses, their scent spilling through the entryway. Now that

Maggie was back on the ranch, the vases were filled again; he knew that when she was gone, it would be just one more thing he would miss. She'd made her mark on this place as well as on him. And nothing would be the same after she left.

His leg was better now, so he knew that she'd be planning to go soon. He couldn't let that happen. Not this time. He had to find a way to make her stay. Not just because of Jonas but also because without Maggie, Justice didn't feel complete.

He shot his cuffs, checked his watch and frowned. Maggie always had kept him waiting. Back in the day, he'd stood at the bottom of these steps, hollering up for her to get a move on, and she'd always insisted that she would be worth the wait.

"Damned if that isn't still true," he murmured when he spotted her at the top of the stairs.

Her long, red-gold hair fell loosely around her shoulders, the way he liked it best. Long, dangling gold earrings glittered and shone in the light tossed from a wall sconce. She wore a strapless, floor-length dark green dress that clung to her curves until practically nothing was left to the imagination. The bodice was low-cut, exposing the tops of her breasts, and the skirt fell in graceful folds around her legs. She carried a black cashmere wrap folded neatly across her arm.

She stood there, smiling at him, and his breath caught in his lungs. Her cheeks were pink and her blue eyes sparkled as she enjoyed his reaction to her. If she only knew just how strong his response was. Suddenly, his tux felt even more uncomfortable than it had before as his body tightened and pushed at the elegant fabric.

"Well?" she asked, making a slow turn at the top of the stairs.

Justice hissed in a breath. The back was cut so low she was practically naked. The line of her spine drew his gaze, and he followed it down to the curve of her behind, just barely hidden by the green silk. His hands itched to touch her. It took everything he had to keep from vaulting up the stairs—bad leg or not—crushing her to him and carrying her off to the closest bed.

She'd been right, he told himself. They weren't friends. They'd never *be* friends. He wanted her desperately and doubted that feeling would ever fade.

But she was waiting for him to say something, watching him now with steady eyes. He didn't disappoint her.

"You're beautiful," he whispered, his voice straining to be heard past the knot in his throat. "Every man in the room is going to want you."

She came down the stairs slowly, one hand on the banister, each step measured and careful. He got peeks of her sandaled feet as she moved and noticed a gold toe ring he'd never paid attention to before. Sexy as hell, he thought, and grimly fought a losing battle to get his own body back under control.

"I'm not interested in every man," she said when she was just a step or two above him.

"Good thing," he told her. "I'd hate to have to bring a club to fight them off with."

She gave him a dazzling smile that sent his heartbeat into overdrive.

"I think that's the nicest thing you've ever said to me, Justice."

Then he'd been a damn fool, he thought. He should have always told her how beautiful she was. How important to him she was. But he hadn't found the words and so he'd lost her. Maybe, though, there was time enough for him to take another shot at it.

He reached out, took one of her hands in his and helped her down the last two steps. When she was standing right in front of him, he inhaled, drawing her scent into his body as if taking all of her in. He lifted one hand, smoothed her hair back from her cheek, touched her cool, soft skin and felt only fire.

"Maggie, I—"

"Well, now, don't you both look wonderful," Mrs. Carey said as she walked into the hall, Jonas on her hip.

Justice didn't know if he was relieved or irritated by the interruption.

The baby kicked his legs, waved his arms and, with drool streaming down his chin, reached for his mother. Maggie moved to take him, but Mrs. Carey stepped back. "Oh, no, you don't," she said, laughing. "He'll have you covered in drool in no time—you don't want to ruin that dress."

Maggie sighed and Justice watched her eyes warm as she looked at her son. He felt it, too, he realized, looking at the baby safe in the housekeeper's arms. A wild, huge love for a tiny child he wasn't even sure was his yet. But the more time he spent with the baby, the more he saw of him, the more he cared for him. He and Maggie were linked through this child, he knew. But would it be enough to start over? To rebuild what they'd lost?

"She's right," he said, keeping a tight grip on Maggie's hand. "We're late anyway."

Maggie lifted one eyebrow at him. "Was that a dig?"

He gave her a half smile. "Just a fact. You always did make us late for everything."

"I like to make an entrance."

"You do a hell of a job, I'll give you that," he said and was rewarded by a quick grin. Her smile sucker punched him, and he had to steady himself again before looking at Mrs. Carey. When he did, he found the older woman giving him a knowing look. She saw too much for Justice's comfort. Always had.

"Goodnight, little man," Maggie whispered as she leaned in to Jonas and kissed his cheek. Then she cupped her hand around the back of his head and just held on to him for a long moment. Pulling back, then she said, "Does he feel a little warm to you?"

"Warm?" Justice repeated, reaching out to place his palm on the baby's forehead, a sudden, sharp stab of worry slicing through him. "You think he has a fever?"

"Maybe we should check before we go," Maggie said. "It won't take long and—"

"He'll be fine—don't you worry." Mrs. Carey shook her head at both of them. "I know how to take care of a baby and if I need you, I'll call your cell."

"You've got the number, right?" Maggie asked, digging in her small cocktail purse to drag out her cell phone and make sure it was on.

"Of course I do, you've given it to me three times just today."

"My number's programmed on your phone, too, right?" Justice asked, patting his pants pocket to assure himself he had his phone, as well.

"I have your number, too. And the police," Mrs. Carey said, herding them toward the front door. "And the hospital and probably the National Guard. Go. Dance. Have fun."

Frowning a little at the bum's rush they were receiving, Justice took hold of Maggie's elbow and steered her onto the porch. "We're going, but we're only a few miles away and—"

"I know where Stevenson Hall is, Justice. Haven't I lived here most of my life?" Mrs. Carey shooed them off with one hand. "Go on, have some fun, for heaven's sake. The baby's fine and he's going to stay fine."

"If you're sure..." Maggie didn't sound at all pleased about leaving now and her gaze was fixed on the smiling baby.

"Go."

Justice took Maggie's wrap from her, draped it over her bare shoulders, then took her arm and threaded it through his. Giving his housekeeper one more look, he said, "She's right. Jonas will be fine, and if we have to, we can be back home in ten minutes."

"All right, then," Maggie said unenthusiastically. She looked at Mrs. Carey. "You promise to call me if he needs me?"

"Absolutely," she said. "Drive safe."

Then she closed the door and Maggie and Justice were standing on the dimly lit porch all alone. Her scent drifted to him and the heat of her body called to him—and Justice could only think he'd never been less interested in going anywhere. It wasn't worry over the baby making him want to stay home. It was the idea of having this elegantly dressed, absolutely beautiful Maggie King all to himself.

But he had an obligation to the charity the King Ranch funded, so he would go. "We don't have to stay long," he said, leading her down the porch and across the drive to where one of the ranch hands had parked the SUV.

"I know." Maggie threw one last glance at the house behind her, then turned to look at Justice. "Jonas is probably fine, and besides, I want a dance with a handsome man in a tux tonight."

His mouth quirked slightly. "Anyone I know?"

She laughed as he'd meant her to, then said, "Maybe Mrs. Carey is right. Maybe we should try to relax and enjoy the night."

"Maybe," he said, sliding one hand down her arm. "But for God's sake don't tell her that."

Maggie laughed again as she swung herself inside the car after he opened the door for her, and Justice told himself to enjoy what he had while he had it. He knew all too well just how quickly things could change.

The charity ball was a huge success.

The banquet hall at the local art center was packed with the county's movers and shakers. A band was playing dance music on the stage, and formally dressed waiters moved through the crowd carrying trays of appetizers. Helium-filled balloons in an array of colors filled the ceiling and occasionally fell limply to the floor below. Women dressed in jewel-toned gowns swirled in the arms of tuxedo-clad men, and Maggie was left to visit with friends instead of dancing with her husband as she wanted to.

She spotted Justice across the room, standing in a knot of people. Even from a distance, her breath caught in her chest just watching him. He was magnificent in a tuxedo. She knew he hated formal wear, but even in a tux, his raw strength and sensuality bled through until most women would have had to fan themselves after a peek at him.

Maggie frowned when she saw him rub idly at his thigh. She probably should have put her foot down about attending this dance, but he was so damn proud. So reluctant to be treated as if he needed help. And the truth was, he was well on the way to being one hundred percent again, so a small ache or pain wasn't going to stop him anyway.

The men clustered around Justice were no doubt asking his advice on any number of things, she thought, while absentmindedly keeping track of the conversations around her. But that was how it had always been. People turned instinctively to Justice. He was a man who somehow gave off the air of being in complete control, and to most people that was simply irresistible.

She was no different. She looked at Justice and knew she wanted him with every breath in her body. He was the one. The only one for her. Sighing, she turned her head and smiled at the still-speaking woman beside her.

So when Justice came up behind her a moment or

two later, she was so startled she jumped as he laid one hand on her back. Heat spilled through her as his fingers caressed her spine with a delicate touch. She closed her eyes, sighed a little and took a breath, hoping to regain her balance. Then, looking up at him, she asked, "Having a good time?"

He dipped his head to hers and murmured, "Hell, no, but it might get better if you dance with me."

Maggie smiled, then asked, "You sure you're up to it? Your leg, I mean."

"The leg's fine. A little achy." He held out a hand. "So? A dance with the guy who brought you?"

"Oh, honey, if he was asking me to dance, I wouldn't hesitate." A few chuckles resulted from that statement by a woman old enough to be Justice's grandmother.

"Mrs. Barton," Maggie said with a teasing laugh, "you'd better be careful. I've got my eye on you."

As Justice led her through the crowd to the mobbed dance floor, Maggie felt a swell of pride inside her. There were any number of women in this room who would give anything to be on Justice's arm. And for tonight, at least, that woman was her.

She went into his arms as if it was the only place on earth she belonged. When he held her so tightly to him she could feel the strength of his body pressing into hers, Maggie nearly sighed with pleasure. Then he turned her lazily in time to the swell of the music, and she smiled, enjoying the moment. All around them, couples swayed in time and snatches of conversations lifted and fell in the air.

When Justice's step faltered, Maggie frowned. "Are you okay?"

He gritted his teeth. "I'm fine."

"We don't have to dance, Justice."

He hissed out a breath. "I said I'm fine, Maggie. The leg aches a little. That's all."

"I'm just concerned."

"You don't have to be, damn it," he ground out, then clamped his lips tightly together for a second before saying, "I don't need you to worry about me, all right? Can we just dance?"

But the magic of the moment was ruined for Maggie. *I don't need you.* His words repeated over and over again in her mind. "That's the problem, Justice," she blurted while still following his lead around the floor.

"What?" He was frowning again now, and damned if that expression didn't make him look more sexy. More dangerous.

"You don't need me."

"I said I don't need you to worry about me—there's a difference."

"No," she insisted, staring up at him as they made another turn. "There isn't. I need *you.* I always have."

"That's good, because—"

"No," she interrupted him, uncaring about the people surrounding them on the floor. They probably couldn't overhear the conversation over the music, but even if they could, that wouldn't have stopped her. "It isn't good, Justice. It's the reason I can't be with you."

"You *are* with me."

His hand tightened around hers and his eyes

narrowed into slits. Maggie shook her head at his fierce expression. "Not for much longer. Yes, I need you, but I can't be with you, because I want to be needed, too."

"What the hell does that mean?" he demanded, holding her closer, as if half afraid she was going to bolt. "Of course I need you."

She laughed shortly, but there was no humor in it, only misery. "No, you don't. You wouldn't even let me help you a second ago when your leg hurt."

"That's different, Maggie. I don't need a therapist."

"No," she said, her temper building, frothing, despite the fact that she was in the middle of a crowd that was slowly beginning to take notice. "You don't want to need anyone. You won't admit that you can't do everything yourself. It's your pride, Justice. It always comes down to your pride."

Justice's voice was low and tight. There were too many damn people around them. Too many who might be listening in. "My pride helped me build the ranch into one of the biggest in the country. My pride got me through when you walked out."

"Your pride is the *reason* I walked out, remember?"

"You're not walking this time," he told her, his grip on her hand and around her waist making that point clear. "This time we *have* to be together."

"Why?"

"Because I got a text from Sean at the lab. The results of the test are in. I'm Jonas's father."

Both of her eyebrows arched high on her forehead as she tried to pull free from his grasp. "If you're waiting for me to be surprised, don't bother."

"I know. I should have listened. I should have believed."

"Yes, you should have."

He felt as if a two-thousand-pound rock had been lifted off his shoulders. He felt change in the air, and it damn near made him laugh with the possibilities of it all. "Don't you get it, Maggie? This changes everything. I'm his father. That means the doctor was wrong. I *can* give you children."

"I already knew that, Justice," she said, glancing to the side as another couple moved in close.

"Which is why we're getting married," he said, the decision made and delivered like an order.

"Excuse me?" She stopped dancing, dragging him to a sudden halt.

"I said we're getting married."

Maggie frowned at someone who jostled her, then turned to him and announced, "I can't marry you. I'm already married."

"You're married?" Justice stared at her as if she were speaking Greek. "What do you mean you're *married?* We've been sleeping together!"

Several heads turned toward them now, and Justice scowled at the most obvious eavesdroppers, shaming them into looking away.

Maggie flushed right up to the roots of her hair, but it was fury, not embarrassment, staining her cheeks. "I'm married to *you,* Justice!"

She spun around on her heel and pushed her way through the crowd. Justice was left staring after her, stunned by her declaration and furious that he hadn't known about this before. He started after her, his steps long and sure. When he caught up with her, he grabbed her arm, turned her to face him and, ignoring the crowd, said, "I signed those divorce papers, Maggie! How the hell are we married?"

"I never filed them, you big jerk." And once again, she pulled free and made her way to the exit. Justice was right behind her, ignoring the wild rustle of conversations and laughter filling the hall behind him.

No doubt people would be talking about this night for a damn long time, he told himself while he took off after Maggie. Mostly, he suspected they'd be calling him a fool, and he'd have to agree.

He and Maggie were still married and he hadn't even known it. When he reached the front door, he raced outside and spotted Maggie walking with furious steps down the sidewalk in the direction of home. Racing for the parking lot, Justice found his car, started it up and chased down his errant wife.

Driving alongside her while she was muttering to herself and bristling with unleashed fury, he rolled down the passenger window and ordered, "Get in the car, Maggie."

"I don't *need* you, Justice." She made sure of the emphasis on the word *need,* and flipped her hair back behind her shoulders. "I'll walk."

"You can't walk it."

"Watch me."

"It's ten miles to the ranch."

She slowed a little, shot him a furious glare and said, "If I get in that car, don't you *dare* speak to me."

"We have to talk about this, Maggie."

"No, we don't. We've said plenty. In front of the whole town, no less. So if you can't promise me silence, I'll walk."

"You're freezing."

"I'm too mad to be cold."

"Damn it, Maggie!" He slammed on the brakes, threw the car into Park and jumped out, racing down the sidewalk to catch up to her. His leg ached like a son of a bitch, but he ignored the pulsing pain in his quest to catch the most infuriating woman he'd ever known. When he grabbed hold of her, he wasn't even surprised to feel her turn into a hundred and twenty pounds of fighting fury.

"Let me go, you big bully!" She wrenched free from his grasp, and when his hand clutched at her forearm again, she swung one leg back to kick him in the shins. He dodged that move and still didn't release her. "Don't touch me. You humiliated me in front of the whole town—"

His eyes went wide. "I humiliated *you?*"

"You told the whole damn room we've been sleeping together."

"And you told 'em we're *married.* Who cares?"

"I do, in case you haven't noticed."

"So, now whose pride is the problem?" That one question delivered in a quiet, reasonable tone did what all of his arguments hadn't. They shut her up but fast, despite how resentful she looked about it.

"Fine. I'll take the ride. But I'm not talking to you, Justice. Not tonight. Not *ever.*"

He smiled to himself as he led her back to the car. One thing in this world he was sure of. Maggie Ryan King wouldn't be able to keep a vow of silence if her own life depended on it.

Eleven

By the time they reached the ranch, Maggie's temper had died into a slow burn. She could still see the shocked, delighted expressions on the faces of the people surrounding them at the ball. She just knew that by tomorrow the story was going to be all over the county.

And there wasn't a damn thing she could do about it. God, she felt like an idiot. She'd been harboring too many dreams about Justice, and seeing them shattered in an instant—in front of an audience—was just humiliating.

She had the door open and was jumping to the ground almost before the car had rolled to a stop.

"Damn it, Maggie! Wait a minute."

She ignored him and marched toward the house. She'd had enough. All she wanted now was to go inside, hug her baby and go to bed. Then when she woke up, she'd pack and get the heck out of Justice's house before he'd even had his morning coffee.

"Maggie, wait for me."

She glanced over her shoulder and hesitated when she saw him limp slightly. But a moment later, she reminded herself that he didn't want her help. He didn't need a therapist. He didn't need her.

Fumbling in her clutch purse for the front door key, she blew out a breath as Justice came up behind her, then reached past her to unlock the door and open it up.

"Thank you."

"You're welcome."

She hurried to the stairs, but his hand on her arm stopped her. "Maggie, at least talk to me."

Turning her gaze up to his, she stared into those dark blue eyes and felt a sigh slide from her throat. "What's left to say?"

"I'm so glad you're home. I was just getting ready to call you!"

They both turned to look up at the head of the stairs, where Mrs. Carey stood, holding a fretful Jonas. Instantly, Maggie gathered the hem of her dress, hiked it above her knees and raced up the stairs. Justice was just a step or two behind her.

Scooping her son into her arms, Maggie cuddled him close and inhaled sharply. "He's burning up!"

Justice came close, laid his hand on the back of Jonas's neck and shot a look at Mrs. Carey. "How long?"

She wrung her hands together. "He's been uneasy all night, but just in the past half hour or so, his fever's climbed. I tried calling the doctor but couldn't get him, so I was going to call you."

"It'll be fine, Mrs. Carey. Don't worry." He plucked Jonas from Maggie's arms and held him close to his chest. With his free hand, he took Maggie's and curled his fingers around hers. She immediately felt better, linked to his warmth and strength. When she looked up at him, she saw the calm, stoic expression she was used to.

Tonight, that was a comfort. She was so scared for Jonas that having Justice beside her, taking charge and looking confident, filled her with the same kind of certainty.

"We'll take him to the E.R.," Justice was saying, already starting down the stairs, taking Maggie with him.

"Don't you want to at least change clothes first?" Mrs. Carey called after them.

"Nope."

The emergency room in any city was a miserable place, Justice thought as he paced back and forth across the pale green linoleum. The smells, the sounds, the suffering, it all piled up on a person the minute he or she walked in the doors. They shouldn't have to be there. Kids shouldn't be allowed to get sick. There should be some sort of cosmic law against making a child who didn't even understand what was happening to him feel so bad. If he had his way, he thought, glancing over his shoulder to where Maggie sat on a gurney cradling Jonas in her lap, he'd see to it that his son was never in a place like this one again.

Everything in Justice tightened as he realized that

what he was feeling was sheer terror with a thick layer of helplessness. And that was new. Justice had never in his life faced a situation that he couldn't fix—except for the time when Maggie had left him. Yet even then, he reminded himself, he could have stopped her if he'd let go of his own pride long enough to admit what was really important.

She'd been right, he realized. At the dance, when she'd accused him of letting their marriage dissolve because of his pride. But damn it, was a man supposed to lay down everything he was for the sake of the woman he loved?

Love.

That one word resonated inside him and seemed to echo over and over again. He loved her completely, desperately, and a life without her seemed like the worst kind of prison sentence.

His gaze fixed on Maggie now, he saw tears glimmering in her eyes. Saw her hand tremble as she stroked their son's back. Then she lifted her gaze to his, and he read absolute trust in those pale blue depths. She was looking to him to fix this. To make it right. She was turning to him despite the hard words and the hurt feelings that lay between them. Justice felt a stir of something elemental inside, and as he held her gaze, he swore to himself that he wouldn't let her down. And when this crisis with Jonas was past, he would do whatever he had to do to keep Maggie in his life.

As soon as they got Jonas taken care of and settled down in his own bed back at the ranch, he was going to tell her that he loved her. Tell her what she meant to him and how empty his life was without her—and his pride be damned.

"Justice, he feels so hot." She cradled the baby's head to her chest and rocked as Jonas sniffled and cried softly, rubbing tiny fists against his eyes.

His heart turned over as he watched the baby and reacted to Maggie's fears.

"I know," he said, "but don't worry, all right? Everything's gonna be fine, and I'm gonna get someone in here to see him even if I have to buy the damn hospital."

Someone out in the waiting room was crying, a moan came from behind a green curtain and nurses carrying clipboards hurried up and down a crowded hallway, their shoes squeaking on the floor. They'd been there an hour already, and but for a nurse checking Jonas's temperature when they first arrived, no one had come to check on the baby.

Maggie forced a smile. "I don't think buying the place is going to be necessary."

"It is if it's the only way I can get somebody's attention." He shot a glare over his shoulder at the hallway and the hospital beyond. "Damn it, he's a baby. He shouldn't have to wait as long as an adult."

Maggie sighed and smiled a little in spite of her obvious fear. "I'm glad you're here with me."

He stopped and stared at her. "You are?"

"God, yes," she said on a choked laugh. "I'd be a gibbering idiot right now if you weren't here with me, pacing in circles like a crazy person and threatening to buy hospitals."

He walked toward her and went into a crouch in front

of her so that he could look at her and his son. He dragged the backs of his fingers across Jonas's too-warm cheek and felt a well of love fill his heart. The baby turned his head, looked at Justice and sighed. A tiny movement. A small breath. And dark blue eyes looking into his with innocence and confusion.

And in that instant, that one, timeless moment, Justice finally completed the fall into an overpowering love for his son. It had been coming on him for days, and maybe it was all instinctual. Like a cow in the spring that can pick out her own calf from the herd.

Nature, drawing families together, bonding them with an indefinable something that in humans was explained as love. A love so rich, so pure, so overwhelming, it nearly brought him to his knees. There was absolutely nothing on this earth that Justice wouldn't do for that boy. Nowhere he wouldn't go. Nothing he wouldn't dare.

"It'll be all right, son," he whispered, his voice breaking as his eyes misted over. "Your daddy's going to see to it."

Maggie reached for his hand and held on. Linked together, a silent moment of complete understanding passed between them, and Justice couldn't help wondering how many other parents had been in this room. How many others had waited interminably for help.

"This is ridiculous," he said. "There should be more doctors. More nurses. People shouldn't have to wait. I swear, I'm going to talk to the city council. Hell, I'll donate an extra wing to this place and pay to see it's better staffed."

"Justice…"

"What the hell is taking so long?" he muttered, squeezing Maggie's hand to relieve his own impatience. "I don't get it. What do you have to do to get seen around here, bleed from an eyeball?"

"Well, wouldn't that be festive?" A woman's voice came from right behind him.

Justice whirled around to face a doctor, in her late fifties, maybe, with short, gray hair, soft brown eyes and an understanding smile on her face.

"I didn't see you."

"Clearly, and as to your earlier question, I'm sorry about the wait, but I'm here now. Let's take a look at your son, shall we?"

As the doctor walked past him toward the baby, she took the stethoscope off from around her neck and fitted the ear pieces into her ears. "Lay him down on the gurney, please," she said softly.

Maggie did but kept one hand on Jonas's belly, as if to reassure both of them. Justice stepped up behind her and laid one hand on her shoulder, linking the three of them together, into a unit.

"Let's just listen to your heart, little guy," the doctor crooned, giving Jonas a smile. She moved her stethoscope around the baby's narrow chest and made a note on a chart. Justice tried to read it but couldn't get a good look.

Then she checked his temperature and looked in his eyes. Finally, when the baby's patience evaporated and he let loose a wail, the doctor looked up and smiled.

"What is it? What's wrong with him?" Maggie reached to her shoulder to lay her hand over Justice's.

"Let me guess," the doctor said, hooking her stethoscope around her neck again before scooping Jonas up in capable hands and swaying to soothe his tears. "This is your first baby."

"Yes, but what does that have to do with anything?" Justice asked.

Jonas's tears had subsided, and he was suddenly fascinated by the doctor's stethoscope.

"Babies sometimes spike fevers," the doctor was saying. "Not sure why, really. Could be a new tooth. Could be he didn't feel well. Could be growing pains." Still smiling, she handed Jonas to his mother and looked from Maggie to Justice.

"The point is, he's fine. You have a perfectly healthy son." She checked her chart. "According to this, his temperature has already dropped. You can take him home, give him a tepid bath, it'll make him feel better. Then just keep an eye on him, and if you're worried about anything at all, you can either call me—" she wrote down a phone number on the back of her card "—or bring him back in."

Justice took the business card she handed him. He glanced at her name and nodded. "Thanks, Dr. Rosen. We appreciate it."

She grinned at him. "It's my pleasure. But if you meant what you were saying earlier, the hospital could use the extra wing and I've got lots of ideas."

Justice stared down at her and found himself smiling. There was so much relief coursing through his veins at the moment that he would have built the woman her own clinic if she'd asked him to. And he had the distinct feeling she knew it. As it was, he tucked her card into his breast pocket and said, "Give me a few days, and we'll talk about those ideas."

Her eyebrows shot straight up in surprise, but she recovered quickly. "You've got a deal, Mr. King."

When she left, Maggie leaned in close to Justice and he slid his arms around her and their son, holding them tightly to him. He rested his chin on top of Maggie's head and took a long minute to simply enjoy this feeling.

He had his family in his arms, and there was simply no way he would lose them now.

The ride back to the ranch was quiet and Maggie was grateful.

There were too many thoughts whirling through her mind for her to be able to hold any kind of rational conversation. Behind her in his car seat, Jonas slept fretfully. Soft whimpers and sighs drifted to her, and she turned in her seat to look at him, needing to reassure herself that he was safe. And healthy.

When she faced the front again, she took a moment to study Justice's profile in the muted light from the dashboard. His eyes were fixed on the road ahead of them. His mouth was firm and tight, his jaw clenched as if he, too, were having trouble relaxing from the scare they'd had. In the shadows he looked fierce and proud and untouchable.

But the memory of his arms coming around her, holding her and the baby, was so strong and fresh in her mind that she knew he was right now hiding his emotions from her. Which was probably just as well, she thought. Now that they were back on solid ground, now that they knew Jonas was fine, everything would return to the way it was. The way it had to be.

God, she could still hear him at the dance. *We'll get married.* Did he actually think that she would stay with him just because Jonas was his son? Or because he knew now that he could give her more children? Didn't he see that a marriage for the sake of the children was a mistake for everyone involved?

She blew out a breath as Justice steered the car down the long drive to the ranch house. Before he'd even turned off the engine, the front door flew open and a wide slice of lamplight cut into the darkness. Mrs. Carey stood on the threshold, wearing a floor-length terry cloth robe, fisted in one hand at her neck.

"Thank goodness, you're back. He's really all right?" she called out. "I've been so worried."

Maggie stepped out of the car. "He's fine, Mrs. Carey."

"Go on to bed," Justice added as he came around the front of the car. "We'll talk in the morning."

The older woman nodded and turned for the stairs, leaving the front door open with the lamplight shining like a path in the darkness.

Maggie went to the backseat, opened the door and deftly undid the straps holding Jonas in his car seat. He stirred a little, but as soon as his head was nestled onto his mother's shoulder, he went back to sleep. Having her child cuddled in close gave Maggie the strength she was going to need when she spoke to Justice. So she held on to Jonas as if he were a talisman as they headed for the house.

Once inside, Justice closed the door and silence descended on them. It had been one of the longest nights of Maggie's life—and it wasn't over yet. She couldn't wait until morning to say what had to be said. She didn't know if she'd find the will to have this conversation in the morning; by then, she might have talked herself out of it, and she couldn't allow that to happen no matter how her heart was breaking.

"Quite a night," Justice said, splintering the quiet with his deep, rumbling voice.

"Yes, it was." She turned her gaze up to his and stared into those dark blue eyes for a long moment. God, how she would miss him. *Say it now, Maggie,* she told herself firmly. *Do it and get it over with.* "Justice…"

He watched her, waiting, and she could see by his rigid stance that he wasn't expecting good news.

"I'm going to be leaving tomorrow," she said, the words bursting from her in a determined rush.

"What?" He took a step toward her, but Maggie backed up, stroking one hand up and down Jonas's spine. "Why?"

"You know why," she said sadly, feeling the sudden sting of tears. She blinked them back, desperate to at least complete this last part of their marriage with a little dignity. "Your leg's nearly healed. You don't need me, Justice, and it's time I actually moved on with my life."

"Move on?" He shook his head, ground his teeth together and said, "Now you want to move on? Now when we know I'm Jonas's father? Now that we can have the big family you always wanted?"

"It's not about that," she said with a sigh.

"I signed those divorce papers a hell of a long time ago, Maggie, but you never filed them. Why?"

She shook her head now. "You know why."

"Because you love me."

"Yes, all right?" She raised her voice and immediately regretted it when Jonas stirred against her. Hushing him, Maggie lowered her voice again and said, "I did. Still do. But when I go home, I'm finally going to file those divorce papers, Justice."

"Why now?" He stared at her, his features shadowed by the overhead light.

"Because I'm not going to stay married to you for the sake of our son," she told him, willing him to understand. "It wouldn't be right for any of us. Don't you see, Justice? I love you, but I need to be loved in return. I want to be needed. I want a man to share Jonas's life with me. I want a man who'll stand beside me—"

"Like I did tonight, you mean?"

"Yes," she said quickly, breathlessly. "Like you did tonight. But, Justice, that's not who you are normally. You don't let people in. You don't let yourself *need* anyone." She blew out a breath, bit down on her trembling lower lip and said, "You'd rather be right than be in love. Your pride is more important to you than anything or anyone. And I can't live like that. I won't."

She turned for the stairs, her heart heavy, her soul empty. She picked up the hem of her dress, took one step and was stopped by a single word from Justice.

"Please."

Stunned to her core, Maggie slowly turned to look at him. He stood alone in the entryway, a solitary man in the shadows though he stood beneath an overhead light. There was hunger in his eyes and a taut, uncomfortable expression on his face.

She'd almost convinced herself she had imagined him speaking when he said again, louder this time, "Please stay."

Maggie swayed in place, shocked by his words, astonished that he would swallow his pride and so damn hopeful she nearly couldn't breathe. "Justice? I don't think I've ever heard you say that before."

"You haven't." Justice went to her then, desperate to make her hear him. Make her understand everything he'd learned in the past few hours. It had been coming on for days, he knew, but the time spent in that emergency room, sharing their fears, standing beside her, wanting to take on the world to help his son, had coalesced everything into a very clear vision.

Without Maggie, he had nothing.

She'd knocked the floor out from under his feet by telling him she was going to leave him again. And if he allowed it this time, he knew it would be permanent. If he clung to his pride and refused to bend, he would lose everything that had ever mattered to him.

So he threw his pride out the proverbial window and risked everything by going to her. Two long steps brought him to her side. He reached for her but stopped himself. First, he would say what she needed to hear. The words he'd denied them both the last time they were together.

"I need you, Maggie. More than my next breath I need you."

Her beautiful eyes filled with tears that crested and spilled over to roll down her cheeks unchecked. Her lower lip trembled, and he lifted one hand to soothe that lip with the pad of his thumb. His gaze moved over her, from her tumbled, tangled hair to the now-ruined elegant ball gown. She was magnificent and she was his. As she was always meant to be. This was a woman born to stand beside a man no matter what came at them in life. This was a woman to grow old with. To treasure.

To thank God for every night.

And damned if he'd lose her.

"Justice, I—"

He shook his head fiercely and spoke up, keeping his voice low so as not to disturb his son. "No, let me say this, so you'll never doubt it again. I love you more than should be humanly possible. The last time you left, you took my heart with you. When you came back, I came alive again. I won't let you leave, Maggie. If you go, I'll go with you."

She laughed a little, tears still spilling down her cheeks, and she'd never looked more lovely to him.

"See?" he asked. "No more pride. No more anything unless you're with me."

"Oh, God…"

"Stay with me, Maggie," he said gently, tipping her chin up so that he could look into those tear-washed eyes of hers. "Please stay. Please love me again. Please let me love you and Jonas and all the other children we'll have together."

She laughed again, a small sound filled with delight and wonder, and Justice could have kicked his own ass for taking so long, for wasting so much time, before setting things right between them.

"It's getting easier to say *please*," he told her, "and I swear, tonight won't be the last time you hear it."

"I don't know what to say," she admitted, staring up at him with a smile curving her mouth and tears glistening like diamonds on her cheeks.

"Say yes," he urged, pulling her and the baby into the circle of his arms. "Say you'll stay. Say I didn't blow it this time."

She leaned her head against his chest and sighed heavily. "I love you so much."

Justice grinned and held them a little tighter. So much relief had flooded his system in the past hour that he felt almost drunk on it. He wanted to shout. He wanted to go call his brother Jeff and thank him for sending Maggie back home where she belonged.

Then she pulled back and looked up at him again. "Am I dreaming?"

He smiled at her, bent his head and placed one quick kiss on her upturned mouth. "No dream, Maggie. Just a man telling you that you are his heart. Just your husband asking you to give him another chance to prove to you that he can be the man you need. The man you deserve."

"Oh, Justice," she said with a sigh, lifting one hand to cup his cheek, "you've always been the only man for me. You've had my heart since the moment I saw you, and that will never change."

He rested his forehead against hers and gave silent thanks for coming to his senses in time.

Then Maggie shifted their son in her arms and handed him to Justice. "Why don't we take him upstairs and tuck him in? Together."

Justice cradled the tiny boy who was the second miracle in his life and dropped his free arm around

Maggie's shoulders. Together, they climbed the stairs, and when they reached the landing, Maggie stopped and smiled up at him. "Once our son is settled in, I think I'm going to need a little attention from my husband."

Justice grinned at her. "I think that can be arranged."

Her head on his shoulder, they walked down the hallway of home, passing from the shadows into the light.

* * * * *

WYOMING
WEDDING

BY
SARA ORWIG

Dear Reader,

Wyoming Wedding resolves the competition of Jared Dalton, Chase Bennett and Matt Rome, three affluent cousins who made a bet to see who could make the most money during the year. Two cousins, Jared and Chase, have been drawn north to their roots in South Dakota and Montana. Ambitious and driven, Matt has opted to have his headquarters in the state where he grew up, thus we travel in this story to the third state, beautiful Wyoming.

Through his college years and shortly afterwards, Matt Rome, the tough former rodeo champion, parlayed a bull-riding fortune into lucrative investments and switched to a finance career. Now Matt needs a wife to acquire more wealth and win the bet with his cousins.

What happens when two people who are poles apart in their backgrounds – and are equally poles apart where they're determined to go in their futures – find a hot chemistry between them whenever they are together? Sparks fly when they agree on a temporary paper marriage that sizzles from the first night together. The temporary marriage is merely a gambit to get what each one wants, yet what happens after they have exchanged vows? Read and see how the conflict spins out and is resolved with the third CEO and the waitress he discovers he can't resist.

Sara Orwig

Sara Orwig lives in Oklahoma. She has a patient husband who will take her on research trips anywhere from big cities to old forts. She is an avid collector of Western history books. With a master's degree in English, Sara has written historical romance, mainstream fiction and contemporary romance. Books are beloved treasures that take Sara to magical worlds, and she loves both reading and writing them.

To David

One

October

Matt Rome sat in one of the best steak houses in Cheyenne, Wyoming. Waitpeople moved between linen-covered tables that held flickering candles. The dim lighting cast a spell over the room. The piano player explored an old tune. Having dined earlier with the woman from his most recent affair, Matt was back for a late-night coffee—on a mission. He'd tipped the maitre d' generously to seat him in the section assigned to Brianna Costin. While he watched her wait tables, hurrying between the dining room and kitchen, he ran his fingers along the handle of his coffee cup.

Whenever he saw her, it only served to reinforce his

opinion that she was one of the most beautiful women he'd ever seen. The fact that she was a waitress was no hindrance to his plans. Just the opposite—her status and income would probably make her more cooperative. She was tall with luscious curves and flawless skin. Her black hair was always thickly coiled at her nape. She suited his future plans fine.

His time and patience both had dwindled and still, he had no more likely a candidate for a paper marriage. Once, he would have given serious consideration to Nicole, the woman he'd had dinner with, but no longer. She was too demanding of his time. Their fight tonight had been the final push for them to break off relations. It had been easy to tell her goodbye when she'd issued an ultimatum to spend more time with her or get out of her life. His thoughts shifted to Brianna as she approached his table.

Usually his waitress now that he'd started requesting her, she was efficient and courteous. Beyond that, she seemed barely to take note of her patrons. Even though Matt always gave her impersonal courtesy—as if he hadn't noticed her, he couldn't avoid watching her as she made the rounds. Sometimes she would glance his way, whether out of professional reasons to keep up with her patrons' needs, or something more personal, he had no idea.

It was half an hour until closing, yet a few diners still lingered. Holding a carafe of coffee, Brianna approached his table to refill his cup.

"Do you want anything else?" she asked. Even

though she never held eye contact long, when he gazed into her thickly fringed green eyes, the contact fueled a primitive reaction.

"As a matter of fact, yes, I do," he replied. "I'm back to see you. I'd like to talk to you after work."

"I'm sorry. I never socialize with our patrons," she answered coolly, all friendliness leaving her voice. "It's better that way," she added without a flicker of change in her expression.

Unaccustomed to rejection, he bit back a smile. "I'm asking for an hour over a cup of coffee. If you prefer, you can meet me somewhere else. I promise you, I'm safe to be with," he said, reaching into his pocket to hand her a business card. "I'm Matt Rome."

"I know who you are," she replied. "I imagine everyone in Cheyenne knows who you are, Mr. Rome." Without glancing at the card, she pocketed it.

"It won't take long," Matt continued. "How's the Talon Club?" It was an expensive private club located at the top of one of the city's tallest buildings.

She smiled. "Thanks, but I don't believe they would allow me in—I'm not a member."

"I belong to the club. If you'll meet me in the lobby of the building, after your shift, they'll let us in. Or if you prefer, since it's three or four miles from your work, I can wait and follow you home to take you from your place."

As if mulling over his offer, she paused. "I have a feeling you intend to ask me something big. I can save you time by saying no now."

Again, he suppressed a smile. "This is not what

you're thinking, I can assure you. Here isn't the place to talk. I would wager a sizable bet you'll be pleased we talked tonight."

For the first time since he'd met her he seemed to have her full attention as her eyes narrowed a fraction. He waited, his amazement increasing. Matt could usually outlast any silence at a bargaining table, though as time stretched, he decided she was sticking by her refusal. "I understand you can't talk as freely here," he said finally.

"That's for sure. My clothes might not be presentable for the club either."

"Yes, they are," he said, glad to find she was considering his offer. She wore what every other waitperson in the restaurant wore—black slacks and a black shirt, only on her, the outfit was as stylish as a high-dollar ensemble.

"Very well, I'll meet you in the lobby at a quarter before midnight."

"Excellent," he said, his eagerness making him laugh at himself. When had it ever been this difficult to get a woman to go out with him? He was more amused than annoyed.

"You don't intend to order anything else now?" she asked.

He raised his coffee. "This is sufficient. As a matter of fact, I'll take the check so they can clear this table."

She left to return in a few minutes with his bill. "Thanks."

"I'll see you in the lobby," he said, and she was gone. Congratulating himself on his victory in getting her to go out, he watched her walk away. The black slacks rode low below her tiny waist that was emphasized by the ties of her white apron. He wondered how her legs looked—they were obviously long and slender. He liked watching her, mentally peeling away the slacks, wishing for a moment this was a restaurant where waitpeople wore skimpier clothing.

Despite the fact that she was reserved, and with obvious barriers, he remained interested.

Time seemed to drag in the lobby of the building that housed the club until the revolving door spun to reveal her. The apron was gone and her straight black hair cascaded over her shoulders. As she approached him, her hips swayed slightly. His desire stirred.

"I'm glad you came," he said, lust warming him.

"I'll reserve judgment on whether I can say the same or not."

He laughed. "I'll admit, the last woman who responded similarly was a little six-year-old girl in grade school, I think. I had some hostile encounters in the first grade," he said, expecting to wring a smile from her. Instead, she gave him another solemn glance and remained silent. "Let's have a drink and then we can talk," he said, motioning toward the dark, glossy elevators.

"Is this why you've asked for my section each time you've come to the dining room lately?" she probed as the elevator sped them skyward.

"Not exactly…maybe partially. You're good at your job."

"Thank you," she answered, giving him the feeling she was hoping to get this meeting over with so she could go home. Her lack of interest was beginning to bother him.

The maitre d' greeted them and escorted them to a table by the window overlooking the city. On the table, a small candle threw a soft glow on Brianna, catching shining glints in her silky dark hair. They gave their drink orders, hers a limeade and his a glass of brandy. As soon as they were alone, she looked at him expectantly.

"I've wanted to meet you," he said, and something flickered in her eyes that made him suspect that she felt the sparks as much as he did. That awareness jolted him.

"Brianna, I've had my staff look into your background so I could learn more about you," he said. This time the flash in her green eyes was unmistakable indignation.

"I'd call that an invasion of my privacy."

"Not really. I only have information that is more or less public knowledge. You're from Blakely, Wyoming, the first of your family to attend college. You're enrolled in Wyoming University in Laramie, commuting from Cheyenne—that one stumped me even though it isn't a long drive."

"I doubt if it gave the information that I found a better job here and I only have classes on campus on Tuesdays and Thursdays this semester, thanks to the convenience of online classes. So tell me what else you know about me."

"You have five siblings, two married sisters and three younger brothers. One brother is still in high school and all three of them work. You are a senior in college and you hope to go to law school."

"So far, you're right. How much deeper did you look into my private life? Do you do this with every woman you invite out?"

"Calm down," he said, noticing her words were becoming more clipped. Her irritation was showing.

"How's school going?"

"I have a suspicion you already know. I like my classes. So far, I have all A's."

"Commendable," he remarked. "And at the moment there is no man in your life. I'm surprised there wasn't one waiting in the wings. You're a beautiful woman."

"Thanks, and there isn't one, waiting or otherwise," she said with the first faint smile since her arrival.

"What do you really enjoy? Tell me about yourself," he said, leaning back slightly.

"I have the feeling I'm being interviewed for something," she said. "I like cold winter nights, roaring fires, roasting marshmallows. I like achieving my goals, living in the city." As she talked, he watched her. They were the closest face-to-face they had ever been, and she was even more gorgeous up close. Her green eyes captivated him, and he could only imagine them filled with passion. Her bow-shaped mouth and full lips made it impossible to avoid conjuring up fantasies of kissing her. She was composed, rarely gesturing when she talked with a soft voice that was as sexy as everything else about her.

"And what do you dream about doing?" he asked,

trying to get through the barrier she kept between them. For some reason, probably out of her past, she had a chip on her shoulder. Or perhaps it was because any man with a pulse would try to hit on her. He knew she had men in her life on occasion.

"I dream about being a lawyer, having complete independence, helping my family."

"But on a more personal level? Everybody has hopes and longings."

"That's easy," she replied, smiling at him. "I want to see things I've never seen in real life—palm trees, seashells, the ocean, tropics with balmy weather. I've never seen the ocean. Actually, I've never been out of Wyoming or even flown in a plane." For the first time, she looked as if she had relaxed with him. "I dream about going to Europe because pictures of foreign places are breathtaking. So, Mr. Rome, what do you dream of doing when you've probably already done everything in life you want to do?"

"It's Matt, not Mr. Rome. What do I want? That's part of what this is about," he said, pausing when their drinks were served. "I hope what I'm going to discuss is something appealing, not something threatening to you."

"Since we've been all around the mulberry bush, so to speak, why don't you tell me why I'm here?"

"I'm not certain being so direct is going to help you in law school," he observed.

"I'm not in law school tonight," she said, and he knew she was waiting for an answer to her question.

"This evening isn't going exactly the way I expected.

I'll grant that while I don't know you, I'd like to. Will you have dinner with me tomorrow night?"

When she stared at him in silence, he thought perhaps she was going to get up and walk out. "You could have asked me that when I was your waitress at dinner. It didn't take all this."

"I want to get to know you. Also, I had a feeling if I'd asked you then, you would have turned me down."

"You're right. I think there's more to this than going to dinner with you. Guys at the club ask me out often and they don't actually take me out ahead of time to do so."

"Let me guess—you've never gone out with any of them."

"You're right," she said. "You and the other men who ask me out want one thing—my body. I'm not in your social class and we both know that. I'm a waitress, you're a wealthy bachelor. Not all the men who've asked me out are even single. I've received explicit invitations when the wife is in the powder room. At least you're not married."

As she looked away, her cheeks flushed a bright pink. The color heightened her beauty, and he knew he wanted her body as much as any other man had. Every inch of her was enticing. So far, he also enjoyed being with her—all reasons to support the argument that he was making an acceptable decision.

Zach Gentner's warning floated in the back of his mind. He could recall too clearly his best friend and chief investment advisor trying to talk him out of even thinking about getting to know her. Zach had his own arguments:

her poverty-stricken background, her lack of education, her lower-class life, her large, uneducated family.

Worst of all, she was three or four weeks pregnant by a man who had run out on her. That last argument had almost carried the day for Zach, until the next time Matt had gone to the club to eat. With Nicole accompanying him, he had surreptitiously watched Brianna, finding he was still drawn to her. Because of her pregnancy she might possibly be an even more likely candidate. She would need the money—no other woman on his list of candidates did. Until Brianna, the women he had taken out since college had been almost as wealthy or wealthier than he was. He knew, too, without any doubts, that all the other women on his list, including Nicole Doyle, would not want a two-year marriage of convenience. Not at all. He and Nicole had fought tonight over how seldom she had seen him. He was tired of her relentless dissatisfaction, which made him leery of choosing her as a candidate for his proposal.

Brianna seemed the perfect choice and when the marriage ended, she would be easier to get out of his life.

Leaning forward, she propped her chin on her fist and seemed to shake off the anger in her previous comment as she smiled at him. "So again, Matt, what's behind all this really?" Brianna inquired in a coaxing voice.

Desire flared. He wondered if lust had completely clouded his judgment as Zach had declared. Perhaps it had, because at the moment, Matt knew he craved her with an intensity that surprised him.

"All right, I'll get to the point. First hear me out. I'm

going to present something to you. Before you give me an answer, I want you to think about it for at least twenty-four hours or even several days if you want. Will you agree to that?"

As disappointment took the smile off her face, she sat up straight, all of her barriers once again in place with a frosty chill settling around her. "I think I can give you an answer right now. It's definitely not."

"You're jumping to conclusions. I'm not going to ask you to be my mistress."

Her eyes widened in surprise. "I can't imagine one other possibility you'd have for wanting to talk to me. I don't have any skills or a degree, so you're not out to hire me. What *do* you want?" Now she was filled with obvious curiosity, and he was satisfied that he finally had her full attention. The first little nagging doubts tugged at him that he might be making a mistake, only not for the reasons Zach had given. Matt didn't care about her background because she could rise above that and, as his wife, she would be accepted. What worried him for the first time was finding out that she had a strong will and a stubborn streak. Sticking with his decision, he pushed away worries.

He took her hand in his. The first physical contact startled him. He was going to make a commitment. "I need a wife. I want a marriage of convenience."

Two

Shock came first. A marriage proposal from Matt Rome, probably the wealthiest man in Wyoming, a man she knew only because she was his *waitress*. Her second thought was—as his wife, she would have money. Real money, oodles of money.

A mansion and a sports car and no more struggling to put food on the table—her head spun. At the same time she was filled with disbelief. She turned icy and alternately awash in heat.

Then common sense set in. Billionaires did not propose marriage to her. Actually, only Tommy Grogan at home had ever proposed and that had been when she was sixteen years old. She knew, down to her toes, that there was a catch to this offer and it must be a whopper.

All her defenses rushed back and she was ready to end the evening and go home in spite of her promise to hear him out. Reeling from it or not, she suspected if she knew the full story, she wouldn't want any part of what he had on his mind.

"Why me?" she asked. "You have beautiful women in your life from the same kind of society background. Why are you asking me instead of one of them?"

"That's your opinion, not mine. For one thing, they bore me. For another, I want this marriage for a short time, two years max. Then I want to be able to dissolve it without an emotional hassle and walk away. I think that will be much easier to do with you than with one of them," he added dryly. The latter reason made sense to her.

"Any other explanations why you chose me?" she asked, knowing that when he found out about her secret pregnancy, he would withdraw his offer. That alone was justification for him to find a more likely candidate for his marriage proposal.

"Why do you want this?" she asked, knowing there had to be something behind his proposal.

"There's an international investment group of men I want to join. I have a couple of friends in it. I'm a likely candidate except for being a bachelor. They're concerned about a bachelor's lifestyle, even though mine is far from wild. If I marry, they'll view me as settled."

She had mixed feelings: caution vied with temptation. She couldn't imagine it was as simple as he presented, yet he was bound to reward her generously. Two years as Matt Rome's wife? The thought made her giddy. Dreading telling him about her pregnancy, she knew she should end this.

"Why would you want to be in the group? You're enormously successful now. You don't need money."

When he smiled, her heart skipped. He was irresistibly handsome with his curly black hair and thick lashes that emphasized his clear blue eyes. She, along with all the other females in the vicinity, had always noticed him when he'd come to the dining room where she worked. Fortunately, she'd never made an issue of it and he didn't seem aware of her reaction to him. She'd heard everyone talk. In a club filled with wealthy members, Matt Rome stood out because he was the richest. And probably the youngest. He was hands-down the best-looking, with a smile to die for.

He had seemed attentive to the different women he brought to the steak house, although she knew earlier he and the woman with him had had a heated, drawn-out disagreement.

"I'd like to get into the group because they're far more successful than I've been. They're international and will open doors for me that won't be opened otherwise. I'll make more money faster."

"You have more money than you can spend. Why would you want to make more?" she persisted, and his blue eyes twinkled with amusement.

"Maybe it's the challenge of making it. There's never such a thing as too much money," he added as she shook her head.

"I can't imagine wealth like yours. If I had that much, I think I'd want to quit striving for more."

"You'll see someday. If you become a successful lawyer, you'll want more money."

"That wouldn't bring me anywhere close to your wealth." She sipped her limeade and put it down. "You don't want me. Even if you may have checked me out, there's a very big reason you will want to look elsewhere."

"Your pregnancy?" he asked.

She stared at him for a moment, at a loss for words. "I thought medical records were private."

"They are. There are other ways to find out."

"One of my friends must have talked," she said, narrowing her eyes and remembering only two of her closest friends, plus the father, had been told what she thought had been her secret. "I suppose once you tell someone, it's no longer a secret."

"A pregnancy is something you can hide for only so long. It might actually be a plus. I understand you're not very far along."

She shook her head, amazed by all he'd learned about her. "No, I went to the doctor two weeks ago and found out. I'm barely a full month."

"It definitely doesn't show," he said.

"No, not yet."

"What about the father?"

"He's out of my life. He's gone and he left no forwarding address—so to speak—which suited me. He legally signed away all privileges and rights." She continued, "He came from a big family and he never wanted kids. Actually, he turned out to be a jerk. He is on a full scholarship, so he's intelligent, which may be a good biological trait for the baby. But he and I didn't part on the best of terms," she answered, giving Matt the same information she'd told her two closest friends. She'd been devastated when the doctor told her she was pregnant. One of her friends had had a party and she remembered how much fun she'd had that night with a guy she saw there and had known from school. She tried to focus on what Matt was saying to her, looking at his blue eyes, eyes the color of the Wyoming sky on a clear summer day. She knew she had to get away from his influence, to think over his proposal with a clear head.

"You've told me what you'll get out of this marriage of convenience. What will I get from the union?"

He smiled, that captivating smile that had probably set too many female hearts fluttering. He was handsome. Handsome and rich beyond dreams. "You'll get half a million dollars when we marry, the other half when we divorce."

"A million dollars!" She gasped. She stared at him, unable to imagine having such money.

"That's right," he confirmed his statement.

"And a divorce later—won't they boot you out if you divorce?"

"They have two men who have divorced and the group let them remain, so I think I can weather that scandal. We'll keep a divorce low-key. I'm willing to take the risk to get this marriage and join the group."

"You expect to get your way, don't you?"

"Why not?" He smiled at her, conveying a cocky self-assurance. "Now back to discussing what you get out of this union. In addition," he continued, "I'll take care of the expenses of your pregnancy and the baby's birth. I'll give you a weekly allowance of a thousand dollars, that's yours for however you wish to spend it. You can buy a new car with my approval of your selection. It's yours when we part. You can get a new wardrobe now with my approval—no mink coat at this point. I want a real marriage as far as sex is concerned and I want you to move in with me."

In spite of trying, she couldn't stifle her laugh. He cocked one dark eyebrow as he surveyed her with curiosity. "You don't know me—you may not be able to stand me after I move in with you," she said. The money kept dangling in her thoughts. A million dollars for her!

"We're doing all right so far. Granted, the past hour has been a little cut-and-dried. But don't worry, I'll move you out if I don't like it," he replied.

She shook her head. "You must want in this group desperately."

His amusement vanished. "Joining this investment bunch is important and I intend to get an invitation from them. If it means I have to marry to do so, so be it."

"I can't imagine any amount of money making it worthwhile to get locked into a loveless marriage."

"That's why you're the perfect selection for me," he said, leaning forward to grasp her hand. "You're gorgeous," he said, and her pulse jumped to a faster speed.

"You're intelligent. You're sexy. You work hard. You're honest."

"You don't know that at all. Sorry, I guess that didn't sound so good on my part," she added hastily and knew her face flushed in embarrassment. "There has to be something to this besides more money."

"No, there isn't. Money is enough."

"Then why the rush? Why don't you wait? In another few months you might fall in love. Why rush into a paper marriage?"

"I'm in a rush because my two cousins and I have a bet that ends next May. It's to see which one of us can make the most money before that May deadline. I want to win the bet. If I join this group, I think I can."

"All this is over a bet?" she asked in disbelief, beginning to wonder if he was as smart as she'd heard and read. "No bet is worth getting married for."

"Ahh, this one might be. I'll win that bet, I think, if I join this group."

"Then it must be for an enormous prize. How much money is at stake?"

"We each put in five million dollars. In May winner gets all and the winner treats for a weekend getaway where we can all be together."

"Five million each!" she echoed. She had always heard about his wealth, to actually deal with it left her dismayed. She counted pennies. He didn't even count thousands. "That's astounding you toss money around like that."

"It isn't exactly tossing. I intend to win, I promise you."

"You're driven," she declared, staring at him and wondering about his life that seemed totally focused on making money.

"The pot is calling the kettle black. You're ambitious yourself."

"On a tiny scale compared to you. And our reasons are light-years apart. My goals are meant to get me out of a life of poverty. Your goals are to achieve a whim."

She smiled to take the edge off her statement, feeling sparks ignite between them. He certainly knew how to charm women.

"How do those terms sound to you?" he asked.

"Like a dream. They don't seem real to me. I've never even been alone with you until we came here," she said.

"So far, so good, I'd say. I'm enjoying the moment."

"To my surprise, I am, too," she said. "How could I not enjoy being proposed to and offered so much money?" she asked and they both smiled.

"It has happened, though. I want you to think about it for a few days."

"Where will I live if I marry you?" she asked, thinking the moment was turning surreal.

"I live here in Cheyenne. I have other homes and I have a ranch near Jackson Hole. Does it matter?"

"Not really. When I finish school, I had expected to move out of state to get a job. Now I'll stay near my family because of my baby."

"You may want to rethink your future. If you marry me and I pay you a million, you won't need degrees. I don't want you laboring over college texts when I need you at my side for parties and travel."

She pursed her lips and ran her finger along her cold, empty glass as she shook her head. "That's a problem because I don't want to give up my education. I can take classes in the mornings when you're at work. Also, I can juggle things and make arrangements with professors to make up the work when we travel."

Now he sat in silence, turning his empty brandy glass in his fingers. He had well-shaped hands, broad shoulders and she knew enough from newspapers that he had once been a champion bull rider. Beneath the slick billionaire façade was a tough cowboy, she suspected and guessed that was why he'd kept the family ranch and still remained based in Wyoming.

Feeling their clash of wills, she wondered how often they would disagree. Even if it would be easier to get her out of his life, he was taking a huge chance by asking her to marry him when he didn't know her.

"I was thinking," she voiced her thoughts aloud, "you'd be better off marrying someone in love with you because she'd do everything you want to try to keep you happy."

"If we agree to this marriage, I think we'll work out our differences," he said, and she could detect the supreme confidence in his tone.

"If this marriage is for two years, you'll have a baby on your hands," she reminded him.

"With my money, I don't see that as a problem. I'd claim your baby as mine as far as the public is concerned. That will make me appear even more settled and reliable to this investment group."

Her indignation flared—he would view her baby merely as a means to achieve his end he wanted. She bit back a retort because she wanted to think about possibilities. He wanted to look married and settled and respectable. Reliable. That might give her leverage for bargaining for more for her baby.

"I can see the wheels turning in your head," he said, looking mildly amused. "What do you want?"

"I'm thinking about what you just told me. You'll look terrible if you walk out on a wife and baby."

"So I will, but I'll probably get some sympathy if you walk out on me and take the baby, leaving me because of the long hours I work."

She shook her head. "I suppose that would bring you some sympathy, especially from men who work as long and hard as you."

"So this all looks viable to you?"

"I'm torn between walking out right now or staying and giving consideration to your proposal. It's the coldest, most hard-hearted marriage proposal ever. On the other hand, you know I need what you're offering."

"So you'll think it over?" he asked.

"Of course I will. In some ways, it's the opportunity of a lifetime."

"Maybe if we can get past the proposal, we can find we're good company for each other. Sooner or later, I would have gotten to know you anyway."

She smiled at him. "I find that one a real stretch. I

don't think I would have been in your future if you hadn't needed this."

"We'll see how it goes between us." He leaned forward and reached across the table. "Let's let it go for now. You can mull it over later."

She glanced at her watch, looking up at him in surprise. "It's after one! We need to get out of here so they can close."

"The club is open until two," he said, coming around to hold her chair. "You need your sleep for the baby. We should go." He walked with her out to her car. "I'll follow you home. It's late."

"I drive alone all the time. It's a wonder I survived before I met you."

"I'll follow you," he said in a tone that ended her argument. He put his hand on the car door to stop her from opening it and she looked up at him.

"Tomorrow night, would you prefer to go out to eat, or to eat at my place where we can have a little more privacy to discuss my proposal? You can see where you might live soon."

"I can't believe this is actually happening to me."

"You'll believe it before long."

"Can I look up anything about this investment group you want to get into?"

"Yes." He pulled a card out of his pocket and wrote on the back of it. "Here are some names. Start with these. This group is real."

"I'm sure it's real. I want to know about it."

"I'll pick you up tomorrow night about seven."

"You know common sense tells me to say no to you."

"I don't see that. You stand to gain a lot and lose very little unless you hate being with me."

"You know full well there isn't a female on this earth whose heartbeat doesn't speed up when you're around, so there's no danger of any woman not being able to stand being with you," she said.

"Until this moment, I was beginning to wonder about you. This is the coolest reception in my adult life."

He stretched his arm out again, placing his hand on her car door and blocking her from opening it. Leaning closer, he lowered his voice. "I've proposed to you tonight and we've never even kissed. That's a giant unknown when there's a marriage proposal."

While her pulse had raced all night, now her heart thudded and she looked at his mouth. "I can remedy that one," she said, tingling at the thought of kissing him. She stepped closer to slide her arm around his shoulders, feeling the soft wool of his suit jacket and beneath it, the warmth of his body.

She moved even closer, stood on tiptoe and placed her lips on his. She had started the kiss as if she were tackling a math problem, yet the moment his tongue slid into her mouth, the kiss changed. Heat suffused her, spiraling down to pool low within her and build a fire of physical longing that burned with scorching flames.

His arm banded her waist, pulling her tightly against him, his fingers tangling in her long hair. He leaned over her, his tongue thrusting deep and exploring slowly, a hot, sexy kiss that intensified desire. She would never again be able to view him as dispassionately as she had prior to this moment. His kiss was melting her, stirring longing for so much more with him, surprising her because never had any man's kisses affected her the way Matt's did.

His fiery kiss made his proposal infinitely more inviting. She suspected she wouldn't think straight in the next few minutes about any decisions.

How long they kissed she didn't know. She ran her fingers through his hair, down the strong column of his neck. His tight embrace pressed his arousal against her, hard and ready.

It was late; the restaurant would close and other patrons would come out into the parking lot. She and Matt weren't kissing in a private place. All the dim arguments nagged, though they were faint inducements to stop.

Her pulse roared and she wanted to unbutton his shirt and place her hands on his chest. Realizing what she was about to do, she gathered her wits and pushed lightly against his chest instead.

Pausing, he raised his head as they both gasped for breath.

"Marry me, Brianna," he said and she opened her mouth to answer. Instantly he shook his head and put his finger on her lips. He seemed to pull himself together.

"Don't rush an answer. Your kiss made me ask you again," he said, his blue eyes focused intently on her with a searching look as if he, too, had been surprised by his reaction to their kiss.

She hoped he had been. She didn't want to fade into

the long line of women in his life—all of whom he seemed able to ignore and get rid of sooner or later. In that moment, she knew if she accepted his offer, she would have to guard her heart with all her being to escape falling in love with him.

Moving his hand away, he took her keys to open her car door, holding it for her before returning the keys. As soon as she slid behind the wheel, he closed the door and leaned down as she lowered the window. "Go to dinner with me tomorrow night."

"Of course I will."

"Thanks for meeting with me tonight. I know you didn't want to when I asked you at the restaurant."

"It's been interesting, to say the least. I'll go home and think over your proposal and see you tomorrow night."

"Sure," he said, stepping back away from the car and heading to his own. Turning on the ignition, she drove out without waiting for him. In minutes when she glanced into the rearview mirror, beneath streetlights she saw him following behind her in his sleek gray Jaguar. She drove to the old apartments that were near her work. She parked in the graveled lot and hurried to the side door, turning to wave at him as he waited nearby in the parking lot where he could see her go inside.

Smells of old fast-food boxes and mildew permeated the halls, the sour odor a permanent one. Climbing the steps to the second floor, she entered her apartment that was on the front of the complex. She shared a cramped two-bedroom apartment with Faith Wellston, one of her closest friends and a classmate.

As she shed her clothes and pulled on a heavy night-gown, she considered Matt's proposal. She assessed her surroundings and wondered how she could question the answer she would give him. He was sexy, handsome and appealing. Yet, from all he had said, money was his first love. Maybe his only love. He was going into a paper marriage that, except for sex, was a coldhearted business deal. Yet what difference should that make to her?

His proposal included sex. After his kiss, the mere thought of sex with him made her temperature soar. She shoved aside a stack of textbooks and papers on the scarred kitchen table and pulled out a blank sheet of paper, drawing two columns to represent the pros and cons of accepting his proposal.

His love of money was number one on her con list. And the only thing on the con side. The pro side, she could fill the page. She heard a key turn in the door and Faith walked in.

"Studying this late? Quiz tomorrow?" Faith asked, raking her fingers through her thick red curls.

"Nope. Did you have fun tonight?"

Faith tossed down a stack of textbooks and her purse, then headed for the fridge, her flip-flops flapping with each step. She leaned over to get a cold bottle of water and wiped it on the tail of her gray T-shirt before coming back to the table to pull out a chair and sit facing Brianna. "No, I didn't have any fun tonight. Cal and I went to the library and studied for an exam we have Friday. So what did you do?"

"You wouldn't guess if I gave you all night," Brianna

said. The excitement that she'd tried to stifle all evening made her wiggle and grin. "Ever heard of Matt Rome?"

"Sure. You've said he comes to the restaurant." Faith narrowed her light brown eyes. "He hit on you?"

"Oh, no. Better than that. He wanted me to meet him after work."

"Wow!" Faith let out a squeal and sat up in the chair. "Tell me about it. So he wants to take you out again?"

"Yes, he does, only there's more—a two-year marriage of convenience!" she announced, excitement bubbling up as she threw the paper in the air.

"Marry him! You've got it made! The baby will be paid for and provided for completely," Faith cried. Springing up, she pulled on Brianna and they both danced wildly for a few minutes, Brianna enjoying the moment and letting go all the restraint she'd struggled to exhibit with Matt.

When Faith sat finally, she leaned forward. "How soon? He must be paying you."

"He's made me an offer and told me to think about it before I give him an answer."

"So how much?"

"Half a million now and the other half when we divorce. And we will divorce."

Faith screamed again, throwing up her hands. "A million dollars! Why didn't you accept tonight?" Instantly, her smile vanished. "Did you tell him about the baby?"

"Yes, I did, although he already knew, Faith, from someone," Brianna said, staring hard at Faith, whose eyes widened.

"Not from me." She raised her hand. "I swear, I haven't told anyone with the exception of Cal and he promised to keep quiet. I'll ask him if he talked to anyone."

"It doesn't matter so much now. Matt knows about it and is okay with it."

"Why does he want a paper marriage?" Faith asked.

"Now you're getting to the point. I'm making a list and giving my reply some thought," she said, retrieving the list she had started and waved it at Faith. "My pros and cons list. His life revolves around him acquiring more money all the time. He wants an in to some international investment group and they're leery of letting in a bachelor, hence the marriage."

"That's okay," Faith said, seeming to think about it.

"Maybe. I think his attitude is cold and hard-hearted and material."

"So what are you? You're as driven as anyone I've ever seen and you want your education with a vengeance. The only reason you had a one-night stand was because you finally let your hair down and had too many drinks and had some fun."

"And accidentally got pregnant," Brianna said.

Faith grabbed the pro and con sheet and ripped it in half. "Marry him and stop even thinking about pros and cons. I've seen the guy—he's gorgeous. All of us in Advanced Statistics got to go to a seminar where he was on the panel. He was engaging and magnetic. He's the most moneyed man in Wyoming, maybe. How could you possibly bicker about that? Two years—spectacular. Marry him, use the money and your life will never be the same. It'll mean care for your baby, no worries for you and all the education you want. You'll get out of the dumps like this," she said without pausing. "Forget arguments. Go for it. I would have said yes on the spot."

"I started to and he stopped me and said to think it over."

Faith snorted, puffing out her cheeks. "What's to think over? If he had a kinky lifestyle, it would have already been in the news, so no problem there. Say yes tomorrow night. What'll you wear? Let's go see."

The following night Brianna was all nerves. Faith had already left the apartment. Taking quick breaths to calm down, Brianna walked to the mirror to look again at her image. Studying her plain, black cotton dress, she recalled the few clothes she'd brought with her when she'd graduated from high school and arrived in Cheyenne with a scholarship to college. She'd had few clothes. One formal dress that was bright blue and yellow, several pairs of worn jeans, flip-flops, T-shirts, one plain brown skirt and one white cotton blouse that she'd worn to job interviews. She wondered how many details of her past Matt knew—if he'd known she'd gotten the job at the ritzy steak house in her junior year. No one could know except Faith, whom she'd told, how she'd studied the female patrons to notice their clothing and she began to change her home wardrobe accordingly. While she assumed Matt would find her clothes too cheap, at least she knew they weren't tacky.

When the doorbell buzzed, she grabbed up her purse and her list of what she wanted if they married. Glancing at it one more time, her heart raced. Would this list cause him to revoke his marriage offer? That's what Faith feared, but Brianna kept telling herself to stick by what she wanted. Matt Rome needed this marriage. Now she'd see how badly.

Three

When she opened the door, the first thing she saw was a smile that made her knees weak. How could she argue with Matt over anything? She wondered if he had a clue about the dreams that now filled her life.

"Hi," he said. "You look great."

"Thank you," she replied. "I'm ready. You can come in if you want. I'll warn you, my place is pretty plain."

"If you're ready, we'll go," he answered easily. His charcoal suit jacket was unbuttoned and while dressed for something fancy this evening, there was an aura of earthy sexuality about him that his suit couldn't tame.

After she locked her door, he took her arm to walk with her to his car, holding the door until she slid inside. As she watched him circle the front of the car, she

slipped her hand over the luxurious tan leather uphol-
stery. The Jaguar's walnut paneling in the interior had a
beautiful sheen and she marveled at the world of money.
This was the most elegant car she'd ever ridden in.

Yet she couldn't shake Faith's warnings. Faith had told
her repeatedly not to make demands on Matt, to accept
what he had offered and enjoy life because it was far
better than she would ever see otherwise. Too true, except
she had no doubt he could afford what she was asking.

As she watched him walk in front of the car, her concerns of money and needs and marriage ebbed. Wind
caught dark locks of his hair, blowing them away from
his forehead. He was incredibly handsome. Her heart
pounded and she remembered their passionate kiss that
had filled her with longing. They would be together all
the rest of the evening. The excitement made her bubbly.
She knew she should get her feelings under control so she
could think clearly. She was the only advocate she had.

As he sat behind the wheel, he glanced at her. "Ready?"

"Of course," she answered, smiling. "Drive me to
dinner in the most opulent car I've ever ridden in."

He laughed. "We're going back to the club—the main
dining room tonight. They have good food, only where
you work is one of the best restaurants in the state."

"That's good to hear from a customer."

"Have you thought about my proposal?"

"I haven't been able to think about anything else," she
admitted. "When I went to classes today, I gave up my
front-row seat in each of them to sit at the back because
I knew I wouldn't hear one word of the lecture anyway."

"I'm glad to know you're thinking about it."

"My friend is blown away by it."

"And I take it you're not," he said, smiling. There was speculation in his gaze as he glanced at her.

"We can talk about it when you're not driving. I need your full, undivided attention. In the meantime, tell me about your day."

"Today was mostly business as usual." While he talked about projects and investments, she gazed at him, thinking she could look endlessly at him. She still couldn't believe what was happening to her. It was a Cinderella story, only the prince was in love with money and she was merely the means to an end. Still, there were such promising prizes for her—she would be worth a million dollars. She couldn't get that out of her thoughts and again, the list in her hand was a fiery torch. She didn't want to get burned by it.

Soon he was relating funny anecdotes, and she relaxed slightly, despite the electric current bubbling in her since she first sat to talk to him last night.

When they walked into the darkened dining room of the downtown club, she wanted to pinch herself to know it was all real. She never had evenings like this and she knew she would remember every detail for the rest of her life. A pianist sang the lyrics to the slow song he played while several couples already circled the small dance floor.

They chose a martini for him and milk for her after they were seated. As he gazed at her, the flickering glow of the candles highlighted his prominent cheekbones. He reached over to hold her hand. "Let's dance."

She walked to the dance floor to step into his arms, and it sent her pulse into overdrive. His legs brushed hers lightly, and every touch stirred a riveting response. Just as his car had been an extension of his fortune, she was aware of everything else that proclaimed his wealth—from his fine wool suit to his inviting aftershave, something men she'd known had seldom worn.

She knew she had to accept his proposal. As fast as that thought occurred, she reminded herself to hold out for her most important demands. When he heard her requests, would he get angry? Could she fit into his world of power and money? So many questions about a future which had spun off into the unknown.

"You're deep in thought tonight," he said, his voice quiet as he held her close to slow dance.

"I'm wondering if I can ever get accustomed to things you take for granted. I've never ridden in a car like yours before. I don't have the table manners or the background to go the places you'll go."

"You'll learn. It won't be a problem, I promise. And my world is filled with regular people, the same as your world."

"Our environments aren't the same at all," she said, thinking now more about their kiss last night. She looked at his mouth, a slightly full lower lip. Two years and then marriage to him would be over. One thing she was absolutely certain about—life in the future would be all new to her and she should avoid ever trying to make him the center of it.

"So what else is on your mind?" he asked, watching her intently.

"I'm still thinking about your proposal," she answered.

"Good. That's what I wanted you to do," he said.

When the music changed to a fast number and couples melted away around them, Matt continued to hold her hand. "Let's keep going."

As she watched his cool moves, she forgot contracts, bargaining and wealth. All she could think about was Matt and how attractive he was. She wanted to kiss him again, wanted him to kiss her. Every move of his was sensual, heating her and causing erotic fantasies, images she tried to banish.

Tossing her head, she circled around him and then met his gaze and she knew he wanted her in his arms. If they had been alone, she thought, by now they would have been in an embrace.

There would be no problems with the physical part of their relationship. She worried about her requests for more money and wondered if she should abandon her demands.

When the song ended, he took her hand to return to their table. A couple approached them from Matt's side and he paused. Brianna stopped to wait and recognized a woman Matt had brought to the steak house in the past. The tall, slender blonde glanced at Brianna and then turned her attention to Matt. She was stunning in an intricately embroidered and beaded black dress and the tall man with her was almost as handsome as Matt. They stopped and the men shook hands, exchanging greetings.

"We're leaving," the tall, black-haired man said.

"Nicole, Ty, this is Brianna Costin. Brianna, this is Nicole Doyle and Ty Bookman."

"I barely recognized you out of your waitress uniform," Nicole said acidly to Brianna. "I believe we already know each other. You work at the steak house, right?"

"Yes, I do," Brianna answered.

"The food here is almost as delicious as it is there," Nicole added, turning to Matt. "We've eaten and are going. It's good to see you again, Matt," she said in a warmer tone.

Ty echoed her greeting and they moved on.

"Ignore her, Brianna."

"She didn't say anything that isn't so, although if looks could kill, I'd be a goner."

"There's nothing between us. Nicole is out of my life," he said, holding Brianna's chair for her.

He sat facing her again, opening his jacket. Dark locks of hair had fallen on his forehead and he looked more appealing than when he was buttoned up with every hair combed into place.

"That was better. You're more relaxed tonight. Last night, I felt as if I were standing outside castle walls with the drawbridge up."

She laughed. "If you're comparing me to a princess in a castle, that's a first. No one has ever drawn that comparison. Cinderella in ashes wouldn't be as wild an exaggeration. I came from nothing. My sisters and I all shared one room."

"Are they all as pretty as you?"

"I don't know about that. We resemble each other and

look like my mother, thank heavens. My brothers look like my dad, who was a charming man, merely unfaithful and unreliable and unable to hold a job. Actually, I don't think my dad liked to work."

"Some people don't. Evidently, he stayed inside the law, so that's commendable."

"Yes, he did as far as anyone ever knew. He liked bars and women. I wasn't getting into that trap. My sisters married early and young. I got scholarships. When I got to Cheyenne I got part-time jobs and here I am."

"I've noticed you since the first time I ever saw you at the steak house. It was a June night last year and I ate on the terrace and I don't even remember who I ate with."

"You remember that?" she asked, feeling her face flush and her pulse jump because she couldn't imagine him noticing and remembering a waitress. "Actually, I remember the night. I was new on the job. When I was assigned to your table, one of the other waitresses who had befriended me gave me the scoop."

"What did she tell you? Not that I'm demanding, I hope."

"Of course not. Not to me anyway," she said, and he smiled.

"You've never given me any indication that you've noticed me more than you do the busboys or the maitre d' or anyone else there. Had I but known," she said, fanning herself and teasing him, getting another smile from him.

She kept waiting all through dinner, over her roasted pheasant and his lobster, for him to bring up his proposal. By the time they had finished eating, there still had been no mention of the offer. Soon they returned to the dance floor where she stopped thinking constantly about his proposal until finally a dance ended and Matt held her hand as they returned to their table.

"Let's go out to my place and have something to drink and talk about my proposal. Is it too late for you?"

"No," she said, thankful she didn't have any early classes.

In minutes they were in his car and she turned in the seat to watch him drive. He glanced at her and back at the road. "What do you think so far? We're getting along."

"I agree. I'm still surprised you're interested. You've never given the slightest indication."

"I'm interested," he said. "And I've spent all day and most of tonight wanting to kiss you again," he said in a husky voice that stirred heat in her.

"We'll kiss, but I'm going home tonight. Alone. I'm not staying over," she said.

"I hadn't planned that you would," he answered easily. "I'm patient."

"I don't know where you live."

"I don't make much of an issue of it because I value my privacy. I won't give interviews at home or let the media photograph my house. That's another reason I like living here. I can maintain a certain degree of privacy without too big of a hassle. I can drive myself sometimes and I don't feel as if I have to have a bodyguard everywhere I go."

She hadn't even given a thought to limos or bodyguards.

He drove through tall iron gates that swung open when he punched a small handheld device. They wound up a drive to another iron gate that was opened by a gate-keeper. Matt spoke to the man before continuing on his way. She turned to look back as the gates closed. "How many people work for you here?"

He shook his head. "I'm not sure. I don't deal directly with my staff. I have someone who oversees the house-hold for me."

With each passing second, she became more amazed as she suspected Matt had intended she would be.

They rounded a bend and the forest vanished, re-placed by immaculate grounds with tall stately pines. "My word! You live in a castle," she said, awed by her first view of a palatial mansion with wings, balconies and a wide portico. A circular drive in front created a border for a well-lit garden of fall flowers. "I didn't know there was anything like this in the state. You guard your privacy well."

"That's right. I don't bring people home with me. There are other places to go and few women I see even live here in Cheyenne. It's easier that way."

"You may be making the most colossal mistake in asking me to be your wife," she said, letting out her breath. "This lifestyle is totally foreign to me. I knew you were wealthy. Now this makes it seem tangible."

"I'd think my offer to you would make it seem sub-stantial," he remarked dryly.

"No, your proposal still has a definite dreamlike quality."

"Your kiss last night didn't. It was very real," he said. "And so were the effects of it."

She smiled. "Maybe I can try again later," she flirted.

As Matt stopped in front, a man had come out to open the door for her. When she emerged from the car, the employee greeted Matt, who introduced her.

Matt took her arm and led her into the front hall. Beneath a sparkling crystal chandelier, water splashed in a fountain. Farther along the hall, two staircases spiraled to the second floor.

"I'll show you around later. First, let's relax in front of the fire where we can talk. What would you like to drink?"

"Hot chocolate sounds tasty."

"That's easy. Come with me," he said and they walked across the hall and into another spacious area with a fire roaring in the fireplace, floor-to-ceiling glass doors that opened onto an enclosed room that held a pool, fountains and flowers.

After placing a drink order on the intercom, Matt led her to a brown leather sofa. As he shed his jacket and tie and unfastened the top buttons of his shirt, she momentarily forgot her surroundings and was ensnared in watching Matt. When she was with him, longing was a steady smoldering fire that now fanned stronger. He looked casual, more approachable, his appeal intensifying.

"If you accept my proposal, this is where we'll live when we're in Cheyenne."

She looked around at one wall lined with shelves with an assortment of books, oil paintings, vases, bronze statues. The room was filled with leather furniture, a hickory floor, the huge stone fireplace, a plasma television. Had he brought her out here to intimidate her?

She faced him squarely. "I can't believe that I could ever be a part of this, even for a brief time."

"All you have to do is accept my offer."

"Did you bring me out here so I'll drop my conditions? It seems ridiculous to ask anything more of you when you're doing something that would enable me to live in this house."

He sat on the leather sofa. "Let's hear what you want."

She reminded herself that the worst he could do was refuse. In reality, the worst he could do would be to withdraw his proposal and tell her to get lost.

There was a light rap at the door and a maid appeared bearing a tray with cups of cocoa and a china pot with a lid, plus a plate of cookies.

"Thanks, Renita," he said. "Brianna, this is Renita, who has worked for me for several years now."

After Brianna greeted the woman, Renita turned to leave them alone, closing the door behind her.

"Now back to our subject," he said. "Your requests."

"I have a list," she said, getting out the paper and he smiled.

She held the folded paper in her hand. "Look, Matt, I'm the oldest child in my family. You are in your family, right?"

"Yes, I am."

"From the time I was about twelve years old, I pretty much had to run things at home for all five of my siblings. My mom has cleaned businesses all her life and she's worn out. When my dad was alive, he drank too much and he cheated on her all through the years. I could never be with someone who cheated."

"You won't have a problem with me on that score."

"Good, can we put it in a prenup agreement?"

"I don't think you need to write that one down," Matt said dryly. "I'll be faithful. By the way, once we marry, and I get into the investment group, I won't necessarily hold you to two years. If you want out sooner, a divorce wouldn't affect my role in that group. They have some members who are divorced."

"Seems a little inconsistent to me, but acceptable. Two years maximum, though, right?"

"Right. That will do."

"No problem there. Now the next thing. You're a very wealthy man. So much so that half a million up front and half a million later seems paltry by your standards."

A smile flitted over his face and disappeared, but amusement still danced in his eyes. "How much do you want, Brianna?"

His name rolling off her tongue gave her a tingle. And she felt a momentary panic for trying to wrest more money from him when a million dollars was a fantastic fortune she couldn't imagine earning on her own. Taking a quick breath, she looked him squarely in the eyes. "Two million up front and two million when we part. In addition, I want you to pay for a nanny for my baby as long as I need one. And put some money in trust for the baby's education."

"That's a lot of money. You're going to make some

more by being married to me, plus the car I promised and the clothes and you'll live in a manner you don't now have. I'll think about it. Anything else on that list?" he asked.

She held it closer to her as if to keep him from seeing it. "That covers it. I have a preference about waiting to sleep together until we've said vows," she said, her palms growing sweaty because he didn't appear to be willing to accept her terms about money. "I want to know each other better."

He looked amused. "I won't push that on you anytime you don't want to. Married or not," he answered easily.

She felt her face flush hotly and wished she could control her blushes. "You might consider that a strange request when I'm expecting. I'm pregnant because I partied and let go, celebrating exams being over. Otherwise, I've had one other guy in my past and that was in high school."

"I'll wait until you're ready."

The hot chocolate sat forgotten and she felt the tension increase. What she wanted and what he wanted were different. There was no mistaking which one of them had the most power. If he took back his proposal, she wondered whether she would ever get over letting a million dollars slip through her fingers. Her heart was pounding so hard and fast, she thought he surely could hear it.

He gave her a long look and she almost blurted out to forget what she had requested.

"While we're into demands, I have one more that we

didn't settle last night when we talked. I want you to drop out of school."

"Now?" She was aghast and he asked the impossible.

"Now. In two years you can pick up where you left off."

The thought of losing momentum on her education set her back. It was the one thing she most wanted. Her degree and a nanny. She'd never had any substantial cash in her life, always living hand to mouth, but school was tangible and she had almost achieved part of her education goal.

"I want to finish this semester," she said. "It ends in December. That's not very long."

"Withdraw from college this week. I'd like to take you on a honeymoon. I'll want you to accompany me to Europe often. Your grades will suffer. You can pick school up again when we divorce and you'll be better off than trying to juggle classes *and* marriage *and* a baby. The baby will be two or more when you go back. Easier to handle."

The prospect hurt of giving up a goal she'd had since she was old enough to realize a degree would get her out of the poverty she'd been born into. Two years and she could go back. She would have a nanny, help and money, which would be infinitely easier.

"All right, I'll drop out," she said, feeling as if she were ripping part of herself away.

"Good. As for my part—I'll pay you *one* million up front and *one* million when we part and I'll provide nannies and that education trust fund," he said flatly.

"Thank you," she said, drawing a long breath as relief

filled her. She would still get two million dollars! Her heart was in her throat over wresting so much money out of him. She and her baby—and the rest of her family—were fixed for life, she was sure. There would be more than enough for all of them to go to college or trade school. Matt would provide a nanny for her baby. Financial worries fell away and she was giddy with excitement she couldn't contain.

Smiling at him, she scooted the distance that separated them to throw her arms around his neck. "I accept your proposal, Matt. I'll marry you!"

Four

The minute Brianna voiced her acceptance, her green eyes sparkled. Reaffirmation that he'd made a good choice swept Matt, sending his own enthusiasm soaring. She looked as if he had handed her the world on a silver tray—and well she should, he knew. It was also a look he never would have received from any other woman he'd considered wife material.

Wrapping his arms around her, Matt pulled her closer as they kissed. Soft, sweet-smelling and eager, she pressed against him, her tongue thrusting deep into his mouth as she poured herself into her kiss and set him ablaze. He wanted her more than ever. The thought that soon she would be totally his fanned the flames already raging in him.

He pulled her onto his lap to embrace her as he kissed her, slowly and thoroughly. Her soft moans, her hands running over his neck and shoulders, heightened his passion. Remembering that she wanted to wait for consummation rose dimly in the back of his mind, but her kisses sent another message.

He wound his fingers in her silky hair and longed to bury himself in her. Thought vanished and only the pounding of his heart and roaring of his pulse enveloped him. Holding her, he ran his hand down her back over the thin cotton of her shirt, lower over her cotton slacks to follow the curve of her bottom.

Continuing to kiss her, he cradled her against his shoulder. All of his senses were steeped in pleasure and she was turned in his arms to where he could caress her slender neck. His hand went lower, lightly across her breast. The instant he caressed a taut peak, she moaned and twisted her hips slightly, clutching his shoulders. Her softness and instant responses inflamed him.

He freed her top button to slide his hand beneath her shirt and bra to cup her breast while his thumb circled her nipple. She moaned again, a sound of enjoyment that heightened his own.

Raising her head, she grasped his wrist and pulled on his hand. "Wait, Matt," she whispered. Her plea halted him and he moved his hand, raking his fingers through her hair to comb it away from her face.

"This is too new," she said. "Slow down a little."

"Whatever you want," he said in a deep, husky tone that happened in passionate moments. His pulse still

raced and he was hot with desire that he tried to cool.
Her lips were red and swollen from his kisses, her face
flushed. Her response to his kisses had been intense
and he had to curb the impulse to pull her close again
and try to kiss away her protests. If she would even
protest further.

Scooting off his lap, she pulled her clothes in place
and faced him on the sofa. "We have plans to make."

She retrieved her cup of cocoa and sipped it, holding
the china cup with both hands.

"We're not in love, Brianna, so I think a small, quiet
wedding would be more appropriate. Family and only
close friends."

"That's all I would have anyway," she said.

"I'll pay for the wedding, so you'll have no worries
there. Get the dress you want, but not formal. This won't
be that big a deal. I'd like to marry as soon as possible.
This is Friday. Can you marry a week from tomorrow?"

Her eyes widened and she seemed to be thinking
about it. "I don't see why not," she replied.

"Excellent!" His pulse jumped again. He'd get into the
investment group before the year was out, he guessed.
"I'll clear my calendar and we'll take a week for a honeymoon." He pulled out his wallet and gave her a card. "Here,
use this to buy clothes. If you can't find the wedding dress
you want here, tell me and I'll fly you to San Francisco,
Dallas or wherever you'd like to look. Monday we can
open an account for you and transfer money."

"You don't waste time, do you?"

"Quit your job in the morning. You don't need it any

longer and they can get a new waitress. Not one as beautiful, though," he said, smiling at her.

She licked her lower lip and inhaled and he was sidetracked. He knew she was thinking about something besides her job. He slipped his hand behind her head to comb his fingers into her long hair. "We'll both benefit, Brianna. You'll see."

"I know it'll be a miracle for me," she said. Her ongoing wonder pleased him because it continued to confirm his choice. Nicole, or any other woman he'd known well, would never be awed. They'd be asking for more of his time and his attention, plus money.

"If you'd like, you can move in here right away," he said, hoping she'd accept.

Her eyes widened again and she looked around. "I can't picture living here."

"It's a home and comfortable and why not? After we marry you can move into my bedroom with me. There are twelve bedrooms in this house, so there's no lack of space," he remarked dryly.

"Maybe I'll move in Monday. It won't take long to pack my things."

"Do it tomorrow. Brianna, you're so early in your pregnancy that we can tell everyone the baby is mine."

She bit her lip and looked lost in thought. "I'd like that, but what happens if we stay together until my baby is a toddler? This baby will see you as Daddy by then. Besides, the baby will have my last name."

"I hadn't thought about that," he said, realizing this wasn't going to be as simple as he'd envisioned and he hadn't given enough attention to the prospect of a baby in his life. "Let me talk to my lawyer and accountant and I'll see what I can do."

She nodded as if satisfied by his answer.

"Maybe I can work it out where your baby has my name. If it reaches the media that it's not my baby, the news won't be earth-shattering anyway."

"Because by then you'll be in your investment group," she said and that cool tone she'd first used returned to her voice.

"That's right. This decision is up to you," he said. "I'd think you'd prefer it, too."

"I do, even though it may complicate our lives later."

"We can call our families right now so they can start making plans," Matt said.

"Are you going to leave the impression that we're in love, or are we going to tell our families this is a temporary marriage?" she asked.

"I'd just as soon say it was the real thing," he replied, having already given thought to what he wanted. "That way, when the press gets wind of this, there won't be a big scandal. Will that be a problem with your family?"

"No. I'm close with my mom and sisters and we'll talk. I'll need to bring them here a few days early so they can buy clothes for the wedding that I will pay for with your money," Brianna said.

"Unless you have a preference, we'll marry here at the house," Matt replied. "I'll get the minister. That way, I can keep this private."

"That's reasonable," she said. The more they talked,

the more he longed to pull her back into his arms and kiss her and forget their planning or waiting.

"Sunday morning I'll take you to church with me and you can meet the minister."

Matt pulled out a card and gave it to her. "Here's a card from the owner of a shop that has pretty dresses. It's a small shop and you see the address. Go look there tomorrow. She'll help you and you might find what you like for the wedding."

"I've seen their ads," Brianna said, taking the card from him, her fingers lightly brushing his. The slight contact added to his yearning to hold her in his arms again. "I couldn't ever afford a dress from this shop."

"Now you can, so go look and buy something if you see what you want. I'd like to have both of my older cousins as groomsmen and my two brothers as groomsmen, also."

"That will work for me because I'll have my sisters and my two closest friends," she said. "We've got our plans set for now, and I can feel the evening catching up with me. I should go, Matt."

"Certainly," he said, wondering if their plans would blow up in his face or work as smoothly as he hoped. Was he letting lust kill all his business judgment?

As if she guessed his thoughts, she gazed at him with a somber expression. "We're both jumping into this as if into a dark well."

"No, we're not," he said, his self-assurance kicking in full force. "I've given this thought. I know my proposal and my plans are new to you, but I've been living with them for a while. I think we'll both come out ahead."

"You're being driven by greed and love of money."

"And you're not?" he asked lightly, amused that she could see her own motives in a better light than his.

"This marriage has to make life better for my baby, me and even my family who'll benefit, too."

He hugged her. "Stop worrying and dwelling on the negative possibilities. We're into it now."

"Not absolutely until we say wedding vows," she said. Before he could reply, she spoke quickly. "I still want to go ahead. Don't misunderstand me. I'm glad you selected me."

He held open the door for her and walked to his car with her. "It's natural to have wedding jitters—and in this case, even more expected."

He closed the door and walked around the car, glad he'd planned to marry soon. If he could whisk her to a justice of the peace tomorrow, he'd do it, but he wanted this to appear to be the real thing for now and a big deal for both of them—which it was.

He drove her home, giving her a light kiss. "Think about the money, Brianna, and forget the rest. It's going to be worth your while and mine."

Matt's words rang in his ears early Monday morning when he went to his office. He'd only been there half an hour when his closest friend arrived and came in to see him.

As soon as Matt announced Brianna's acceptance of

his proposal, Zach glared at him. "You'll regret this more than anything you've ever done. You can pick stocks, but choosing a woman as you would a stock is going to be a disaster." Beneath a tangle of wavy blond hair, Zach's pale brown eyes filled with irritation.

Matt calmly faced him. "It's a done deal. We're engaged."

"You can get out of that and you know it. Get out fast. Marry Nicole. She's gorgeous, a socialite who moves in your world. She's wealthy in her own right, so she won't be after your money and she's not pregnant with another guy's baby. Another guy who may show up when he gets wind that the mother of his baby has landed a rich guy."

"The minute I get into that investment group, I don't care. I'm not worried about him, anyway. They went to an attorney and he signed away all rights to the baby. He's long gone from Wyoming."

"That can be broken in court and you know it."

"That's their fight. Not mine. But if it'll shut you up, we can have him found," Matt said, entering his schedule for the day into his BlackBerry.

"As your friend, I'm pleading with you not to marry this woman. She isn't in your social class. She only has waitress experience. She won't know how to deal with your lifestyle."

"Don't be ridiculous," Matt said with amusement. "You think I was born into this lifestyle?"

"You weren't as far removed from it as she is. She's from a tiny little town and plain."

"Her family is honest, aren't they? Never been in any criminal trouble?"

"No, but that's about all you can say for them. That's not the kind of person to lock yourself into a marriage contract with. She'll want more, I can promise you."

"She already has. She demanded more money."

"You've got to be kidding. And you agreed, didn't you?"

"Yep, I did. It's done, Zach. Now, get me a list of places she can put the money I'm about to give her. I'll meet with her later this morning and discuss what she wants to do."

Zach raked his fingers through his hair that sprang back in thick waves. He shook his head and threw his hands in the air. "I give up. I've said all I can say. I suppose you've told Nicole goodbye."

"She walked on me. She was unhappy that I wouldn't give her more of my time. I don't expect those demands from Brianna. I promise you, she's not going to bore me," Matt replied, smiling at his friend. "Think you can have a list in an hour?"

"Sure. I'll get someone working on it right away and I'll go over it... I wish I could dissuade you."

"I'm grown, Zach. I know what I want. She's perfect."

"I'll try to avoid saying 'I told you so' later," Zach grumbled and left the room.

Matt gazed at the empty doorway and wondered if Zach would prove to be right. He couldn't imagine being bored by Brianna. At the moment, he couldn't wait to be with her. He picked up the phone to call his chief attorney.

* * *

Twenty-four hours later, seated in a quiet, high-priced restaurant, Matt glanced at his watch impatiently. After Matt's lunch appointment with Zach, Brianna was going to meet him at the restaurant at one. If Zach didn't show soon, Matt realized he was going to run late for Brianna. Zach was already ten minutes behind. Zach had asked for the lunch appointment away from the office and Matt couldn't imagine the reason. It was uncharacteristic of Zach, who was as much of a workaholic as Matt.

"Matt?"

He heard the familiar voice and glanced around to see Nicole slide into the seat facing him. She looked as gorgeous as ever in a white designer suit with bright red accessories that complemented her pale blond hair. She smiled at him. "Don't get angry at Zach. I asked him to do this because I want to talk to you."

Matt kept his temper in check over Zach's high-handed interference, wondering how much of the blame Nicole shared.

A waiter appeared with glasses of water, took their order and left.

"I ought to walk out now," Matt said easily.

"Please don't. I want to talk to you. I really am responsible for this. I heard from someone that you're thinking about getting engaged to that waitress."

"Nicole, we're through."

Nicole shuddered and gulped. "I suppose I deserve this for getting in such a huff the last time we were together, but I know you're not in love. I know the only

thing keeping you out of that investment group was
your bachelor status."

"Not any longer."

"Matt, don't do this. You can break the engagement.
We had a wonderful relationship for a while and we can
have it again," she said, beginning to sound desperate.
He wished Zach hadn't set him up for this encounter.

He shook his head. "You should have just phoned
me, Nicole, and saved yourself the trouble. I intend to
marry her. It's over between us. You made that abundantly clear."

"Matt!" she cried, interrupting him. "I'm sorry if I
demanded too much of your time. Stop and think how
wonderful we were together. She means nothing to you.
You barely know her."

"This is my decision," he answered patiently, wishing
lunch were over and he could escape. He looked at her
flawless skin and wide eyes. She was a stunning woman
and once upon a time, she'd set his heart pounding, but
she didn't mean anything now, nor did he find her de-
sirable. He realized it was finished—if he'd ever truly
cared for her at all. Idly, he wondered how long it would
be until he would feel that way regarding Brianna.

"Give us another chance," Nicole urged, leaning
across the table to caress his hand lightly while she
talked. "It was incredible between us—you know it was."

"Nicole, this is an absolutely useless conversation."
Matt stopped talking as the waiter approached with a
tray of food. He placed a salad in front of Nicole and a
sandwich in front of Matt.

She smiled at him and raised her water glass in a toast. "Then here's to the happy bridegroom. May your future be filled with joy."

"I'll drink to that one," he said, touching her glass with his and sipping the icy water.

As they ate, Nicole was her most charming, switching totally from the subject of Brianna, yet Matt knew she was deliberately trying to entertain and charm him as a reminder of how good things could be between them. He struggled to pay attention to her conversation and tried to avoid being obvious when he glanced occasionally at his watch. He had to get rid of Nicole before Brianna appeared.

To his consternation, Nicole selected a dessert. Matt asked the waiter for the check and then as soon as they were alone, Matt faced Nicole. "I'm sorry, I have an appointment. I'll get the lunch and you can take your time. I have to leave."

She smiled at him. "That's all right, Matt. I still wish you'd think about what I've said to you. It's not too late to get out of this engagement. You'll be incredibly bored with her."

"That's for me to worry about," he replied easily.

Their waiter returned and Matt settled up.

As the waiter turned away, Matt glanced across the dining room and saw Brianna approaching the table. As he started to stand, she looked from him to Nicole and then back at him and he could see her surprise. She stopped and then turned, rushing away from him.

"Nicole, I have to go," Matt said.

"*She's* your appointment?" Nicole protested, stepping to block his path as she grasped his wrist.

"Move out of my way, Nicole," he said quietly.

"Don't leave. Stay here, Matt. Give us another chance together because what we had was great."

"Goodbye, Nicole," he said.

"Matt—"

In spite of her calling his name, he rushed through the restaurant and outside, to watch Brianna climb into her car. He ran across the lot in the warm sunshine. When she backed out of the parking place and turned, he stepped in front of her car to prevent her from leaving. She honked as he stood with his hands on the hood of the car. Certain she wouldn't hurt him, he had no intention of letting her drive away until he talked to her.

In seconds, she opened her window and thrust her head out. "Matt, move out of my way."

"No. I want you to promise to listen to me."

She glared at him a moment and then cut the motor. He knew she could start up and race away and he wouldn't be able to stop her, but he wasn't going to get anywhere by standing in front of her car. He walked around to climb in on the driver's side. "Move over," he ordered.

With another glare at him, she did as he asked, climbing over the gear shift to sit on the passenger side. He slid behind the wheel, started the car and pulled back into a parking place, where he cut the motor once again and turned to face her.

"That wasn't what you're thinking. You pay attention

to my explanation," he said, determined to get her to listen to the truth. He had no intention of allowing an unwanted encounter with Nicole to harm his future.

Five

Brianna locked her fingers together and nodded. She had feared all along that Matt wouldn't be faithful to her, but she hadn't expected to find him with someone else before they were married.

"I didn't plan that lunch with Nicole," he said firmly, gazing into her eyes. "I thought I was having lunch with Zach, a guy who works for me."

Brianna didn't believe him and waited in silence.

"Nicole said she asked Zach to get me to lunch so she could talk to me. I was already there when she appeared and we went ahead and ate lunch. That's all it was."

"I find that difficult to believe. You forget I've waited on your table when you're together."

"Brianna, do you think I'd make a lunch date with

another woman when I knew I was meeting you at the same restaurant? I've got more sense than that if I'd intended to do any such thing."

She gazed at him, realizing that was probably true. As she began to believe him, her hurt eased. She had been shocked and furious to discover him with Nicole, but she knew what he'd said was logical. Now she really looked at him without a haze of fury. Black curls tumbled on his forehead and his jacket was unbuttoned, revealing a crisp white shirt. His navy tie was slightly askew. Otherwise, he appeared as composed as ever.

"All right, Matt. I believe you," she said. "It shocked me to see you together today. I know she's been a big part of your life."

"That's past. I promise you, she's out of my life now and she won't be back in it."

"But she wants in it, doesn't she?" Brianna asked, hoping she was wrong. Disappointment surged when he nodded.

"Yes, she does. I told her, and I promise *you,* it's all over with her. You and I have a deal. I feel nothing when I'm with her."

Brianna studied him, wondering if he would be saying the same words about her someday. It was decided that their marriage would be over in a maximum of two years. In the future would she be referred to as casually as he dismissed Nicole now?

He leaned forward to tilt her chin up so she looked into his eyes. "You're the woman in my world. By this time next week you'll be my wife. I don't want any other woman. Okay?"

"Okay," she said, her gaze lowering to his mouth. He was only inches away now and her irritation had been replaced by desire. "I don't intend to share you," she said.

"You won't have to," she dimly heard him say, but her pounding heart was dulling his words and she raised her mouth to his as she slipped her arm around his neck. His mouth came down on hers and her lips opened beneath his. His kiss was hot, demanding, confirming that she was his woman in a way words never could.

Worries and concerns about other women in his life ceased to exist. Now all she wanted were Matt's kisses. They were leaning over the gear shift of her car and she realized they were still in the parking lot of the restaurant, so she pushed lightly on Matt's chest.

"We're in public," she whispered. "And this is less than the perfect place to kiss," she added, scooting away from him.

"We have appointments this afternoon, but I would like to cancel all of them and take you home with me."

"You can't," she said, smiling at him. "Not if you want to stay on schedule for a wedding this weekend."

"There's something else, Brianna. We will honeymoon in Rome because there's a charity ball I want to attend. I'd already agreed to appear and I'd still like to go because members of the investment group will be there and I'll have a chance to chat with them and introduce you as my wife. I'm telling you so you can buy a dress for the occasion. Get something elegant and don't worry about expense."

"Rome…?"

Intimidated by the thought of participating in a charity gala with him and meeting his investment acquaintances, her smile vanished. She knew she would be out of her element.

"Matt," she said hesitantly, and his eyes narrowed. "Are you certain you want me to accompany you to something like that immediately after we get married? I haven't ever attended a charity ball."

"You'll dazzle them," he said. "And I'm very sure about taking you. I want you there with me. If you need someone to coach you, I can get someone."

"Not at all," she answered, trying to cover her uncertainties and fears. As soon as possible, she knew she should start getting ready for the ball and practicing her Italian.

She reflected that he would also be working in Italy. As carefully as he'd charted his marriage to help him get into his investment group, so his honeymoon would give him a chance to promote his marriage and show her to the European investors. His constant eye on his goal jarred her until she reminded herself that she had a contract with him. There was no love in this union, so why wouldn't the honeymoon be a business trip?

Brianna glanced at her watch. "We're going to be late for our meeting at the bank today. After that, I see the wedding planner."

"Given the amount I put into accounts for you yesterday, the banker won't mind if we're a few minutes late," Matt said, his heated expression conveying his fervor. "I'll drive and we'll come back to get my car."

Gazing out the car window, she thought about having to stop by the university again today. Even though she'd dropped out of her classes, she wanted to figure some way by next semester to continue her education because Matt would be often occupied with his work. She suspected after their honeymoon, she would have huge chunks of time when she could study. He might want her out of his life as soon as he was accepted into his investment group. She intended to get all she could out of this brief union.

Wednesday, she stopped at Matt's office.

She stepped into the lobby that had enormous planters with tall, exotic greenery, palms, banana trees, tropical plants that were at least eight feet tall. A fountain splashed in the center of the lobby.

First she had to deal with security, but her name was on a list and she was ushered toward the elevators.

As she walked away from the security desk, she heard the low voice of the employee telling someone that she was headed toward the top floor and Matt's office.

When she stepped out into a thickly carpeted hallway, light spilled through the glass walls. More potted plants and leather benches lined the hallway. A stocky blond man stepped out of an office and approached her.

"Miss Costin?" he asked, his gaze raking over her as he frowned. "I'm Zach Gentner. Matt has been momentarily detained in a meeting. If you'll come with me, I'll show you into his office. You can wait there."

"Thank you," she said, smiling and relaxing slightly beneath his friendly smile.

They walked through a large reception area where she met a receptionist and then through a smaller office where she met Matt's private secretary.

She followed Zach into a spacious office with light spilling through two glass walls. The carpet was plush, the dark walnut paneling a complementary backdrop to the brown leather furniture with oil paintings of Wyoming landscapes on the walls and the two tall bronze statues of a stalking mountain lion and galloping horses on tables.

"Congratulations on your engagement, Miss Costin," Zach said.

"Thank you," she said, feeling uncomfortable in spite of his congratulations.

"Your family should be extremely proud of you—you have money now for your baby, a comfortable future and endless opportunities. I hope you can always remember the sacrifices Matt has made to take a total stranger as his wife, in a less than satisfying business arrangement that locks him into a loveless marriage."

His sarcastic words hit her with the pain of a knife thrust. Her smile vanished and she chilled. "It was his choice," she replied stiffly.

"I know it was. I heard you made even greater demands, which he caved to. I hope you don't ruin his life. Of course, if he doesn't get in that group, he'll dump you so fast your head will spin. How long this fake marriage will last anyway, is anybody's guess. Until he tires of your body or you are quite large with child."

She clamped her hands together and bit her lip, trying to keep calm and think before she replied to his hurtful words. "You obviously don't approve of me," she said, forcing her voice to stay low and controlled, determined she wouldn't let him goad her into losing her temper.

"Not at all," he said, "but it isn't my choice. While I've told him what I think, he's stubborn. I hate to see him hurt or watch you ruin his life. You're pregnant with some other guy's baby from a one-night stand, not the best recommendation for marriage. Only you know if that guy is really the father or if it's someone else."

"He's the father," she said quietly, livid with fury that she was determined to keep in check. "Are you overstepping your bounds as an employee, Mr. Gentner? Aren't you afraid Matt will be furious to learn about this conversation?"

"Not at all," he answered coldly. "He'll know I did it for his own good. We go back a long way. Almost as far back as those cousins of his whom I almost called to see if either of them could talk sense into him. That confounded bet is the reason for this ridiculous proposal you have.

"Of course, they're so competitive, they'll see this marriage as a way of eliminating Matt from the running. They'll know he'll get out of this marriage eventually. I hope it doesn't cost him too much money. I know it won't cost emotionally because he doesn't have one shred of love for you. I'm sure that's no secret. Matt is up-front about business deals he makes and that's all this sham marriage is."

"I don't want to listen to this," she said, heading toward the door. "You tell—"

Matt strode into the room. "Brianna, I'm sorry I'm late." He broke off his words as his eyes narrowed. Looking back and forth between Zach and her, he focused on her. "Is something wrong?"

"Maybe for him—"

Zach spoke in a slightly louder tone, drowning her out. "I was congratulating your fiancée on her engagement and upcoming union. I'll leave you two alone," Zach said, leaving the room in haste.

Matt watched him go and then turned to study Brianna. He walked to her to place his hands on her shoulders and continue to gaze at her with a probing stare. "What's happened? What did he say to you?"

"He hopes I don't ruin your life," she answered quietly. "I simply assume you're doing what you want to do and you've given your proposal thought."

"Damn!" Matt said softly. "Forget Zach. Damn straight I've given it thought and I'm doing exactly what I want. Don't think about him or what he's said. I'll talk to him about it later."

"Don't get into a fight over it. I'll forget what he said," she stated, knowing in reality she would never forget.

As she looked up at Matt, it was easy to forget the past few minutes and Zach's hurtful words because Matt gazed at her with such desire in his expression that Zach no longer mattered.

"Brianna, there's something else. I've talked to my lawyer and thought over what I want to do. I'll adopt your baby so the child will have my name, the same as if it were my own."

She gasped with surprise. "You'd do that?"

"It seems the best way. Sooner or later, we'll divorce, but the baby will have my name and I can pay child support."

"Matt!" The enormity of how badly he wanted this marriage made her weak in the knees. "You'd do all that to get more money?"

"I'm doing a lot of it to get you," he said in a husky voice, drawing her closer to him.

She couldn't believe that he really meant what he said. They weren't in love, but whatever his reason, she was going to accept before he had time to reconsider. There was no way his adopting her baby would be bad. "Matt, I hope you really know what you're doing," she said. "It's acceptable to me."

"I thought it would be. I don't see how else we can deal with your baby."

Once again, she wished love was in the mix. Matt's words should have been thrilling, but his offer sounded too businesslike to give her a deep joy. Even so, she was glad for her baby's sake, and his offer gave her another degree of security.

"Now don't worry about Zach or your baby or our future," Matt said.

She wound her arms around Matt's neck. "This is what's important. If you're content, then I'm satisfied."

When he picked her up, she tightened her arms around his neck as he gave her a long kiss that shut out the world.

* * *

Before the rehearsal dinner Friday night, she took deep gulps of air and tried to relax as she waited in her suite for her family to gather before leaving for Matt's. His family was staying with him. She had moved to the hotel where she had booked suites for her family and herself. Members of both families and friends in his wedding party and their spouses planned to gather at Matt's home for hors d'oeuvres and to get acquainted. Then after the wedding rehearsal, they'd leave for an extravagant restaurant.

She was incredibly nervous over Matt meeting her family for the first time. Her family had never been far from Blakely, where they'd grown up. She was the first and only to finish high school, the first to attend college and they knew little about etiquette or table manners. She had spent the past three days getting them new clothes and haircuts, which Brianna could easily afford now. At each meal she had coached them on table manners, with an etiquette book open in front of her for quick reference.

Her family was to meet in the sitting room of Brianna's spacious suite and her mother was the first to arrive.

Adele Costin had been transformed and Brianna gazed at her mother with joy. "Mom, you look great!"

"I have you to thank for it," she replied, smiling at her daughter. "Look, my first manicure. I can't recognize my own hands or my hair or my image in the mirror, for that matter," she said, laughing and holding out her hands. Her mother had spent a lifetime cleaning and Brianna could remember her red, chapped hands.

Now they looked lovely with a pale pink polish on her well-shaped nails.

Her mother's tailored navy suit was attractive and flattering. Her black, slightly graying hair was cut short and combed straight to highlight the soft contours of her face.

"You look wonderful, Mom," Brianna said again and kissed her mother's cheek.

"I hope you are pleased, Brianna, although at the moment, I don't see how you could possibly keep from being joyous. But money isn't everything."

"Mom, I'm happy," Brianna said. "I'm doing what I want to do. We're alone for a minute now, and there's something I want to tell you, but it's not for the rest of the family yet."

"What's that?" Adele asked.

"I'm expecting a baby."

"Oh, Brianna! A baby!" her mother exclaimed, smiling at her and hugging her briefly. Stepping away, she frowned and then leaned closer to study Brianna intently. "Are you happy about the baby?"

"Oh, yes! Of course. And now I'll be taken care of so well and I can help the whole family."

"The whole family isn't what you need to be concerned about. I want you to be really pleased," Adele said quietly.

"I am," Brianna replied, smiling at her mother. "I really am, Mom. I wouldn't be getting married if I didn't want to."

Her mother studied her as she nodded her head. "I hope so, and I want you to tell me if you need me."

"I will, I promise," Brianna said. "Now you'll be a grandmother again."

Appearing to relax, her mother had a faint smile, and Brianna was relieved that the worried look had vanished, at least for now. "A grandmother!" Adele said. "Ah, Brianna, that fills me with more hope for the future and gives me another purpose in life."

Brianna laughed. "You have plenty of purposes in life because you already have grandchildren."

"Each one is precious. Is Matt happy about the baby?"

"Yes, he's okay with everything," she answered carefully, trying to stick as close to the truth as she could. "Now don't start looking worried," Brianna said. "I'd rather not tell the rest of the family until after we've had the wedding. I'll tell them soon afterward, but I wanted you to know."

"That's fine. I can keep the secret, and you don't look as if you're pregnant. How far along are you?"

"Not far at all. The baby is due next summer—late June. We'll announce it soon."

"I understand. I want to meet this man who'll be my son-in-law."

"I think you'll like him," Brianna said, knowing Matt would probably charm her mother and all the rest of her family. "I'm nervous about tonight and meeting his family," Brianna admitted.

"You look beautiful, and he's lucky to get you as his bride."

Brianna smiled and brushed a kiss on her mother's cheek. "I love you, Mom."

"Your sisters are probably going to guess anyway, but your brothers never will. They won't say anything to me about it, though, nor will I to them."

"That's fine," Brianna said, feeling better now that she'd shared her news with her mother and wishing she could tell her everything about this marriage that was really a loveless union.

A knock at the door interrupted them, and Brianna's sister Melody entered with her children in tow.

Brianna smiled broadly, holding out her arms to hug the children. "Everyone looks so great!" Melody's hair had been cut as well, hanging straight with blond streaks, and her plain black dress was short enough to show off her long, shapely legs.

"So do you, Brianna," Melody replied. "Thanks for the dresses, the hotel, the haircuts. Everything is a dream."

Dressed and subdued, Phillip, who was four, and three-year-old Amanda, as well as the other children, would have two nannies to watch them after the rehearsal while the rest of the family went out to dinner.

"You think I look good," Melody said. "Wait until you see the transformation of the guys. You won't know them."

"I hope so," Brianna teased, "since they're usually working on cars in overalls covered in grease."

When her brothers and brothers-in-law entered, she saw what her sister had been talking about. Shaved, shorn and attired in conservative suits with white dress shirts and navy ties, the men had been transformed.

"Mercy! You guys do clean up well."

"So does everyone," said her youngest brother, Josh,

whose black hair was spiked in the front and combed down smoothly otherwise.

"I'm so proud of my family," she said, smiling at them. "And I want all of you to have a good time. Matt is a wonderful guy. Now, if everyone is ready, let's go."

"I can't wait to see this place," Melody said. "I've threatened the kids to behave and not touch anything."

"She's not kidding," Melody's husband, Luke, said. "She threatened me, too."

Laughter followed his announcement and more joking until Brianna raised her voice.

"Matt has limos waiting to take us to his house. Shall we go?"

As they rode through Cheyenne in the limousines provided by Matt, her nervousness returned. Once again, she experienced the same trepidation that she'd felt upon arriving in Cheyenne and again, on her first visit to the university campus. She was too aware of the limitations of her early years, her lack of cosmopolitan experiences or experience with a polite, more sophisticated segment of society. Momentarily, she envied Matt his background and his colossal self-assurance. Yet if they'd been born into the reverse circumstances, so Matt had come out of the backwoods, she couldn't imagine that he wouldn't carry off the transition to an urbanite with the same confidence and aplomb he exhibited daily now.

Her stomach churned with something worse than butterflies. Her palms were damp and she wondered if she could get herself and her family through this evening intact, or if Matt would rescind his proposal.

A uniformed man opened the door, but the minute she stepped inside, Matt was there to greet her. As soon as she saw him, her worries evaporated. Her heartbeat raced for a different reason and eagerness replaced worry.

"Am I glad to see you," he said softly, walking up to her to smile at her. "You are breathtaking and I wish we were alone for the night."

"Matt, I'll confess, I'm so nervous about tonight. You know this entire week is new to my family."

"Relax, Brianna, my family won't bite. We're here to have a good time and get ready for a wedding. Let me make an announcement to everyone and then we can do the introductions."

"Sure, whatever you want to do," she said, thankful to turn the moment over to him.

"Folks," Matt said in a deep, authoritative voice. To her surprise, he got everyone's attention and the room became silent.

"I'm Matt Rome and welcome to Cheyenne and to our rehearsal dinner. I want to thank you for coming to share this time with Brianna and with me. Now, why don't we go around the room and say our names and what relation we are. Brianna, we'll start with you."

When each of Matt's relatives spoke, she paid close attention, noticing Jared Dalton and Chase Bennett, the cousins she'd heard so much about. As her family introduced themselves, she watched each one, assessing her handiwork. Again, she focused on Danielle, whose brown hair was twisted and pinned at the back of her head. Danielle's three-year-old, Hunter, and two-year-old Emma, were as subdued as their cousins.

Finally the last person spoke, and then everyone's attention returned to Matt.

"Thanks again for coming and let's all enjoy the party! Help yourselves to drinks and hors d'oeuvres. In about an hour we'll have the rehearsal. Dinner will follow at a restaurant," Matt announced and then turned to her and people began to talk.

"Brianna, meet Megan and Jared Dalton and Laurel and Chase Bennett."

"Ah, the famous cousins," she said after greeting each in turn. Jared and Chase grinned.

"And our infamous bet," Chase added. "I think some family members are taking bets on who'll win," he said. As the men began to talk and joke about their bet, Megan took Brianna's arm. "You come with us. We've heard enough about that bet to last a lifetime," she said, pulling Brianna aside while Laurel nodded and joined them. "I suspect Megan and I wouldn't be married if it hadn't been for that bet," Laurel added dryly. "Whatever happens, the winner treats the rest to a weekend getaway, so we'll all have a wonderful weekend together."

"Those three are so competitive, yet they are truly close," Laurel said, glancing at her husband, who was nearby. The love in her gaze gave Brianna a pang, because she didn't feel that way with Matt, nor did he love her. This marriage simply secured her future. A future alone with her baby.

"This is exciting," Megan said, "and a big surprise to us. Jared didn't expect Matt to get married ever."

"Nor did Chase," Laurel added with a smile. "But then not too long ago, neither Jared nor Chase expected to marry. Life is filled with surprises."

Brianna listened as the two women talked and it was obvious that they were becoming friends although they seldom saw each other. She was glad to be included in their friendship, even though she knew it would be short-lived.

Soon she excused herself and began to circulate, going to talk to Faith, her friend who would be a bridesmaid.

"I'm so happy for you," Faith said, her light brown eyes sparkling. "This house is a dream home! I can't believe this is your house now—except I know it is."

Brianna laughed at Faith's exuberance, a relief after the tension she'd felt around her family who didn't really know the whole story.

"This is it," she said, realizing she was losing her awe about it since she'd moved in with Matt. "My first time here, I felt overwhelmed—as you should remember."

"This is the best thing that could possibly happen."

"I don't know so much about the best, but it will be good."

"Good. Stop being so pessimistic and such a worrier. He'll fall in love with you. And how could you possibly keep from falling in love with him? He's charming."

"He is that," Brianna agreed. "I'm glad you're here. I hope you're always close by. And I hope we always stay friends."

"I'm going to love having a friend like you. Have me over for a swim sometime. I've seen that pool. Mercy!"

Brianna laughed. "Wait until the honeymoon is over, and I'll call you and we can swim. Weather won't matter. Thanks for being in my wedding."

"I wouldn't miss this for the world. Thanks for inviting Cal to this, too. He likes your brothers."

"I'm glad. I hope Matt does. And vice versa, but then I expect all my family to like him. Let's get together soon. I've missed seeing you."

"Just call."

"I better go talk to Matt's family because I haven't yet."

"Get going. I'll see you later," Faith said, smiling at Brianna.

Moving through the guests and relatives, Brianna stopped to meet and talk to Matt's mother. Penny Rome put her arms around Brianna to hug her lightly. "Welcome to the family!" she said warmly. "We're so happy to see Matt marry. His dad and I'd given up on him."

"Thank you," Brianna said, smiling at Matt's tall, slender mother.

"You must be good for him—he seems more relaxed now. He's too much like his dad—constantly working whether it's necessary or not. Both of them are driven, as I guess you know about Matt by now. This marriage is good for him and we're thrilled."

"I'm glad," Brianna answered. Guilt assaulted her for the fake marriage, but she pushed it aside in her mind. If it hadn't been her, it would have been another woman.

She met and talked with his father—seeing instantly that was where Matt got his handsome looks as they both had the same coloring and features. "Welcome to our family. Mom and I are happy to see Matt settle and marry. He needs that in his life."

"Thank you," she replied politely.

"I hope you'll bring him to see us. We don't see much of him, but I understand that better than his mother does."

"We'll do that, Mr. Rome," she said.

"Brianna, you're in our family now. Call me Travis, or call me Dad if you want."

"Yes, sir. Thank you." She chatted a few minutes longer with him and then they were joined by one of Matt's sisters and Travis Rome moved away. His relatives seemed to accept her into their family and they were all friendly enough that her nervousness ebbed.

She discovered her own relatives were also enjoying themselves and at ease with Matt's side of the family. To her delight, she realized that the men in both families had a down-to-earth common thread of being cowboys, which cut across all levels of society.

Time passed quickly until they boarded limousines and were driven to dinner at an elegant restaurant. As she sat in the restaurant, she gazed at the array of silver cutlery and the crystal and was thankful she had bought an etiquette book and had been studying and coaching her family. Reaching for a shrimp fork, she felt more relaxed and assured than she would have a week earlier.

The one flaw in a perfect evening was Zach Gentner. He shook hands with her, greeting her with a coldness that mirrored her own. She hadn't given any thought to Zach being present, but if he was as close to Matt as he'd said, then he would be included in the wedding party.

During the evening, there was never a moment alone with Matt and she returned to the hotel with her family, going to her suite where she was finally alone. Long into the night she sat up. The next morning would be her wedding, and she was already too far in now to back out of the agreement even if she had wanted to. To her relief, her family had made it through the evening without too many obvious blunders. Hopefully, Matt's money would help give them the opportunities they needed to better their lives.

Tomorrow night the wedding would be over and she would legally be Mrs. Matt Rome. Merely thinking about it gave her a flutter of anticipation.

Finally the moment arrived to step into the large room where they were to be married. Both families and a few close friends were standing as an organist played and Brianna walked in with her arm linked with her youngest brother's. She met Matt's gaze. In a navy suit and tie, he looked handsome, confident and pleased. She felt assured about her appearance—having checked a dozen times before leaving the room where she dressed. Even though her knee-length white silk suit was plain, she liked its simple lines. A diamond and sapphire necklace wedding gift from Matt sparkled around her throat and a gorgeous diamond engagement ring sparkled on her finger. Tiny white rosebuds bedecked her pinned-up black hair.

Her brother placed her hand in Matt's and then she turned to gaze into his eyes as she said vows that she knew would be broken eventually. How hollow the words rang in her ears! For an instant guilt assailed her over the farce they were perpetrating, but then she remembered what each one was gaining. If it hadn't been her, it would have been another woman. She reminded herself again of the things she intended to do to care for her mother, the things that she would be able to do for herself.

After a brief kiss from Matt, they walked out of the room together as newlyweds.

The party commenced in one of his large reception rooms. Outside, flakes of snow swirled while fires blazed in each big fireplace and a band serenaded them.

When Matt drew her into his arms for the first dance, he smiled at her. "For a small wedding, we gathered quite a crowd. We each have sizable families."

"I can't imagine what a large wedding would have been like. This one is huge to me," she said, barely aware of her conversation because most of her attention was on the handsome man dancing with her. Her pulse raced and she was eager to be alone with him. She was conscious of their legs brushing, of her hand enclosed in his warm grasp. As she gazed up into his eyes, she could see the change from the polite smile he had been giving friends and family all day. Desire blazed in the depths of his crystal-blue eyes.

"This is great, Brianna," he said.

"Yes, it is. I'm still overwhelmed and overjoyed. Matt, you've been so good to my family. You were nice and patient with them."

"They're friendly people," he answered.

"Unless they get snowed in, they're all leaving to-morrow morning to drive home. This snow is supposed to stop soon, so it shouldn't amount to much."

"Have you told any of them about our arrangement?" he asked and she shook her head.

"No one. They've heard of you and now they've seen your house and had this weekend, but they don't know the extent of the wealth. They think I'm fortunate, but they have their lives and they'll return to their routines tomorrow. This weekend will be a memory."

"I thought maybe they'd want a bit more after this weekend."

"No. I don't think they've guessed quite what I can do."

"My family is staying here and we can leave before the party breaks up. Why don't we in an hour?" he suggested, and her heart missed a beat. They were leaving here and tonight this marriage would be consummated. She tingled with anticipation.

"Whenever you say," she whispered. "We still need to cut the—"

"I'll come get you at an opportune time," he broke in. He moved on in the crowd and after cutting the cake, for the next hour, she chatted and smiled constantly and hoped she didn't say anything that was nonsense because her attention was half on the handsome man she had married. She had never liked the Cinderella fairy tale because it seemed the antithesis of real life. Prince Charming didn't come along and transform the life of his love, someone poor and uneducated. She didn't

expect that to happen, couldn't even imagine it happened. Yet today, the moment she became Mrs. Matthew
Rome, it had occurred. She now had money, a hefty
savings, investments and a large bank account plus more
cash in her purse at one time than she'd ever had in her
life.

She watched Matt with a circle of friends, women
gazing up at him adoringly, men laughing and joking
with him. A beautiful brunette stood close to him with
her hand on his arm while she told him something and
the group laughed. There was no reason for any jealousy.
Married or single, Matt would always have other women
after him, but she expected him to keep his promise to
remain faithful as long as they were married.

As she watched, Matt took a cell phone out of his
pocket and walked away from the crowd to head toward the hall. A couple came up to talk and then a
friend appeared who asked her to dance and she lost
Matt in the crowd.

Matt listened to one of his analysts discuss an acquisition while he threaded his way through the guests and
into the hallway. Replacing the phone in his pocket, Matt
heard a familiar voice and turned to face his cousin Chase.

"I thought you might like a drink," Chase said, handing Matt a glass of wine.

"Thanks. One glass of champagne is about all I can
bear."

"You have a beautiful bride."

"Thanks, I think so. So do you."

"Thank you. The difference is, I'm in love with mine," Chase said quietly.

Matt gazed into his cousin's green eyes that were steady and filled with what looked like pity. "How'd you know?"

"When you know someone as well as you and I and Jared know each other, it shows," Chase said, flicking his head slightly so stray locks of his straight brown hair would go back into place above his forehead.

"My folks have been fooled."

"They probably don't want to know the truth. I think I can guess why you did it. Jared told me he asked Megan for a marriage of convenience, but she wouldn't have any part of it, and then later they fell in love all over again."

"So Jared knows, too," Matt said, wondering how many others in his family realized the truth.

"Yep, and I didn't tell him. We both came to the same conclusion before we ever said anything to each other. In some ways maybe this bet wasn't such a great idea. If our wager thrust you into a loveless marriage—"

"Whoa," Matt interrupted. "I'm delighted and she's thrilled. She's getting two mil for this marriage and I'm having a dream affair that I would have pursued anyway, wedding or not. We're very content."

"You may be pleased, but you're not in love. There's a vast difference. Even so, it's good to hear that this isn't quite the business arrangement Jared and I assumed it was."

"It isn't remotely a purely business arrangement. I think she's fantastic."

"She's a beauty and very charming. Maybe before too long you both will be in love. Here's hoping you are."

Matt smiled. "Don't count on that one."

"I'm glad she's getting money out of the deal, and I hope that she thinks it's worth it to be hitched to you."

"If I do say so myself, I think the lady looks happy."

"That she does. And may you both be fulfilled in your bargain." Chase held out his drink. They touched glasses and sipped their wine.

"Where'd you find her? What debutante list? She looks younger."

"She's twenty-three. She's been going to college, she's from a tiny backwoods town, she's never been out of Wyoming and she's never flown in a plane."

Chase laughed. "So both of you are in for big changes."

"One of us is."

Chase chuckled. "You may be caught in a bramble bush of your own making. She told me she wants to get a law degree."

"I have no doubt that she will. Now she can easily afford to enroll."

"No problem there. She could have a zilch IQ and with her looks and as your wife, it wouldn't matter." Chase's mouth curled in a crooked grin. "Unless—"

"Unless what?" Matt narrowed his eyes, knowing he shouldn't even ask.

"Unless she's really smart and gives you a run for your money." Chase chuckled. "That would be fun. At least for Jared and me to watch, although you'll never let us know if you come out holding the short end of the stick. Or if you fall in love and she dumps you. 'Course that one, we might know."

"Right. Quit wringing your hands with glee—it won't happen. And I intend to win our bet."

Chase had a wide grin this time. "Sure, coz. We all aim to do that. And one of us will. We each have our own idea about who it will be."

"Speaking of my wife, I want to find her. Where's Laurel?"

"Dancing with an old friend the last I saw. I wish you luck, coz," Chase said with a grin as the two men went in search of their wives.

Brianna listened to someone who was speaking in the cluster of people around her, yet her mind was on Matt.

Soon now they could escape the party, get away to themselves. Anticipation continued to grow. A dark cloud loomed on her horizon—this marriage was as loveless as it was temporary.

She knew the one thing she had to constantly remember was Matt's true nature and love of money.

And then she caught his gaze and her pulse jumped. Across the large room, too far apart to communicate, someone who had been a stranger to her only a short time ago, now could exchange a glance with her and send her pulse into overdrive.

Still watching, she knew when he excused himself and began to move through the crowd toward her. Soon her life would really begin as Mrs. Matt Rome.

Six

That night, Matt carried her over the threshold of his Manhattan penthouse overlooking Central Park, a mere private jet flight away. Setting her on her feet, he wrapped his arms around her waist. "Welcome home, Mrs. Rome," he said and her heart thudded and she wished with all her heart that they had a real marriage.

She struggled to let go of all worries about his cold heart in order to try to make this wedding night a thrilling memory, untainted by reality.

She wanted to love him, to have him make love to her, wondering if this night would be any better and not the disappointment that lovemaking had been in the past. She stood on tiptoe to kiss him.

His arms tightened around her, crushing her to him

while she combed her fingers into his thick mass of curly hair and wrapped her other arm around his neck. Leaning over her, he kissed her possessively, groaning with longing, his tongue a slow, hot exploration.

She thrust her hips against him, knowing they could take hours, certain he was the kind of consummate lover that would be deliberate, tantalizing, infinitely sexy.

Each kiss and caress heightened her appetite for him. She poured herself into her kisses, wanting to obliterate the stream of women that must have been in his life.

Shoving away his jacket, she unfastened the studs of his shirt. His fingers tangled in her hair, sending pins flying and he combed out her long locks slowly while he continued to kiss her.

She pushed away his shirt and ran her hands across his broad shoulders, sliding them down to tangle in his soft, dark chest hair. She freed him of his trousers that fell away.

As she traced kisses over his muscled stomach, he groaned and lifted her to her feet. Unzipping her dress and pushing it away, he held her hips while lust darkened his expression.

He stood in his low-cut, narrow briefs that couldn't contain him while he looked at her leisurely, a heated gaze that was as tangible as a caress.

"You're gorgeous," he whispered, unfastening the clasp to yank away her lace bra. Cupping her breasts in his hands, he rubbed his thumbs over her nipples lightly in an enticing torment.

She gasped, gripping his narrow waist and closing her eyes while streaks of pleasure streamed from his touch.

"This is a dream," she whispered, winding her fingers in his thick curls as he bent down to take her nipple in his mouth, to kiss and suck and tease, his tongue circling where his thumb had been.

"No dream," he said, the words coming out slowly as his ragged breathing was loud. Hooking his thumbs in the narrow band of her thong and her pantyhose, he peeled them away and she stepped out of the last of her underclothes. He held her hips again, straightening and leaning away to look at her as she stood naked before him.

"I've waited too long for this moment," he whispered.

"There should be more to it," she whispered, unable to refrain from letting her bitterness slip about this loveless night. If he heard, he didn't acknowledge it. She peeled away his briefs and he stepped out of them, leaning down to pull off his socks.

As he straightened he picked her up and she raised her face to his, winding her arms around his neck, without looking to see where he carried her.

Still kissing her, he placed her on the bed. He was astride her and he leaned over to shower kisses to her breasts, his tongue stroking each pouty bud. His fingers drifted across her belly, down over her thigh and then so lightly, back up between her thighs. Her cry was loud in the silence, the tantalizing need building in her. Matt was loving her and she could make love to him in return, man and wife for tonight at least.

Reaching to caress him, she opened her legs to him. She kept her eyes closed as Matt explored and teased slowly, his caresses feathery touches, his tongue hot and wet, her need intensifying swiftly.

Driving away her thoughts about a loveless union, he moved lower, raining kisses down the inside of her leg, holding her foot as he caressed her and his hands played over her. Beneath his touch, she arched her hips and writhed.

His muscled thighs were covered in short, curly black hairs that gave slight friction against her skin.

"Turn over," he whispered, rolling her over without waiting. And then he moved between her legs, his fingers playing over her, touching, caressing and exploring, discovering where he could touch to get the biggest response from her. His tongue followed where his fingers had been and when he slipped his hands along the inside of her thighs, sliding higher until he touched her intimately, she gasped and attempted to roll over, but he placed his hand in the middle of her back.

"Lie still, Brianna," he ordered, his fingers driving her to dig her fists into the bed and spread her legs wider.

She moaned, crying out, attempting to turn until finally he allowed her to and then his hand was back between her thighs, touching, rubbing, exploring, another constant tease.

Losing all awareness of anything except his hands and mouth on her, she arched wildly, spreading her legs so he had full access to her.

"Brianna, love, you're beautiful!" he gasped, but she barely heard what he said and paid no heed. She had to have him inside her, wanting his heat and hardness.

With a cry, she raised her hips higher. "Love me!" she gasped as she fell back and he kissed her deeply. She returned his loving, but then pushed him away and down on the bed to climb astride him and pour kisses down across his belly as she stroked his hard rod.

She shifted to take him in her mouth, her tongue circling the velvet tip while he clenched his fists in her hair and groaned, letting her kiss and caress him for minutes until he sat up suddenly to pull her to him and lean over her, kissing her thoroughly.

She kissed him in return until he placed her on the bed and started the loving anew, his hands playing over her lightly, caressing while her need climbed to a fever pitch.

He moved between her legs, hooking them over his shoulders to give him access to her as he kissed and stroked her.

Her eyes fluttered open and she saw him watching her when she gasped with gratification.

"Do you like this?" he whispered, his tongue flicking over her and she moaned softly.

"Yes, yes," she whispered, caressing his strong thighs, stroking his manhood. "Love me, Matt," she whispered, placing her hands on his hips, to tug him closer as he continued to caress and kiss her.

When he moved between her legs and she opened her eyes to look at him, her heart thudded with longing. He was handsome male perfection, ready and poised. Tangles of black curls fell on his forehead and his face was flushed. His body was lean, hard muscles and his manhood thick and ready.

She held her arms out to him. "Love me, Matt. Become part of me."

He lowered himself, wrapping an arm around her as he kissed her passionately again.

Slowly, he entered her, the hot, hard tip of his manhood plunging into her softness, making her cry out with longing. Still kissing her, he withdrew. His kiss muffled her cry as he entered her again, hot and slow, filling her and withdrawing, tempting and stirring desire to white heat.

The teasing heightened enjoyment while driving her wild with wanting him to love her, reaching a point she'd never known where she was desperate for his loving.

She tore her mouth from his. "Matt, I want you!" she cried, arching against him, her hands sliding over his firm bottom trying to draw him closer, her legs tightening around his waist.

He entered her slowly and she moved beneath him, and then they rocked together.

With her blood thundering in her ears and her eyes squeezed tightly closed, she held him, crying out for him to keep loving her. When she climaxed, spasms shook her and ecstasy consumed her. Lights burst behind her closed eyelids and she couldn't stop moving with him until she climaxed again and heard him cry her name.

As she clung to him, he thrust wildly in her. Enjoyment she'd never known before rippled with aftershocks of pleasure.

Finally, they quieted, their ragged breathing returning to normal as he showered light kisses on her face and shoulders and murmured endearments she couldn't believe.

Turning his head, he kissed her fully on the mouth, a long, slow kiss of gratification. They had shared the time with a mutual pleasure but love was missing. Even though he acted like a man in love, she knew he wasn't.

Holding him close, she caressed him while they continued to kiss until finally he raised his head. "You were worth the wait, Brianna. My decision is justified."

Once again he focused on himself, reminding her she was locked into a businesslike bargain. "I can say the same." She was unwilling to think beyond the present moment.

This time with him was fleeting and false. On the plus side, if they had been wildly in love, she couldn't imagine they would have had better sex. He truly was the consummate lover she had expected.

Finally, holding her close against him, he rolled onto his side.

"I don't want to let you go. I can't believe my good fortune in finding you," he whispered.

"I suppose we can both feel fortunate," she said lazily, enjoying being held in his arms and feeling euphoric, trying to keep at bay all the hurt over the lack of love in their relationship, yet feeling an emptiness behind the pleasure.

His hands played lightly over her and he showered kisses on her temple, throat and ear, all faint touches that rekindled her desire.

"Ah, Brianna, you're the best," he murmured, yet

she paid little heed, assuming he was repeating what he'd said before. Deep inside, along with desire for sex, was a hungry need for a true relationship that she couldn't dissolve. She should be more like Matt and focus on the money involved in this arrangement, but it was turning out almost from the first that she couldn't.

"Come here, darlin'," he said, leaning down to scoop her into his arms. Wrapping her arms around him, she combed locks of his hair off his forehead.

"Where are you taking me?" Without waiting for his answer, she pulled him closer to kiss him.

When he raised his head, he crossed the room with her and entered a huge bathroom that held a sunken tub. Matt set her on her feet and turned spigots. "We'll bathe together," he said, testing the water and then turning to pick her up again and carry her into the tub.

Setting her on her feet, he kissed her while water rose and swirled around their legs. Finally, he stopped and took her into his arms again to sit down, holding her close against him.

"You've got an insatiable appetite," she whispered. She could feel his manhood, thick and hard and ready for her again.

"What can I say? You make my blood boil."

"I can do something about that right now," she said in a sultry voice, turning and sitting astride him to lower herself onto him. Desire ignited again, a hungry need that she couldn't believe had been so totally satisfied only a short time earlier, yet now she wanted him with a desperation that seemed fiercer than ever.

He kissed her as she moved on him and in minutes she cried out when she climaxed and felt him shudder from his own orgasm.

Soon she was seated between his legs in a tub of hot, swirling water.

"Better and better," she murmured and felt a rumble in his chest when he laughed softly.

"Before the night is over I'll show you better and better," he promised and her pulse jumped at the prospect.

"This is temporary," she said without thinking.

"Shh," he commanded. "It's not temporary tonight and it won't end anyway, not until we want it to end."

"Until you want it to end," she corrected. "But no matter. Tonight I don't want any angst. This is the best ever," she said, trying to ignore that nagging inner voice.

When they climbed out and toweled each other dry, as she lightly rubbed the soft terry cloth over his body, she looked into his hungry blue eyes. A flame started low inside her.

While he continued to watch her, he rubbed her nipples lightly with a dry towel. Then his towel slipped between her legs as he stroked her.

She gasped, closing her eyes, and he tossed aside his towel to pull her closer, one arm circling her waist and his other hand stroking her soft feminine bud while he kissed her.

In minutes she had her eyes squeezed tightly shut as she held him and moved, his hand driving her wild.

"Matt, I want your love," she said, meaning it literally, knowing he would think only in terms of passion.

He picked her up to carry her to bed and finish what he'd started. Midmorning while they lazed in each other's arms in bed, he combed her hair from her face with his fingers. Caressing his chest, she curled the tight hairs around her forefinger.

"Matt, I'm beginning to have hunger pangs. I think the meal yesterday on the plane was the last time we ate."

"Could be," he drawled in a lazy, satisfied voice. "The only hunger I have is for you," he said, his voice thickening as he rolled on his side and gazed at her. "A penny for your thoughts."

"You'd have to pay a lot more than that. Besides, you can probably guess my thoughts," she drawled in a throaty tone and saw his eyes darken. Could he possibly surmise what she was contemplating, or what she really wanted? If she could, would she trade his money for his love? The question came out of the blue and was one she didn't want to pursue. Why did it matter so much to her? Yet she knew exactly why, and the closer she drew to him in physical intimacy, the more she wanted an emotional relationship. Love was never part of the equation, she reminded herself.

He drew his finger along the top of the sheet where it curved over her breasts, a faint touch that stirred tingles and aroused her again.

She caught his hand. "You wait. You're going to have to feed me before you have me again, mister."

"You think?" he asked, sounding amused. "There's a challenge that I might have to rise to."

"You've already risen and you need to cool it," she

said, knowing she was fighting a battle she didn't even want to win. "How easily you can manipulate me," she said. "Shameless!"

"I'll show you shameless," he retorted, rolling her onto her back and moving over her to lick and kiss until she forgot about food and only wanted him.

"Matt, come here!" she cried, pulling him over her and wrapping her long legs around his waist.

He lowered himself into her, thrusting hard and fast this time as she rose to meet him.

With another burst of satisfaction, she climaxed. Rapture enveloped her while she continued to move with him until he climaxed and called out her name.

"Brianna! Love! My love!"

She knew the endearments were meaningless and she should ignore them, but for today, she relished knowing he wanted her.

Later, she curled against him in his arms with her hair spilling across his chest. She could hear the steady beat of his heart, feel the rhythmic thumping beneath her hand. She was satiated, lethargic.

"I can't move," she whispered, running her forefinger in slow circles through his thick chest hair.

"We'll bathe and then go eat."

"I think we had the same plans earlier, but they went awry. Perhaps we shouldn't bathe together this time."

"Perish the thought. A simple bath and food. The simplicities of life."

"It doesn't seem to work out that way. This time, I'll tip the scales in favor of getting to eat," she said and slipped out of bed, gathering a sheet around her as she hurried away from him to the bathroom to shower alone. She locked the bathroom door behind her, certain if he came and pounded on it, she would open it at once.

To her surprise, he let her go and she showered and dried in total silence. Wrapping herself in a thick maroon towel, she went to find him.

She located Matt with glasses of orange juice, a pot of coffee, a tall glass of milk and covered dishes, some on the table and some still on a nearby cart. He wore jeans and a T-shirt and his hair was wet.

She walked up behind him to slide her arms around his waist. "You're a fast cook."

"I used my powers of persuasion to get room service to deliver on the double. Now feast away, my love. I ordered everything I could think you might like."

His "my love" stung. She wasn't his "love" and it bothered her more than she'd expected it would. She tried to focus on all she was gaining, but love was turning out to be far more important than she'd expected.

With her appetite suddenly diminished, she sat down, opening dishes and discovering tempting omelets, scrambled eggs, hot biscuits, slices of ham, strips of bacon, bowls of strawberries and a fruit plate with grapes, melons and pineapple slices.

"This is the ideal way to start the day," he said, and his tone took her attention from food. She looked up to see him seated, watching her with his head propped on his fist.

"Aren't you going to eat?" she asked.

"Yes, but I was thinking about last night."

She waved her fork at him. "Do not think lusty thoughts until I've had breakfast. I really forbid it!"

"Yes, ma'am, sexy wench."

She laughed. "Not really. What's our schedule?"

"Tomorrow we fly to Rome," he said.

"I hope I see it. I haven't seen anything of New York City. Not even the park, which is right across the street."

"We'll be back here soon, I promise. Then I'll take you anywhere you want to go."

She set down her fork and took a drink of milk. "You've given me paradise and allowed me to do things I could only dream about before."

"It's a good arrangement," he said. She hoped she hid her disappointment, because he could have been discussing a business transaction he'd made.

In minutes she forgot her disappointment as she returned to eating breakfast, determined to get a glimpse of Central Park before he carried her back to bed.

With each passing mile of their flight to Rome, Matt was pleased to see she was captivated. She hovered at the window, looking at little more than clouds and water, yet she seemed totally engrossed. "Flying is the best possible means of travel!" she said.

"If you'll save all that enthusiasm until we're in bed, this will really be a memorable day."

She smiled. "I'll remember this flight always," she said, and he wondered how long they would stay together. Right now, he was unable to imagine tiring of her, but he always eventually grew bored with women. Yet he suspected Brianna would last longer than any of the others ever had.

"I'll bring you back plenty of times, Brianna, so you'll be able to fly more often than you'll want. You'll see Europe to your heart's content."

"I can't envision such a thing. You take this for granted. Even if I moved here to live, I can't imagine ever being that way."

"You'll be a jaded traveler, I promise."

"Don't make promises you can't keep. We'll never know who's right, but I feel certain I am."

"I'll tell you what I want—I want you in my arms in bed."

"Later, later," she said, waving her fingers at him without tearing her gaze from outside the window. "I want to see everything."

"I figured you would," he answered with amusement. "Enjoy it. Rome will be more fascinating than ocean and clouds."

"I'm scared to even think about Rome," she said.

"You—scared? I don't believe it. You'll be fine, and as my wife, you'll be totally accepted."

"I want to see as much as possible in the short time we'll be there."

"I'll repeat—I promise to bring you back, so you don't have to try to see and do everything this time," he said. He suspected he was going to have to do the tourist things sometime this week for her sake, but he'd be thinking about how he couldn't wait to make love again.

* * *

In Rome, they moved into a luxurious suite in the hotel where Matt usually stayed. She gawked only slightly at the elegant lobby, and then they were locked in their suite and could have been in a tent as far as the outside world was concerned.

Matt had intended to show her Rome, but his intentions were lost in lovemaking until Friday, when he left her a limo and driver while he attended a meeting.

She had a whirlwind tour, stopping at the Colosseum and at St. Peter's. As she stood in St. Peter's Square and admired the beauty of the ancient Basilica, she thought how some of her dreams had become empty and disillusioning.

All through the years of growing up with hardships and only hopes of becoming affluent, and then through the generous bargain with Matt, she had thought riches would give her all she wanted. Matt's money would give her, her baby and her family comfort, education and security—but the rest was empty.

She had been thrilled over the prospect of a honeymoon in Rome, but now that she was here, it was not the pleasure she had expected. She wished she had someone with her to share each discovery—there would be no great memories to take home from this trip. She'd brought her camera, yet she didn't care to keep any pictures. Love was missing and it made a difference.

The real disappointment was Matt. There were moments he was charming company. How easily she could fall in love with him if only—

She stopped that train of thought. Matt was who he was, and she had to accept it. He was at a meeting today, working to get even more wealth. Yet she had been guilty, too, of placing too much importance on money.

She stood in the square, combing her breeze-tussled hair away from her cheek with her fingers, and realized she would never feel quite the same about what was truly important in life.

Strolling around, she only half looked at her surroundings, still lost in her thoughts and hurting because she had locked herself into a situation where she lived with a charming man who didn't even know she existed except in bed.

Finally, she turned away to head back to the limo, wanting to stop her sightseeing for the day, wondering if she would ever return to Rome with someone she loved.

Later in the afternoon, Matt arrived, sweeping in the door and kicking it closed as he pulled her into his embrace.

"How did you like Rome?" he asked, and her half-hearted answer was lost in his kisses, her sightseeing report forgotten.

Getting ready for the charity ball, Brianna took her things to the large bathroom. She knew Matt had already showered and was dressing which would take him no time. When she finished bathing, she expected to have the bedroom and bathroom to herself. She didn't want distractions from Matt while she got ready and she con-

tinually ran through the list of names of the investors
and facts about them.

As she dressed, she wondered if Matt had concerns
about his new wife's inexperience. So far, he'd ex-
pressed absolutely none. She felt as if anyone could
glance at her and sense her background, her lack of
experience and sophistication, yet she reminded
herself that Matt's monumental self-assurance would
cover a lot.

Repeatedly during the trip, she had been thankful for
the honeymoon being in Italy and the ball being in
Rome, because for the past two years she had been
studying Italian in college. Since she felt she might be
interested in international law, she wanted a minor in
languages. The day she learned about the ball, she'd
even gone out and bought a crash course in "Teach
Yourself Conversational Italian" to practice further.

Finally, she went to find him at his desk, poring over
something. The desk light caught glints in his thick
black hair. She wondered how he could tune out the
world and concentrate on business when he had only
minutes before leaving for a glamorous evening with
people he intended to impress. Her palms were damp
with nervousness and she felt the same as she had on
the first job interview in Cheyenne.

"Matt," she said softly.

"One minute, Brianna," he answered, his head still
bent over figures. "I want one more minute to finish this
list," he said. "I'm in the middle of—" His words died
as he glanced up at her and he stared at her. "You're

gorgeous," he said, his voice becoming husky as it did when he was aroused.

She let out her breath. One hurdle passed. Her pulse speeded when he circled the desk toward her, never taking his gaze from her.

When he crossed the room, she tingled. Fighting the urge to smooth her skirt, she knew she was dressed as flawlessly as she could in a scarlet sleeveless dress that was the most expensive dress she'd ever owned with the exception of her wedding outfit. Cut in a low V neckline, the skirt split up one side to an inch above her knees and she wore matching sandals.

"You look too beautiful to waste the evening at a ball," he whispered, walking up to her and slipping an arm around her waist. As he leaned toward her, she pushed lightly against him, wiggled out of his embrace and stepped away.

"Not so soon. You don't know how long I worked to achieve this look. Let's go. When we return tonight, you can do as you please and I promise I won't protest."

He groaned. "You make things so difficult."

"You'll manage," she said, smiling at him while her pulse raced.

"Shall we go?" he asked, offering her his arm. She nodded and stepped close to loop her arm through his.

The streets of Rome were congested. Traffic was busy, and her case of nerves returned, but not as threatening as before because now she was at ease with Matt and he was the one person who mattered.

"This city is beautiful," she said, knowing this

night would remain a vivid memory for the rest of her life.

"Yes," he answered, smiling at her. "Did you enjoy the sights? I haven't heard about your day."

"Of course I did. I hope yours was successful—whatever your meeting was about."

"About an investment I have. Yes, I had a productive meeting. And now we're going to impress some people tonight," he said, still smiling.

"Rome seems incredibly noisy. Scooters are everywhere," she said, barely aware of her statement, trying to stop reflecting on Matt's ambition.

"Here we are," he said. "I want you to have a memorable evening."

The limo halted in front of the canopied door of a luxury hotel where lights blazed. As she emerged, her nervousness climbed. She inhaled deeply, glancing at Matt, who looked drop-dead handsome in his tux. Smiling at her, he turned to hold her hand. Squaring her shoulders, she decided to simply enjoy herself and to stop worrying over the impression she might make.

Her heart twisted because he was still thinking about work and the investors.

They entered the large ballroom, where a waltz played and couples danced.

From the first moment in the door, Matt greeted people and introduced her to too many to recall. The names of the investors she finally had firmly in mind and within minutes she saw the first one approach. He was a tall, black-haired man with a beautiful black-haired

woman was at his side. His dark gaze was on Brianna.
"Here comes—"

"Signore Ruffuli and his wife, Letta," Brianna said
quietly to Matt. "And his wife doesn't speak English."

"Very good!" Matt smiled broadly, turning to greet
the couple.

"Buona sera, Signore Rufulli e Signora Rufulli,"
Matt acknowledged his friend and his wife. *"Vorrei
presentarle a la mia sposa,"* Matt said in fluent Italian,
turning to make introductions to Brianna.

*"Buona sera, Signori Rufulli. Piaciere di fare la loro
conoscenza. Che bella serata."* Brianna smiled as she
greeted them.

While the men talked, the two women conversed
until Matt took her arm as they walked on to meet others.

"You surprised me," he said. "You didn't tell me you
speak Italian."

"It's very limited. In college I had two years and I
studied a little in one of those crash courses on a CD,
'Teach Yourself Conversational Italian,' before we
came tonight."

"I'm impressed," Matt said as he gave her an ap-
praising study and she wondered what he was thinking.

"I intended you to be," she said, turning to smile at
a blond man who approached them and shook hands
with Matt as he greeted him.

"Brianna, please meet Sven Ingstad. Sven, I want you
to meet Brianna Rome."

"I hoped to meet your lovely wife," he said in a
courtly manner while he smiled at her.

Gradually, they circled the fringe of the dance floor and she met all the men from the investment group who were present. She knew from beforehand that three wouldn't be present at the charity ball.

Finally, she was in Matt's arms to dance, and as they whirled across the floor, he studied her. "You have facets to you I know nothing about. I may have to reassess my expectations."

"If you think that, from my standpoint, the evening just became a success," she said, flirting with him.

"Then I think we can both count tonight as a big accomplishment. You've captivated them."

She laughed. "I hardly think 'captivated' is the correct description. I hope they like and approve of me," she said, refraining from adding that he was the one whose opinion of her was important.

"There isn't another man on this earth who wouldn't approve of you," Matt said, and his voice dropped a notch lower. "Wait and see, as the evening wears on, who wants to dance with you."

Except that approval by others was important to Matt, she hardly cared about his business acquaintances. Matt was pleased with her because it moved him closer to his goal, but she still had the feeling that he saw her only in those terms—and through desire. Matt never seemed to miss the women who had gone out of his life. Why did she expect to be different? Was there any way to break through that total focus he had on wealth and make him see her as part of his life? And since when had she started wanting to? Was she already falling in love with him in spite of fully knowing what he was like?

"How long do you think it will take before they invite you to join?" she asked.

"I can't answer that. I don't think they will for a couple of months at the earliest. Anxious for this marriage to end?" he asked and she wondered how much he was teasing and how serious he was.

"Not at all," she said. "Why would I be? I'm doing the Grand Tour. I don't want this to end."

"That wasn't the answer I hoped for," he said, gazing at her with a questioning speculation. "I wanted a reason that included me," he said and, again, she wondered at his statement.

"So do you want to hear that I think you're the sexiest man on earth and I can't wait to be back in bed with you?"

His blue eyes darkened. "The first possible moment, we're out of here," he said.

The music ended and Sven Ingstad appeared to ask her to dance, followed by another Italian acquaintance of Matt's who was widowed.

Wide doors were opened on an adjoining reception area where long tables were covered in fancy dishes of caviar, foie gras, truffles, brandied fruit, crepes, tempting chocolate extravagances and other exotic dishes she couldn't recognize. Throughout the evening, talking with wives, or in clusters of people she had met tonight, it was her tall, handsome husband who took her attention. Even when separated, she was aware of where he was, glimpsing him while he danced one time with each of the investors' wives and she knew he charmed each one and probably impressed on them how delighted he was to be married.

Most of his time was spent at her side; he poured the attention on her and she suspected it was for the benefit of those investors he hoped to convince that he was happy in his union. Who would think a man on his honeymoon wasn't wildly in love with his new wife? Whatever his motive, she enjoyed Matt's undivided attention, his flirting, his amusing anecdotes.

When the band took a break for an intermission, a dignitary stepped to the microphone and introduced the planners of the ball. Then awards were made to the six largest contributors and Matt was called forward to receive a plaque, which he placed on their table.

"Matt, that's terrific!"

He barely glanced at the plaque. "It was a good cause and it's tax deductible," he said and she guessed he contributed to impress the investors.

In a short time the band commenced playing again and Brianna was swept back up into the fray.

Later, dancing with Matt, Brianna was surprised to discover it was midnight. "The evening has flown, Matt. I'll always remember this night and every detail of it."

"I'm glad. And I think we've stayed as long as newlyweds should be expected to. We're leaving," he said.

Her pulse jumped because as successful as the evening had been, the prospect of making love with Matt was vastly more exciting. She'd had her night in Rome, but now it was time to return to the privacy of their suite with a man who had to be the most fantastic lover possible.

Seven

When they were seated in the limousine and on the road with the partition to the front of the limo closed, Matt pulled her onto his lap.

"You were an asset tonight," he said, thinking she had been. She had surprised him and he was certain charmed many others. "I've been waiting to do this." He removed the pins from her hair and dropped them into his pocket.

Her green eyes were clear, fringed with thick black eyelashes, her lips full and soft. He wanted her with an intensity that seemed to increase each day.

"You wait until we get home. This is far too public and we might have to stop for some reason."

"I won't wait to kiss you," he said, knowing that would be an impossibility. For hours he had been ready to leave the ball, but he had known he should stay to shmooze with the investor group. He wanted them to know Brianna and to see that he was happily married.

He wondered if he would be invited into their group soon. If so, what about Brianna? He wasn't ready to dissolve their marriage. She was looking out the window of the limo, lost in her own thoughts. He toyed with long locks of her hair. "I haven't heard much about the places you went today. All you said was you enjoyed the sights."

"St. Mark's was beautiful." She studied him. "I'd guess that when you look at it, you are simply trying to estimate the value of it."

He smiled. "I'll have to admit, I've given thought to its monetary value because the amount would be staggering."

"Not to you. And if you could turn a profit, I think you'd go after even a famous landmark."

"Never a sacred one. No, I don't think I would. Usually, famous landmarks are national treasures or otherwise off-limits or not financially feasible. Is something bothering you?"

She gazed impassively at him. "Marriage, even a businesslike paper one, is complicated. Living with another person is a big change."

"I take it that's a convoluted yes. Is this because I haven't taken you sightseeing?"

She shook her head. "Just little adjustments. It's good between us, Matt," she said, smiling at him. "You know it is."

Puzzled, he appraised her. "It's spectacular between us," he answered.

"Watch out, you'll get accustomed to having me in your life," she said with a twinkle in her eyes, and he smiled at her.

"I know I want you here now for damn sure," he replied. "Don't tell me you're getting emotionally tied up in this marriage?" he asked.

"I know better than to do that," she answered easily, running her hand over his knee, and he forgot their discussion.

Matt wrapped his arms around her and nuzzled her neck. She smelled sweet and was soft and he wished they could get home faster because he wanted to take her to bed. He raised his head to gaze into her eyes, seeing desire dance in their depths.

"Brianna," he said and she looked into his eyes. He leaned the last few inches to kiss her, a long, lingering kiss that she returned with fire.

"This damn drive is too long," he said, once, and then bent to kiss her again. His fingers sought her zipper, but she caught his wrist.

"I'll remind you. We wait until we get back to our suite. This limo isn't the place."

"It is for me," he said. "I'll do what you want, but once we're in our suite, then I get my way." He pulled her close, cradling her head against his shoulder as he returned to kissing her.

The moment they entered their suite, he caught her to pull her into his embrace.

"Now, beautiful, I get to make long, slow love to you." He kissed her again and stopped thinking.

* * *

Around noon the next day, Matt gave Brianna a list of stores she might like and she left in the limo to go shopping.

The phone rang and he answered to hear Zach's voice.

"We acquired the property you wanted in Chicago," his friend said. "The contract is on your desk and you can sign when you return. They know you're on your honeymoon."

"Good."

"How'd the ball go?"

"How do you think? She wowed them," he answered without waiting for Zach's reply. "She was stunning, brilliant, charming the investors. She even conversed in Italian."

"I'm glad," Zach said. "Matt, if I'm wrong, I'll admit it. You know that. Maybe I underestimated her."

"I think you did," Matt said quietly.

"Be funny if you fall in love with the little woman."

Matt laughed. "No danger. And the 'little woman' has her own plans for the future."

"Sure," Zach said as if Matt had stated that Brianna could fly to Mars. "No morning sickness?"

"Nothing. If I hadn't heard her talk about her doctor's appointment, I wouldn't believe that she's pregnant. It doesn't show yet even slightly and she feels great. She's pumped up about the travel because she's never been anywhere, so that makes it fun."

"Will wonders never cease," Zach muttered.

"Matter of fact, Zach, see if you can clear my calendar next week. I think we'll stay longer. We might as well take one more week."

"Am I talking to Matthew Rome?" Zach asked, suddenly sounding puzzled.

"You heard what I said. Clear my calendar and I'll be in touch. Let me know if anything urgent develops."

He broke the connection and waited with his hand on the phone, lost in thought about Brianna and the night before. His gaze went to the empty bed and he wished she were still here. He wanted her as if they'd never made love. He couldn't concentrate on business for thinking about her, and he was thankful he'd taken another week off, but he wanted her back in his arms immediately. Recalling their conversation on the drive back to the hotel from the ball, he reflected on her warning to watch out, that he might get accustomed to having her in his life.

He gazed into space, wondering if such a thing could happen. And her remarks about her sightseeing had carried a slightly jarring undercurrent. It was obvious she recognized his life was focused on making profitable deals. He had more money than he could spend, but he liked the challenge of competing and acquiring lucrative assets. When she agreed to this marriage, she had known that much about him. So why would it disturb her now…unless she was becoming accustomed to his commitment and wanted it to continue?

His entire being was dedicated to acquisition and success. If she couldn't cope with that, she knew the conditions of the bargain she'd made.

Tossing aside worries about their relationship, he swore softly and looked at his watch, counting the hours until he'd be alone with her. His cousins, Zach, no one close seemed to think it was going to work out between them in this temporary marriage. Ridiculous. His union with her was already dizzying in its success, and any negative feelings on her part were insignificant. Her slight disapproval of his lifestyle would have no effect. Yet even as he came to that conclusion, he had an uncustomary ripple of dissatisfaction. Surely he wasn't getting bothered because he didn't have her one hundred percent approval. He refused to consider such a possibility.

On Saturday, daily life returned as they flew home, only her real life had changed forever. The first of the following week she spent two days drifting around his mansion while Matt flew to Houston to work and by the third day, she had already looked into online courses for next year. She was restless, bored and didn't have a circle of friends who had time on their hands.

Within five minutes after Matt returned home Friday night, they were naked, making love and she forgot boredom and loneliness.

The next morning she was in his arms listening to business deals he had transacted while he was away.

"Matt, you talk about your Texas ranch and property in Houston and Dallas, your property in Chicago and New York, and your Wyoming ranch. Other than the block your office is in here in Cheyenne, do you own any other Cheyenne property?"

"No. There's never been any particular reason to want any."

"I'd think you'd want to invest in more in Cheyenne since you live here. It's sort of an investment in the future."

"You might be right," he drawled in a lazy voice as he combed his fingers through her long hair. "I'll get someone to look into it."

"There are some old areas that could be fixed up and utilized and you have a lot of interest in cowboy life— it might be nice if you'd look into building a museum."

"I'll think about it. You look into museums and see what we have. I don't even know. Here's what I'm far more interested in," he said, his hand drifting along her slender throat and then lower.

"There's something else I want to discuss with you. While you were gone I looked into some online courses for next year." His hand stilled.

"I thought we'd settled the school situation. You'll go back after we part ways."

"You were gone three days. You'll be away a lot on business. I've worked all my life since I was eleven years old. I'm bored just sitting around here."

"There are charity jobs you can do that will keep you as busy as a full-time job, if that's what you'd prefer. I don't want you tied into something where you can't travel with me. I'd think you'd want to travel with me when I go to Europe or interesting places."

"Whether you are in Europe or here, you work. But I have a lot of time on my hands until the baby comes and charity work—a little will go a long way. Even after the baby is born, I'll have some time to myself and if I don't, I can drop the course. What's wrong with an online course if it doesn't interfere in any way with you?"

He rolled over to prop himself up on his elbow. His blue eyes had darkened and this time she recognized irritation. A muscle worked in his jaw that was thrust out stubbornly.

"We had an agreement. You're backing out of it and next thing I know, you'll be too involved in school to do what I want."

"I did agree. But I didn't realize how much time I'd have. I promise to drop classes instantly if they interfere in any way. Otherwise, what's it to hurt if I enroll?"

Scowling, he opened his mouth, but she put her finger over his lips. "You wait," she urged. "Think it over and then tell me your answer. If I make sure it doesn't interfere and you never even know I'm doing it, then what's the harm?"

"It's the principle."

She smiled. "That's ridiculous, Matt. That simply means you want your way in this whether it's sensible or not. You think about it calmly and rationally and then give me an answer. You have excellent judgment."

"How long am I supposed to give this thought?"

"How about until this time next week?" she suggested.

"Very well, but I can't imagine changing my feelings on it."

"We can both change our minds if it's mutually agreeable, don't you think?"

He glared at her. "All right, you get your way. I'll think about it."

"That's all I want you to do. And in order to keep you happy in the meantime," she said softly, running her hand down his smooth back and over his bare, hard bottom, letting her fingers play on him. "I'll do my utmost to please you," she whispered, wrapping one arm around his neck and pulling him closer as her tongue flicked out to trace his lower lip.

With a groan he rolled over on top of her, sliding one arm beneath her to hold her while he kissed her and ran his other hand along her bare thigh.

In minutes she knew his annoyance with her had vanished and she did her best to pleasure him until he rolled her onto her back again. Lowering himself between her legs to enter her, he filled her swiftly and then pumped as if driven and unable to take his time while she cried out with pleasure, moving with him.

Later, when they lay in each other's arms, he showered her with light kisses and caresses. "This is great, Brianna," he said.

"But not as great as a business deal and making money. You get a high from gaining more wealth, don't you?"

He studied her with a penetrating look. "Thank heaven I don't have to choose between sex or making money," he replied.

Solemnly, she shook her head.

As snow swirled and fell outside, they spent the weekend in bed together and Monday, the last week of October, when she kissed him goodbye, she had a pang because she was going to miss him badly.

Watching him drive away, she wondered if he would consider her enrollment in online courses. She thought he was being ridiculously stubborn simply because he wasn't accustomed to anyone telling him no or even giving him bad news, much less wanting to go back on a promise.

She hoped he thought about it. In the meantime, she had plans for now. Her entire family was coming to town and this time she would put them in the mansion.

It was time to get them enrolled in colleges or trade schools, as she'd intended. If they wanted to return to the life they'd had before, they always could, but she suspected each one of them would move on to something better than they'd had in the past.

She planned to talk to her mother and set up an account for her. She could afford it easily and she knew her mother was accustomed to a simple life and would keep confidential what Brianna did.

That night, she sat at the large informal table in the breakfast dining area and gazed around the table while everyone ate and talked. Her mother sat at the other end of the table and was talking to Brianna's youngest sister, Danielle. She watched Danielle laugh, her eyes sparkling while she and their mother took turns helping Emma and Hunter, Danielle's children.

"I still think this bubble will burst and I'll find out it never was true," Melody said.

"It's very true," Brianna replied. "Matt has been liberal with my allowance and about letting me do what I want to do," she said, having no intention of telling any of them the actual situation at this point. So far as she could tell, both her family and Matt's had accepted their marriage and thought they were in love, which suited her fine.

Through the weekend and into the next week, they pored over college catalogs, made calls, sent e-mails and contacted schools, searching for places for her relatives to attend school. All the men except her youngest brother enrolled in the University of Wyoming. Both sisters had picked two-year schools in Laramie, solving their search quickly and were looking for places to live in Laramie.

Wednesday night as they all sat in one of the large recreation rooms, Matt called and said he'd arrived in town and was on his way home.

Brianna excused herself and met him at the door when he came in. Snow dusted his topcoat and flakes melted in his hair, drops glistening in the light. He stomped his booted feet.

Rushing to throw herself into his arms, she pulled him close for a long, heated kiss.

Finally he raised his head. "What are all the cars out there? Do we have company?"

"Yes, as a matter of fact—"

"Damn, I've been waiting to get home to you. Who's here and when are they leaving?"

"Actually, they're not leaving for a while. My family is here. I invited them and I'm getting them enrolled in colleges."

"Brianna, they're not *living* with us, are they? You have a nice family, but I don't want them underfoot while they get an education."

"I know you don't," she replied coolly, stepping away from him. "They came when you were away."

"I'm back and they're here now."

"They are. If I remember correctly, you are going out of town again Monday morning."

"Right. But my house is mine and I like solitude. I'll be glad to put them up in any hotel they want, but I want our house to ourselves."

"I hope you're not saying to get them out of here tonight," she said, growing angrier with him by the second. "It's snowing."

"No, I'm not," he replied with a long sigh. "But I hope you can have them moved when I return from the next trip."

"Matt, this is a huge, enormous mansion."

"Right. I like space, solitude and privacy. That's why few people have ever been here. I have guards, gates, high walls, a privacy fence and a gatekeeper. That's it, Brianna. I asked you to marry me. I did not marry your family or intend to share my home with them. Frankly, I'd feel the same about my own family."

"Matt, you're a coldhearted man with only one love."

"So be it. You knew that much when you married me. Your family goes. I can tell them or you can."

"I'll tell them because I can do it in a nicer way than you will."

"True enough. I hope you put them in a wing other than the one we're in," he stated, giving her an intent look.

"Of course I did. I could have hidden them in this castle, and you'd never even see them and you know it."

"Mentally, it isn't the same as having the place to myself."

"You are really unreasonable on this subject. I can't believe you would do this to your own family."

"I certainly would. Ask my dad which hotel he prefers. Enough said on that subject. I'll go greet them, but first, come here," he said, slipping his arm around her waist and drawing her to him to kiss her.

The minute his mouth touched hers, her annoyance with him evaporated. She kissed him in return.

Finally, she pushed away. "Right now, I'll admit, I wish we were alone. But I'm not tossing my family into the cold in the middle of the night."

"I didn't ask you to do any such thing. Come on and I'll go see the family," he said in a resigned voice and she shook her head.

"Heartless cad," she said under her breath, and he turned to smile at her.

"Although lovable, right?" he teased and she glared at him, but she knew she couldn't stay irritated with him. She could move her family and they'd be so excited over hotel life they wouldn't care. They'd probably think he was giving them a great welcome.

Matt charmed her mother and sisters. He played with her little nieces and nephews, counseled her brothers and brothers-in-law on schools and courses and performed a convincing act of enjoying being with everyone.

It was eleven o'clock when they finally closed the door to their bedroom suite and had complete privacy and hours later before she turned on her side to run her fingers over him while she talked to him.

"You charmed my family tonight, I'm sure. They don't have a clue you're the coldhearted reason they will be moved out."

"So be it, Brianna. A person knows what he wants."

"I'm reeling in shock from how nice you can act when actually, you're not in the least bit friendly."

"Your family isn't going to mind if you'll find a really fine hotel," he said, smiling at her.

"No, I know you're right. A hotel will be delightful for the little kids. Actually, all of them except Mom enjoy a pool."

"Your mom might, too. Buy her a swimsuit."

Brianna made a mental note to take her mother shopping.

"Come to town tomorrow and meet me for lunch."

"It's a date," she said.

The following day at eleven, Matt heard a small commotion outside his office door. His door swung open and Nicole entered his office a step ahead of Tiffany, who was protesting loudly. "I'm sorry, Mr. Rome," Tiffany said.

"Don't worry, Tiffany. It's fine," he said, although it wasn't fine at all and he didn't want to see Nicole.

As the door closed behind her, leaving them alone, Nicole smiled at him. "Don't be angry with her or with me. I was in the area and I thought I'd see if you wanted to do lunch."

"No, I don't. Or anything else, Nicole. I thought I made that clear last time we were together. My wife is meeting me soon and I'd as soon she didn't find you here in my office."

Still smiling, Nicole sat in a chair facing his desk. "Don't be such a bear. I'm sure she really doesn't care what you do. Come on, Matt. You and I know each other well and I know why you married. I also know you don't want me to talk to the press about it." She smiled at him.

"Don't try in any manner to blackmail or intimidate me," he said in a quiet, cold voice. "It isn't going to work."

"Sit down and relax, Matt," she said. "I seem to have a knack for picking the wrong days."

"Wait until you're invited and then you won't have that problem."

"I might have a long wait," she said, standing. Relieved that she looked as if she were going to leave, he lost some of his antagonism. He glanced at his watch.

"Don't worry about the little wife. She isn't going to raise too much of a fuss. I'm sure she never wants to go back to being a waitress."

"She won't ever have to do that," he said, waiting for Nicole to leave and aware of the passage of time. "Nicole, this is pointless. It's time for my appointment," he said, growing more impatient with her because he didn't want to have to explain her presence once again to Brianna. They'd had enough of a disagreement over her family at his house and she was due to arrive soon.

* * *

Brianna stepped off the elevator and a door opened. Zach emerged, stopping when he saw her. "Good morning."

"Hello, Zach," she answered coolly and hoped her wariness didn't show.

"You look very nice this morning."

"Thank you," she answered in a cold tone, waiting.

"I should admit to you that perhaps I made judgments too swiftly. I thought your marriage to Matt would be a disaster, but to the contrary, he seems happier than I've ever seen him. I think you're a good influence on him. It's only fair to tell you."

Surprised, she stared at him. She wondered if Zach actually meant what he was saying or if there was some ulterior motive. "Thank you," she answered quietly. "I'm glad to hear that, although marriage is a big uncertainty, whether it's one like ours or a real one."

He smiled at her. "I wanted you to know."

"Thank you," she reaffirmed cautiously, still wary of the turnaround in his views toward her. "I appreciate that and I hope you're right."

"I'm right about Matt. I've worked with him almost since the day he went on his own. Of course, life is filled with change and I know this is a temporary union. If you ever need me, call," he said, handing her his card.

"Thank you," she said again, more warmth in her voice this time. "A friend is always a good thing to have. I'll go now. I'm a little early, but I may as well get Matt and maybe we'll beat the lunch crowd."

"Brianna," he said, and she paused. "I heard you carried off the ball in Rome quite well and impressed Matt and others."

This time she gave him a full smile. "I'm glad to hear that," she said, feeling better and deciding Zach meant what he was saying. Surprised and pleased, she walked away.

The moment she stepped into Tiffany's office, she knew something was amiss. Tiffany's eyes widened and she knocked over a stack of books.

"Mrs. Rome," she said.

"Please, Tiffany, call me Brianna," she said patiently, wondering how many times she was going to have to ask his secretary before she would relax and address her by her first name.

She headed toward his office. "Is he in his office?"

"Yes, he is. If you'll wait, I'll announce you."

"You don't need to, thanks," she said, wondering what was the matter with Tiffany, who was growing more flustered and nervous as she crossed the room. Had Zach merely been trying to stall her, too? Brianna knocked and opened the door, coming face-to-face with Nicole Doyle.

Eight

"I'm going now," Nicole said, smiling broadly at Brianna.

She glanced past Nicole at Matt, who approached her with impassive features but blazing blue eyes. "Nicole is leaving, Brianna. Come in," he said, taking his wife's arm and brushing a kiss on her lips lightly. He draped his arm across her shoulders.

"Goodbye, Nicole. Please close the door as you go," he added in a cold tone.

Blowing him a kiss, she left, closing the door behind her.

Brianna couldn't keep from being annoyed, but common sense told her that it had to be like the last time.

"I didn't know she was coming," he explained.

"Then we'll drop the subject. I have a feeling if you wanted her around, I'd never have seen her at all."

He smiled, kissing her lightly. "Thanks and you're right. You're the woman for me, and I'm busy trying to get you to myself before I leave town."

When she chuckled, his smile faded. "You look gorgeous today, except when you entered my office, I wished there was absolutely nothing beneath that leather coat."

"In this weather?" She laughed. "It's a cold November day and I'm not visiting your office naked beneath my coat."

"I can still imagine. Let's have lunch," he said, taking her arm. "I want you. If we go home, your relatives are all over the place. This office is as private as the street outside."

"It's difficult to work up a lot of sympathy since we made love half the night last night. Besides, I'd guess you have appointments later today and we should have lunch and let you get on with your work."

In his secretary's office, she paused. "Tiffany, what time does he have to be back?"

"Actually, not until two o'clock."

"Thank you," Brianna said sweetly, smiling up at him. "We should go before every restaurant gets crowded."

She left with him, noticing Nicole's perfume still lingering in the air and wondering how persistent Nicole would be in trying to get back into Matt's life. And how successful.

When they were in his car, Matt watched the road. "Brianna, have you told your family about moving?"

"Not yet. You're leaving Monday and you'll be gone the rest of the week. I'll tell them then and they'll be gone when you return."

"Not sooner?"

"I'm afraid not. That would be difficult."

"How difficult to make a hotel reservation? I can do it and they'll like it."

She didn't answer and rode the short distance to the restaurant in silence, wondering about him and how solitary he was and how little he seemed to care for anyone else or anything else except money.

When they were seated in the restaurant and had ordered, she took off her coat and looked up to see Matt watching her and desire had ignited in his gaze. A tingle jolted her from her reverie and made her aware of her tight-fitting, plain navy sweater and skirt.

"You look gorgeous as usual. If I didn't have that appointment—"

"But you do," she finished. "I'll make you a deal. If you're not going to let my family stay at your house, the least you can do is help my brothers by giving them job advice. You have a lot of contacts, so you should know places to send them."

Matt groaned. "Brianna, I don't do job placement. I pay people who work for me to deal with hiring."

"Then it will be a good experience for you and broaden you to look beyond yourself a little. You're kicking them out of your house—so this is the least you can do," she persisted, knowing she was badgering him, but determined to get him to help her family.

"I didn't help my brothers—Lance works for me, but that was different, and Christopher is off playing football and doesn't give a rip what I'm doing. Your family will manage. Heaven knows, you do."

"They will manage much better with your help and you owe them."

"I don't think I owe them anything when I'm footing a giant hotel bill for six adults and four little kids."

"The little kids cost nothing. Now look, Matt, your mansion will easily hold all of them and they can stay out of your sight."

"Don't go back to that. They're out and I'll get Zach to look into helping them with jobs. How's that?"

She only hoped Zach would do his best for them. "I hope Zach will," she said, wondering whether he would actually help or merely go through the motions. He had seemed sincere in his compliments to her, but she didn't know him well, so she had no idea if he had been truly sincere.

As Matt drove, she stared at his long, lean frame and knew she was falling in love with him. He had been good to her and kind and generous to her family. He was the most fantastic lover. She thought she'd be able to guard her heart so easily and never fall in love with him because she still thought he was heartless when it came to work and money. And whatever happened, their union was temporary. She had no illusions about Matt changing his mind regarding the length of their marriage.

* * *

True to his word, Matt talked to some of her family about their future plans and gave them his business card, telling them to call his office to set up appointments to talk to Zach, who would help direct them where to turn in applications and resumes. Also, Zach would see about having their resumes professionally done, something Brianna had planned on doing herself, but she was relieved to see Matt take this on.

Again, that night when they finally were alone in the east wing of the house and closed in their bedroom, she wound her arms around his neck. "Thank you for today and all you're doing."

"If I can keep you happy and showing me how grateful you are," he said in a husky voice, "it's worth it to me."

"I wish you didn't have to go Monday and be gone so long. I'll miss you."

"I miss you more each time we're apart," he said.

"Have you ever thought about not traveling quite so much?" she asked, knowing even before she finished her sentence that business came far ahead of everything else.

"I'm doing what I have to do, but it's not quite the same," he said in a solemn tone that made her heart miss a beat. Could she possibly be growing more important to him?

He tightened his arms around her, leaning down to kiss her, and ending conversation and her curiosity.

* * *

Monday she kissed him before he left for Chicago
and then she turned her attention to her family. As she
had expected, news of the hotel move excited her family.

She began to plan a nursery, drawing sketches and
studying magazines. Her pregnancy still seemed unreal
to her because she couldn't see any change in her
shape. Trying to stay fit, most days of the week she
walked on Matt's track in his exercise room and swam
in his indoor pool.

If she could take even two courses each semester, she
would get four out of the way in a year. She was a senior
and needed eighteen more hours for an undergraduate
degree. She suspected after a few months, Matt wouldn't
care what she did. His fascination with her would surely
dwindle and she could take more than two.

She looked into some local charities that she could
give a day to and miss when Matt wanted her to go with
him, finally agreeing to give a day each week to helping
in the local food bank.

When it was nearly ten o'clock Friday evening, Matt
arrived. She'd spent the late afternoon and early evening
getting ready for his return and had her black hair
pinned up on either side of her head, to fall freely down
on her back and on her shoulders. She'd selected new
red silk lounge pajamas and matching high-heeled
sandals and her excitement mounted with each passing
hour. They'd talked half a dozen times during the day
and she knew he was anxious to get home. Her pulse

rate increased when she heard the beep of the alarm as a door opened and closed.

She rushed to meet him when he swept into the hallway bringing cold air with him. At the sight of him, her heart thudded even faster.

Dropping his briefcase, he shook off his thick, black topcoat and let it and his charcoal suit jacket fall on the floor with his briefcase. Hurrying toward her, he shed his tie.

She ran the last distance to throw her arms around him and he caught her up, crushing her in his embrace and kissing her hotly.

Beneath his cotton shirt and wool pants she could feel the warmth of his body. Running her fingers through his tangled curls, she kissed him. As her heartbeat speeded, her desire was a blazing fire. "I've missed you so!" she gasped and returned to kissing him.

"Not anything like the way I've missed you, Brianna," he declared. "Love, you look luscious enough to eat," he said and kissed her, scooping her into his arms to carry her to the bedroom.

Saturday she lazed in his arms. "Matt, look at the sun coming through the windows. It has to be midmorning, I have things to do, and so do you."

"You're complaining?"

She rolled on top of him, smiling at him. "Hardly. I'm euphoric and lusty, but I need to eat for the baby."

He smiled as he wrapped locks of her hair around his fingers and pulled her to him to kiss her.

His cell phone rang and he continued to kiss her until she broke it off. "Answer your phone. Only a select few have your cell phone number."

"It better be important," he grumbled, picking up his phone and saying hello. In moments, he sat up and she rolled away, grabbing her robe and going to shower, guessing it was a business call. She dressed in jeans and a T-shirt and went to the kitchen to get breakfast.

Soon he joined her. He had showered and dressed in chinos and a tan knit shirt. His damp hair was in tight curls. His eyes were bright with excitement and she realized the phone call had been something that pleased him. As she poured orange juice, she said, "You look like that cat who caught the mouse. What's happened?"

"I'm meeting with four members of the investment group Tuesday, so I'll fly to France Monday. They all but told me outright they want me to join their group."

First she felt excitement that he had achieved his goal. That quick flash was replaced by cold fear that he would be through with her and ask her to pack and go.

"Congratulations!" she cried, hugging him, letting him have his moment and wanting to avoid any dissonance.

"It'll only be overnight, they said. Come with me. They told me to bring you along."

He continued talking about Paris, but the joy at hearing he wanted her along was immediately crushed. He was taking her because they'd told him to.

He leaned down to look her in the eyes. "Are you with me? Paris? You look like you're thinking about something else."

"No, I'm delighted for you, and yes, I want to go."

"You don't sound as if you really do. I'm not twisting your arm," he said, studying her.

Smiling, she hugged him. "I'm just wondering if you join their group now, if you'll tell me goodbye," she said, but that wasn't really what had made her joy disappear.

He hugged her. "Hardly," he said, winding his fingers in her hair and pulling her head back to gaze into her eyes. "I want you in my life for a lot longer," he said and kissed her.

And she intended to be, she thought as she kissed him in return. She would make him want her for a long, long time—long enough that he might not ever want her to go.

In spite of his all-important drive for wealth, she loved her handsome husband. She reminded herself no one was perfect, but Matt's flaw was a gigantic one that could affect everything he did.

She pushed away from him. "We should eat and then let me plan what I have to do to get ready."

"They're taking us to dinner Tuesday night and I'm sure it'll be a celebration dinner."

She shook her head over his exuberance and absolute confidence. "Matt, I've never known anyone who has the self-assurance you do. My word, you believe in yourself!"

"I suppose I do, but why else would they be calling and asking me to meet with them and bring you and plan on dinner? It stands to reason. Go buy a new dress and we'll stay Wednesday. I'll take you out for our own little celebration the following night."

She took a breakfast casserole from the oven. As

they ate, she listened to Matt talk about his plans, but her mind was still on their future together and if she was important to him in any manner other than as a means to get him into this group, or in his bed.

She realized he was telling her about problems at work with acquisitions he wanted and the difficulty he was having with one of his vice presidents, and she began to pay close attention, pushing aside her worries as she absorbed what Matt was saying.

It was three in the afternoon when he left for an errand and she went shopping for a dress for her Paris dinners.

She arrived back home before Matt and began to pack and sort through clothes, knowing Matt could take all of her time when he returned home.

She finally heard him at six-thirty when it was dark outside and a cold wind howled around the house.

He rushed inside and her heart thudded, desire instantly igniting because he looked irresistible. His broad-brimmed black hat was pushed to the back of his head and his thick leather and lambs-wool lined jacket swung open. He carried two huge boxes and she wondered if he'd purchased a suit for himself.

"So you've been shopping, too," she said. "I'd hug you, but I can't get close to you."

"Let's go to the family room," he said and, though he had four rooms the description would have fit, she knew which room was his favorite.

She already had a roaring fire blazing in the mammoth fireplace. She turned, waiting for him to set down his packages, and then she was in his arms and the world vanished.

It was hours later when she stirred and sat up in front of the fire. "I'm burning on one side, cold on the other and this floor is hard."

"It's not all that's hard and that's your fault," he said with amusement, pulling her to him to kiss her.

"Stop and let me move to higher ground. A bed and a warm shower first. And tonight, I get dinner at a decent hour. You know, it isn't healthy for a pregnant woman to miss meals."

Matt looked stricken. "Darlin', I'm sorry. I swear you won't miss another one—"

She placed her fingers on his mouth and smiled at him. "Stop. I feel fine. But food would be good right now."

"Steak it is. You go upstairs to shower and I'll shower in another bath and get dinner on the table."

Smiling at him, she left to do what he suggested. It wasn't until after dinner and they had moved back to the family room that she remembered his packages. He knelt to get the fire built up again, the scent of the burning logs filling the room. His jeans pulled tightly on his muscled legs and he straightened, setting the screen in place.

"Did you buy yourself a new suit?"

"I shouldn't have forgotten all about this," he said, picking up a long, narrow box that was the smaller of the two. He brought it to her to hand it to her.

"I should have had that sent out, but they were on the verge of closing and the truck had gone for today."

Curious, she opened the box to look at dozens of red and white and yellow roses. "Matt, these are gorgeous!" she said, taking out the card and pulling it open swiftly to read. "Thanks for helping me reach my goal. Love, Matt."

She set down the box and kissed him, pushing away from him in a moment.

"Wait now. I want to put these in water. They have them in those little vials, but I need to get them into a vase."

Rushing to get them in water before he tried to stop her, she had seen the look in his eyes and his thoughts weren't on the flowers.

He followed her into the kitchen, talking to her about Paris, and when she finished her arrangement in a large crystal vase, he carried it back to the family room for her.

As soon as he set it on a table, he crossed the room to pick up the largest box to give to her. It was tied with a red silk ribbon.

"I thought this was a suit for you," she said.

"They don't tie my suits up with silk bows. I have them custom-made by my tailor."

He placed the box on a leather sofa and she leaned down to untie a beautiful bow. She raised the lid and pushed away tissue paper to gaze at a box filled with dark fur.

Startled, she glanced at him.

"It's your present," he reminded her.

Burying her fingers in the soft, silky fur she lifted out a full-length mink coat. A card fell out and Matt picked it up off the floor to hand it to her. "Thank you, love, Matt."

SARA ORWIG 145

"Matt, this is beautiful," she said, running her fingers through the thick fur. Yet instantly she wondered if the coat was a bribe to smooth the way and get her to go quietly when he told her they were through.

"It's elegant," she said, slipping it on, but feeling stiff and cold, knowing she should steel herself for what was to come. She turned to face him.

"You look gorgeous, but I really like you better with nothing," he said, smiling and walking up to slip his hands beneath the coat and wrap his arms around her.

Putting her arms around his neck, she stood on tiptoe to kiss him, a thorough, heated kiss. She wanted him and didn't want to be tossed out like old shoes, yet she couldn't believe that wasn't the exact reason for the gift.

She leaned away. "You don't even know for certain that they'll invite you to join. If they don't, do I lose my coat?" she asked in a teasing tone, trying to cover the chill she still suffered and the dread that had consumed her.

"You'll keep the coat no matter what, but I'm sure I'm in."

"Congratulations, again," she said quietly. "This is an extravagant gift."

"I want you to have it," he said, drawing her back into his embrace and leaning down to kiss her, yet even his hot kisses couldn't drive away the demons that tormented her.

Arriving in Paris late Monday afternoon, they checked in to another luxurious suite in a hotel near the Arc de Triomphe.

Matt had attributed her sober manner to jitters about
dinner with the group of foreign investors and their
wives again. Letting him continue to think that, she
smiled politely at his reassurances that she shouldn't
worry about Tuesday night.

While she unpacked in their bedroom, Matt walked
up behind her and took clothes out of her hands.

"Stop working the instant you arrive. We have the
rest of the day. I'll show you some sights and take you
to dinner," he said, nuzzling her neck.

She turned to wrap her arms around him and kiss him
passionately, still certain the mink coat had been a
farewell gift and a bribe.

Matt's arms tightened around her, and sightseeing
and her fears were all pushed aside.

After making love far into the night, they slept.
Brianna woke after only a couple of hours and couldn't
go back to sleep. She kept thinking about leaving Matt
and it hurt. She loved him. There was no turning back
and reversing her feelings for him, yet she was certain
he would end their sham marriage soon now that his
goal had been achieved.

She wrapped herself in a robe and moved to a window to look at the twinkling lights of Paris, knowing this
wasn't the way to see or remember the city. How soon
would he tell her they were through?

Sometimes she wished she had never met him. She
rubbed her stomach, thinking about her baby. Matt was
good with her little nieces and nephews. She had
thought he would be around for a while for her baby.

She knew she needed to adjust and pick up and go on with her life, but Matt was dynamic and had swept into it, changing her world. He wasn't going to fade away or be forgotten easily.

She pulled her robe closer around her and closed her eyes, wanting sleep to come so she could stop worrying about her future.

"What are you doing, Brianna?" Matt asked, his deep voice a rumble in the dark room.

"Enjoying the city at night," she replied.

"I want you here in bed with me," he said sleepily. "I'm glad you like Paris," he added. "I can't work up the same enthusiasm."

"You miss a lot in life," she whispered, torn between annoyance that he was so totally focused on what he wanted and hurting because she had fallen in love with him in spite of it. She didn't receive an answer, but she went back to bed, slipping beneath the covers. He reached out and pulled her close against him, holding her tightly. For now, she held him, reassuring herself that she would be in his life a while longer.

The following afternoon, she shopped while Matt met with the investors and she was the first to arrive back at the hotel.

When he walked into the suite and tossed aside his topcoat, she knew he was in the group. Looking triumphant, he scooped her up into his embrace to kiss her passionately. "I'm in," he finally said. "We did it, Brianna. With thanks to you, who made this possible. I'll take you out for our own celebration tomorrow night, but tonight, they're taking us to a very expensive, very exclusive restaurant."

"Congratulations!" she said, wondering again how long their sham marriage would last now that the reason for it had vanished.

The evening should have been a warm memory in a restaurant with exotic French fare. She enjoyed sitting beside Signore Rufulli. All seemed happy to have her join them and everyone celebrated Matt becoming part of the group.

Flying home on Thursday, she had memories stored away, but along with them was the chilling knowledge that Matt no longer needed their union.

Before sunrise Friday morning, his cell phone rang and Matt stretched out a long arm, picking it up and flicking it open. He answered in a sensual, satisfied tone while she continued to run her fingers lightly over his chest and lower.

He listened such a long time she looked up. When she saw he was scowling, she guessed he was hearing bad news. Had a stock market somewhere in the world dropped during the night?

"How bad is it?" he asked quietly.

She rolled away and sat up to look at him, her curiosity growing.

"When did it happen?" he asked in a solemn voice and she wondered what calamity had transpired.

"How's he doing now?" Matt asked.

She wrapped her arms around herself and waited. It was worse than she'd imagined because someone was hurt and from Matt's tone, it was someone important to him.

"Thank God for that," he said, glancing at her and she wondered if he wanted privacy for his conversation. She grabbed a robe and slipped out of bed, leaving the room for a few minutes.

When she returned, he was propped in bed, still talking, but his voice sounded normal and he smiled over something. She let out her breath because it evidently wasn't too dreadful.

She had put on a red lace gown and, shedding her robe, she slipped beneath the covers and saw him watching her. He pushed away the sheet, but she immediately pulled it back and sat up cross-legged to stare at him, holding the sheet to her chin.

Finally, he broke the connection and looked at her. "Sorry to wake you with that call. It was Lance. My dad has had a heart attack."

"Oh, no! I take it he's doing better."

"Yes, he is. It was mild. He had chest pains and Mom took him to the E.R. From what I understand, Lance indicated there were changes in Dad's EKG and he had elevated enzymes. They want to keep him for observation, so he'll stay in the hospital for now. The prognosis is very good. Later this morning I can talk to Dad. In the meantime," he said, reaching out to pull on the sheet she grasped beneath her chin.

"Wait a minute!" she said, keeping the sheet waded tightly in her fist. "Aren't you going to Miami?"

"No. Lance said Dad's doing fine now and I don't need to come."

"You've got to go," she said, aghast that he was brushing aside his father's rush to the E.R. "Your father had a heart attack and you have a plane at your disposal. You can drop everything to do as you please."

"I need to work. There's no need for a trip to see him, Brianna," Matt restated patiently. "I'll see Dad at the next family gathering. In the meantime, there is someone I want to see," he said, reaching out again, but she scooted back quickly and pushed away his hand.

"Matt, that's the coldest attitude I've ever known. You go see your father."

"I'm all grown up now and have my own life and he's supposed to have a full recovery. It wasn't that serious."

"No wonder you don't want any children!" she snapped, staring at him intently.

He scowled at her. "Brianna, my dad is doing fine. There's no reason for me to go traipsing off to Florida to see him when he's okay."

"He's had a *heart attack*. He's older. My word, Matt, don't you care?"

"Of course I do, but I cut the apron strings when I left home for college. I don't go running home to them with every little thing, nor do they with me. We're not that kind of family."

"Well, thank heavens, mine is," she said, thinking how they all rallied around whenever there was a crisis. "We may not have money, but we love each other."

"I love my parents," he said patiently, but she could hear

the note of irritation in his voice and knew she was aggravating him, but she couldn't stop. His parents seemed warm and nice and had welcomed her into the family.

"Brianna, I am not going to Florida, so drop it," Matt said forcefully.

"You really don't have a heart, Matt," she said and left the room, going to the bathroom where she could shut him out. He didn't care about family, not his or anyone else's. He was nice and generous and giving to people as long as it didn't involve him too intensely and personally.

Her first assessment of him as heartless, in love only with money and perhaps himself, had been accurate. That's all he was about. She was in love with him and she couldn't stop loving him, but she knew it was time to move on. She had money now, enough to do as she pleased. What was the point in remaining with Matt? Their philosophies of life were poles apart. She wasn't going to change him, wasn't going to influence him. He knew what he wanted and went after it with a ruthless determination that shut out the rest of the world. And he really didn't care about anything else except success and the acquisition of wealth. She didn't even think he truly cared around the trappings of wealth or the power it gave him. He lived for the sheer accumulation of money.

It was a cold way to be and he would never love anyone in the fullest sense of the word. Nor would he be a good father. She knew he would shower a child with gifts and give a child some attention, but that all-accepting love that she already felt for her baby was something Matt could not attain. Nor did he want to.

He was selfish to the core and the sooner she moved on, the better off she would be. The cold realization hurt and tears stung her eyes. She thought about her future. If she stayed he would shower her with care throughout her pregnancy and childbirth. She knew he would be at her side for that—unless some crisis arose in his business. Then he'd be off and gone and return with presents for her to make up for his absence.

Did she want to give that up this early? Stay and enjoy his attention and help. It was tempting because it would be lonely and more difficult on her own even with money to buy whatever she wanted. Also, his very generous allowance would end if she walked away.

Yet the thought of making love to him had soured. Could she turn off her feelings about his coldness? She rubbed her neck, torn between going and staying, knowing she shouldn't rush into a decision she would regret later.

She recalled the night she'd met his parents and his father, Travis, saying to her, "I hope you'll bring him to see us. We don't see much of him, but I understand that better than his mother does." As far as Brianna was concerned, that meant that they'd like to see a lot more of their son than they did.

She heard a knock at the door and went to open it, looking up at Matt. Her heart thudded and for an instant, all her thoughts of leaving him vanished. How could she walk out when each time she saw him, she wanted to kiss him?

"Come in, Matt," she said, stepping back.

"I thought I'd see if you'd like to go downstairs with me to get something to eat. I think we were headed that way when we were interrupted by the telephone."

She nodded. "I'm going to shower. I'll be down shortly," she said, noticing his jeans and T-shirt and knowing she should shower and dress.

"Fine. See you downstairs. I'll get breakfast."

Closing the door, she waited for him to leave and then she stepped out to go to the closet, where she selected jeans and a blue sweater, got underwear and went to shower.

Downstairs she found him in the kitchen with egg casserole, ham, oatmeal and a platter of fruit on the table. He had orange juice and milk poured for her. While snow fell outside, they sat at the table near the fire. "If I go to Florida now, it's close enough to Thanksgiving that they'll want us both to come and stay."

"That wouldn't be the end of the world," she said, picking at her food and still thinking about her future, feeling cold and forlorn. "You can take some more time off."

"Look, if it would make you feel better about my dad, we can call Lance and you can talk to him."

She lowered her fork. "You don't get it. If your father was going to be released from the hospital tonight and go home and I could talk to him right now, I would. Or to put it another way—if this were my mom, I would be packing right now to go and I'd probably leave within the hour to see her. So talking to your brother really doesn't matter. I know your dad is going to survive this and I believe you when you say that the prognosis is good. But people are more important to me than money. You've always known that. Family is way more important than career."

"Brianna, you'd do anything short of a criminal act to get that degree. You wouldn't let your family interfere with you getting it and you didn't stay home with them. You moved to Laramie to get an education and you've stuck with it."

"I'd go home to see Mom if she had a heart attack," she replied, knowing she was being stubborn with him, but still aggravated by his cavalier attitude.

"Admirable, but in my case unnecessary. And I would understand if the situation were reversed."

"I recall your dad telling me that he was happy to see you marry and maybe now they would see more of you," Brianna replied.

"My dad said that?"

"Yes, he did."

"Mom I can understand. She would be happier if none of us had ever left home. She likes having us around, but we all grew up and moved on and it would have been odd if we hadn't."

Brianna turned to look at the fire and think about the coming week when he would be gone. She could take her time to contemplate her future and decide what she should do. She was tempted to tell him it was over now, but she knew that would be foolish. She had too much to gain by staying if she could get a better grip on her emotion and let go some of her affection for him.

They ate in silence until she thought she couldn't get down another bite. "Excuse me, Matt," she said, getting up and carrying her dishes to the sink to rinse them and put them in the dishwasher.

"You don't need to do that," he said.

"I know. It's habit and I don't mind." The room became silent again and she suspected their quasi-marriage was over.

"Dammit, Brianna, I'm not going and that's the end of the matter. Dad doesn't need me."

"Watch out, Matt. If you're not careful, someday, no one will need you," she said softly and one dark eyebrow arched.

"As long as I have a fortune, a lot of people will want and love me," he said in a cynical tone.

"Yes, that's true and you'll always know your fortune is exactly why." Her hurt deepened at his self-absorbed, callous attitude.

"I'm such an ogre?"

"Of course not. You're charming and irresistible in too many ways, and you'll always have women who love you and men who like you, so you'll never be lonely," she said, thinking all his relationships would be as shallow in the future as they had been in the past.

"Your arguments are contradictory," he stated, assessing her intently. "Someday you plan to be an attorney. You need to get your argument tight and to the point."

She smiled stiffly. "I'll remember that bit of advice. I know you'll find as much happiness in your future as you have in your past."

Something flickered in the depths of his eyes and a muscle worked in his jaw while he clenched his fists. "I'm not going to Florida. My dad doesn't need to see me, nor has he asked me to come."

"You've made that more than clear," she said and watched him turn and leave the room.

Tears threatened, but she fought shedding them, knowing they had been headed for this moment from the start, but never expecting it to hurt so badly.

In many ways she wanted to give his money back to him and walk away, feeling free from a bad bargain. Yet she knew that would be foolish and hurt not only herself, but her baby and her family. Too much was at stake, and Matt's money would secure the future for all of them. And he would never miss it because he had already amassed enormous wealth and was primarily engrossed in the acquisition of more, not the enjoyment of having it.

That day as she went about her exercise routine, she considered her decision. She loved Matt and she wanted to be with him, but it was ridiculous for her to stay and hope he'd someday change his basic nature. As much as it hurt, she wanted out of the fake marriage, wanted to tell the truth to her family, wanted to go on with her life. A life that had been transformed by Matt.

She knew he would protest and she was equally certain he wouldn't want her to go despite the temporary nature of the whole arrangement. And how much harder it would be to leave after the baby came. Yet that might be the time when Matt would have grown tired of them. So why wait until there were two hearts to break?

She had to get out of this fake marriage now.

Monday morning, she was determined to get up before he was out and gone so she could break the news to him that their marriage was over.

Matt had already showered and gone down to breakfast. She showered and dressed quickly, hurrying downstairs to catch him before he left.

She found him in his study, poring over papers in front of him at his desk. His suit jacket was tossed on a chair and he hadn't tightened his navy tie. A fire blazed in the fireplace and the crackle and pop of burning logs was the only sound in the room. In spite of her thick blue sweater and jeans, the heat from the flames was welcome. She was chilled to the bone.

"Knock, knock," she said as she entered and he looked up, tossing down his pen before he leaned back in his chair. "Matt, I want to talk to you," she said, crossing the room to stand by the fire. "I'll be brief. I know you have to go soon."

"Come in. You look upset. What's up?" he asked. He leaned back with his hands behind his head and his long legs stretched out in front of him.

"I've given thought to the future and to us," she said. "I guess it started when your father had his heart attack. We married with an agreement and we've both fulfilled our part of the bargain. I helped you get into the investors' group and you paid me the money you promised—part of it still due. Therefore this marriage has accomplished its purpose. It was never intended to be a permanent arrangement. Right?"

"Right," he said, lowering his hands and coming to his feet to rest his hands on his hips. Thick curls fell on his forehead and he was handsome, sexy and appealing. Her heart gave a twist, but this was inevitable. Better to get it done and over.

"When we discussed a marriage of convenience, I recall you saying that once you're invited into the investment group, you wouldn't hold me to two years. You told me that I can stay that long, but if I wanted out sooner, I could go."

"You're walking out?" he asked in disbelief, and for once, his total self-assurance looked shaken.

"Yes, I am," she answered, hurting and hoping she wouldn't cry in front of him. "I see no reason to stay longer. You've achieved your goal and got what you wanted. You're through with me—"

"Not really, Brianna. We have a good thing going here—and you've acted like you thought it was great."

"The physical relationship between us is fine, but my emotions are tangled up in it. I haven't had enough relationships to make comparisons. It's been wonderful, Matt, and you know it, but it's time to go. Look how distant you are with your blood relatives. If I stay, I'll fall in love with you and then it'll be the same way with me and with the baby."

"I can't believe you want to do this."

She ran her hand across her cheek. "Thanks to you, I have sufficient money to live comfortably and pro-

vide for my baby. My family will be with me for the
baby's birth. I find it difficult to imagine you being
interested in a baby or wanting to go through this pregnancy with me."

"I think you're jumping to conclusions," he said
quietly. "I don't want you to go," he said, walking closer.

"All we're having is an affair. A legally contracted
affair. It isn't a real marriage and you never intended it
to be," she said softly as if she were explaining something to a child. Tears still threatened, and she swiped
her eyes again as she gazed up at him.

"You don't even want to go—"

"Of course I don't want to go!" she cried, finally losing
her control. "I'm probably in love with you and even
though you're charming and sex is the best, there's no
future here. I don't want to end up like Nicole, dragging
around after you and trying to recapture your attention."

"That's entirely different. You're unique and
maybe we'll both fall in love. Isn't that worth waiting
to let happen?"

"Maybe? *Maybe?* No. I think I'll get hurt worse and
I don't want to have all the upheaval of moving when I
have an infant to care for. It'll be much easier now to
find a place, get settled and get ready for my baby."

Closing the distance between them, he wrapped his
arms around her and kissed her for a long time. As she
remaining stiffly in his arms, her resistance melted until
she responded, aware of the salty taste of her tears.

He raised his head, wiping away her tears with his
thumbs. "Don't cry. Stay with me. We're happy together

and have a good thing going. If it makes you feel better about it, I'll promise to keep this marriage together for the full two years and then you won't be so worried about the future. How's that?"

She shook her head. "Not enough. I guess you made me want it all, Matt. I want a real marriage and if I can't have a real one, I don't want one at all."

His eyes darkened and he clamped his jaw closed. "There's not going to be a real marriage. You've known that from the start."

"Yes, you've made it abundantly clear," she replied, gazing steadily into his eyes.

"You know what you want. I'm not going to stick around and argue. If you want out, you're free to go," he said and the words cut with the sharpness of a knife. "I'll help you move any way I can and do what I can for you about the baby. I'll still pay for nannies when the time comes. We should part friends, Brianna."

"Thank you," she said quietly, once again fighting to keep from crying.

"You can call me whenever you want anything." He slipped his hand behind her head to caress her nape, moving closer again. "If you change your mind, let me know. I'll welcome you back into my life—anytime in the near future."

He looked handsome, appealing, as irresistible as ever and she wanted him to tell her to stay and let it be a real marriage.

Instead, they stared silently at each other, each one wanting something different, each one with conflicting desires that were impossible to resolve. Suddenly, he pulled her into his arms again for another passionate kiss.

Leaning over her, he held her tightly while his tongue thrust deeply into her mouth and he kissed her long and thoroughly.

Her heart thudded and she clung to him, kissing him in return, knowing this was his goodbye. She ran her hand across his broad shoulders that felt warm through the thin cotton of his shirt. She was tempted beyond measure to cry out that she would stay and take her chances on the future with him. She didn't want to go. She loved him and might forever.

Finally, she pushed against him. He released her only a fraction. Breathing hard, he gazed at her. "Don't go," he said.

"I love you," she whispered and he flinched. The gesture was harsh and cut as much as his words had. He shifted away a few inches, tucking her hair behind her ear.

"I can't do the permanent marriage, Brianna. I'm not into long relationships, much less a lifetime commitment. You've known that from the first night."

"I know. Saying that it's been wonderful sounds woefully inadequate for all you've done. I hope you make back your investment and oodles more. May you make another billion or so, Matt." She slipped her arm around his neck and kissed him again, long, heated and final. When she drew away, she was crying.

"Don't pay the rest of the money you and I agreed on. There's enough invested to take care of me, my baby and my family sufficiently. We have a fortune now."

"Don't be ridiculous. We have an agreement—a written contract. You've lived up to your part of the bargain."

"If you give me more, I'll send it to charities."

"That's foolish, Brianna," he stated. "Spend the money on yourself and your family. With a child to raise, you can use it. Charity begins at home."

"So does love, Matt," she said solemnly. "You're missing what's important in life."

"I'm not certain you would have made that statement when you first met me. With a couple of million, your perspective has changed."

"Not my basic feelings about family and love."

"Remember, you can change your mind about this. All you have to do is let me know," he said.

"This is officially goodbye," she said, hoping she could be out of his house when he returned from his New York trip.

"Sure. But I intend to keep in touch."

She nodded, letting him think what he wanted. He gave her a long, hard study and then turned to pick up his jacket and leave, closing the door behind him.

"Goodbye," she whispered again. She had no intention of turning into another Nicole, someone pursuing him when he didn't want to be pursued.

Shaking and cold, she walked to the fire to warm her icy hands, knowing flames probably couldn't remove the chill that enveloped her. Matt had gone out of her life. Would she ever stop loving him? How long before he replaced her and forgot her?

She suspected it wouldn't take him long at all. All

week he would be taken up with business and making more money.

When she entered her enormous closet and looked at the array of clothes she now owned—a mink coat, designer dresses and shoes, purses that at one time would have paid her rent for months—she had another pang for the life she was tossing aside.

She would need help moving her belongings. Her brothers and brothers-in-law could do it without difficulty. The first and most important thing was to find somewhere to live. The next thing was to let her family know that she was leaving Matt.

She wanted out of Matt's house immediately and finding a comfortable hotel suite became top priority. Wiping her eyes, she went to the computer to check out hotels.

Since Laramie was where all her family would be, she thought about looking there later for a house. Melody had already purchased a house and was moving in another week.

Brianna got down the one small suitcase she'd brought when she'd moved in with Matt. Now she owned so much it would take an entire set of luggage and probably more than one trunk. She wanted him home and in his arms and their lives together to go on the way they had. This time when tears came, she gave vent to them, leaning against the doorjamb and crying, knowing it was over with Matt.

Matt immersed himself in business and stayed busy every night in New York. Even so, he couldn't get

Brianna out of his thoughts. Occasionally he would spot a tall, leggy woman with black hair like hers, and his heart would skip a beat.

Too well, he remembered being there with her and the first time she had seen Saint Patrick's, her first trip to Central Park. He saw her too many places, too often, and he couldn't shake thinking about her.

He called her each night, but she never answered. For the first time he realized she really might be gone out of his life completely. She wasn't predictable or like any other woman he'd ever known. If she wanted to vanish out of his life, she would. He was sure he could track her down, but as far as seeing her socially or even taking her out again, he faced the fact that might be impossible now.

The realization she had really cut all ties hurt. He'd had her final check deposited into her account at the bank and he expected he would hear from her about it. Matt wondered if Brianna would ask his suggestions about investing the money. Or would she stick to what she'd said and give her final payment to charity? He couldn't imagine her doing any such thing.

Wednesday evening his cell phone rang and he answered instantly, hope flaring that he would hear Brianna's voice.

Instead, it was one of the investors discussing an opportunity that had arisen. Matt's attention was taken by the prospect and he worked into late hours, sleeping little and getting up to check on the market.

By Friday, he had made over a million from the investment. That night in the hotel he wrote down the figures, staring at them. For the first time the return gave him no great satisfaction. What he really wanted was Brianna in his life—even more than money. The realization shocked him, and he wondered when she had become so damn important to him that everything else diminished.

Had she been right that money wasn't the all-important facet of life, less meaningful than love? He couldn't answer his own question except for that in this case, he would have given not only the million but more to have her with him again.

He'd never thought anything could be as great as the accumulation of wealth, the challenge and success of making a big deal, but now it wasn't his prime need. He had a huge fortune. Even the bet with his cousins had lost its priority.

Disgusted with life and with himself, he pushed away and paced the room impatiently. He strode to the window to look out over the city. Lights sparkled in every direction. What was she doing now?

He missed Brianna and her exuberance and enthusiasm. She was a good listener and he'd grown accustomed to talking freely to her about business— something he didn't feel would be wise to do with anyone else, even Zach. He wondered if she'd ever know that he'd taken her suggestion about investing more of himself into Cheyenne. Now he wished he had told her that he'd asked Zach to check into some particular properties.

Matt knew he'd get accustomed to life without her, just as he always had after a breakup, but at present, it bothered him.

Turning to his usual solution after a breakup, he intended to immerse himself in work. Tomorrow, Saturday morning, he would fly to London and work there all next week.

Late Thursday he returned home, where he worked until he fell asleep over his desk before he finally went to bed. He was exhausted, yet still unable to sleep peacefully, dreaming about Brianna and waking to want her in his arms.

It jolted him the following week when he received the first thank-you from a nonprofit literacy group. Any donations he made went through the foundation set up in his name. He realized this was Brianna's doing, and she was giving the last payment to charity just as she had said she would.

Staring at the note in his hand, he stood a long time wondering about her and the depth of her feelings. He hadn't really thought she would turn down his money under any circumstances. Had she done this to emphasize to him that love was more important and he was far too material?

He spent long hours at his office and exercised several hours each day, but nothing filled the emptiness he felt. He hated missing her and reassured himself that with time his longing would fade away.

One night in his office at home, he sat thinking about

Brianna. He missed her dreadfully and he'd never missed anyone before. She had changed his life and he couldn't get his old life back. She was everywhere he looked, yet not really there, only a phantom of a memory. He missed her and wanted her and realized he had fallen in love with her, something he had never expected to have happen. Through affairs and friendships, women had been secondary in his life. Even his family had always faded to the background, but Brianna wouldn't fade away or diminish or get out of his thoughts.

He began to wonder if her family was settled in Laramie, going to school as they had planned and if she had moved there to be near them.

He'd been to the steak house where he'd first found her, but no one there had seen her. He knew he could hire someone to find her, but there wasn't much point in it. Unless he wanted to make a permanent commitment. Wouldn't that be far better than this hellish misery he was going through constantly?

Brianna tried to keep her mind on the booklet in front of her. She was trying to decide on courses for the spring semester at the University of Wyoming. She sat at a desk, poring over brochures and selecting classes, trying to get a schedule that would work. Because of her marriage to Matt, she would be behind schedule now on graduating, but only by a semester. She wanted to make certain she got her degree and she knew the baby would throw her timetable into upheaval.

Now because of Matt, she would have all the help she

wanted to hire and her mother lived here in Laramie and would be available and eager to help.

Her thoughts wandered to Matt. She missed him more than ever and wondered how long it would take her to get over him and to stop thinking about him constantly. She was lonely, hurting and missing his vitality and loving.

She had told her mother everything about her marriage and agreement with Matt.

There were moments she wished she had stayed until he walked out on her, but she knew she was better off making the break now.

She finally talked to a counselor about the courses she wanted to take and left to return to the sprawling condo she had purchased in a gated area that was in a relatively new area of Laramie.

When she turned onto her street, she saw a sleek black car parked in front of her house. As she turned into her drive, she wondered whose it was. Glancing over her shoulder, she saw Matt step out of the car.

Her heart missed a beat. He looked handsome in a leather jacket, jeans, western boots and a wide-brimmed Stetson. She stopped her car and climbed out to go meet him while her racing heart speeded even faster.

"What are you doing here?" she asked, watching him approach, snow crunching beneath his boots.

Nine

He walked up to her and she threw her arms around his neck at the same time he pulled her into his embrace. And then he kissed her.

Holding him tightly and forgetting all her resolutions, she wanted him more than ever.

She longed to push away his thick coat and heavy clothes to run her hands all over him. She kissed him hungrily while Matt tightened his arms around her.

He picked her up. "Door key?" he asked and then kissed her before she could answer him.

He held her while she unlocked the door and then carried her in, kicking the door shut behind him.

"Why are you here?" she asked, refusing to think about telling him goodbye all over again.

"I missed you," he said, glancing beyond her. "Where's your bedroom?"

She pointed as he kissed her again while he walked where she had directed.

An hour later she stirred in his arms as he rolled on his side and propped his head on his hand to look at her.

"I wasn't going to do this," she said quietly, gazing up at him solemnly and brushing his jaw lightly with the tips of her fingers as if to reassure herself that he was real.

"I wasn't, either. I've tried every way I could think of to forget you."

"Every way?" she asked, wondering if there had been a woman in his life.

"Maybe not every way," he said in a husky voice. "I want you back. What do I have to do? We're already married."

"Not really," she answered. "That's a technicality and our contract was for two years only."

"Will you marry me for real?"

Her heart missed a beat as she gazed up into his blue eyes. "Is that a proposal?"

"It is. I'm asking you to be my wife now and forever. I don't like being without you. I think about you constantly and miss you all the time and I don't want to go on like this."

"Do you mean it?" she asked, sitting up and tugging up the sheet beneath her chin.

"Will you marry me?"

"Forever?" she cried.

"Forever," he stated emphatically.

"Yes! Of course I will. I already have. I love you!"

"Darlin', I love you."

"More than money?" she asked, squinting her eyes and looking intently at him.

"Much more than money," he mused. "I found out that you were right about so many things, particularly what's really vital. Now let me see. What advantages are there to you over money? Soft, curvaceous, best kisser on earth, sexiest woman, a necessity for me to exist and function. Should we have another wedding?"

"I don't think so. Just another honeymoon."

"I'll vote for that one," he said. "You name where you want to go and I'll take you for as long as you want. I'll do anything to keep you happy."

She brushed his thick black curls away from his forehead and let her fingers slide down his cheek and along his jaw, feeling the faint stubble. "I didn't think you'd ever be back."

"I didn't, either. It was as big a surprise to me as to you to find out that I can't get along without you," he said solemnly and she smiled.

"I'm glad. I wasn't doing so well myself."

"Speaking of how you're doing. You still don't look pregnant. Are you sure you didn't make all that up?"

"Absolutely. I've been to see the doctor and I'm fine. I don't show yet and I guess part of it is because I'm tall. I don't know. He said everything is okay. I'll get bigger sometime so enjoy my skinny looks now."

"I intend to. Every way possible."

She held his jaw. "What about the baby? Do you mind?"

"I'll adopt the baby and it'll be mine. This baby will know me as its daddy. A daddy who loves it very much."

"Do you care whether I have a girl or boy?"

"Nope. As long as everyone is healthy and if you're happy, I'm happy."

They gazed into each other's eyes and she smiled at him, joy bursting in her. "I can't believe you're here and I'm so happy you are."

"I love you, Brianna, love you with all my heart."

She turned to kiss him, pausing to look up at him. "I never thought I'd hear you say that."

"I love you, darlin'," he said. "My wife. Decide where you want to go for a real honeymoon."

"Anywhere with you will be paradise," she said, pulling him closer to kiss him.

Epilogue

The following October...

"Bye, Mom, thanks," Brianna said, completing her call home to her mother. "Matt, will you stop a minute!"

He chuckled as he nuzzled her neck and she turned in his arms to hug him. "Let me talk on the phone, for heaven's sake!"

"All I was doing was holding you and kissing you a very little bit," he said innocently. "How's Jenna?"

"Jenna is fine and Mom is having a wonderful time with her and my sisters are there now so everyone is happy." She held up the baby's picture and they both looked at it.

"Brianna, I'll swear if I didn't know better, I'd think

this is my own flesh and blood. She's got my black curly hair and my blue eyes."

"Indeed, she does, but she also looks like me," Brianna said, smiling at him and looking back at their daughter. "She's beautiful. It was wonderful of your cousins to put off this weekend until Jenna was a couple of months old."

"We're great guys," he declared smugly and she laughed. She glanced around their large bedroom with bamboo furniture and plank floors. A ceiling fan turned lazily overhead. "This is really grand, but only because you're here," she said. Her smile faded as she gazed up at him. "Thank you for getting out of your investors' group so you'd be home more."

"You were right about what's important in life. And I'm glad you postponed law school indefinitely."

She kissed him lightly. "We have enough money for a good life in Cheyenne."

"That's a little bit of an understatement," he remarked dryly. "But it is good, and so was spending a week with my folks last month."

"Speaking of spending time with someone—it's past when we were supposed to join the others for the dinner party. We're already twenty minutes late," she said, glancing at her watch.

"They won't care," he said, continuing to nuzzle her throat and shower kisses on her temple and ear.

"I care. Now come on and let's join them."

"Sure," he said, straightening up and watching her cross the room. "You barely ever looked pregnant and now no one can guess by appearance that you had a baby a few months back. You look gorgeous."

She glanced in the mirror. "Thank you. You look good yourself," she said. "C'mon, Matt, and we'll go see your friends."

He groaned. "And listen to Chase crow over winning this bet."

"That's what you get for making such an extravagant bet," she said as he caught her hand and they left their island house for the large community building they all shared. Music carried on the night air from the band and outside flames danced beneath the grilling meat being turned by a cook.

Holding her hand, he led her up the steps into the large open room where a band played and the others danced.

The music ended and Brianna and Matt joined the other two couples. Brianna felt lucky to be Matt's wife and to be included in this group. From the first moment she met them, both Laurel and Megan had been friendly. Their handsome husbands had been, also.

"Finally, the newlyweds join us. A waiter should come by with drinks," Chase said.

The music commenced and Matt turned to take her into his arms to dance as the other couples paired off to dance.

Later in the evening the women sat in a cluster while the men stood nearby.

"This is a wonderful weekend," Brianna said.

"Wonderful and wacky," Megan added, "with their crazy bet, but it got us all together and that's good."

"They'll think up some new scheme," Laurel stated.

"I guess we can be glad for that bet though. I think that's what got us all together with our husbands. Right?"

"You're right," Megan said.

"What's happening?" Matt came up to join them and pulled a chair close to Brianna while the other men came to sit by their wives.

Matt raised his glass in a toast. "Here's to the winner of the bet—Chase. I never thought you'd win," Matt said. "I have to tell you."

"My oil beat out your investments and your businesses," Chase said, smiling at his cousins.

After a slight cheer, they all touched glasses and sipped their drinks.

"We were thinking about another possible bet this next year—" Jared began, but the women shouted and finally he looked at his cousins and threw up his hands.

"No more wild bets!" Megan declared, and they all laughed.

The band commenced playing again and Matt asked Brianna to dance. He wrapped his arms around her to dance slowly. "I love you, darlin'. My life is complete with you in it."

"Chase rented this island for the weekend and all this came with it?"

"Not all. The winner had to take care of the weekend, so this is Chase's deal. It's been fun, but I'm ready to go back to our own place. I want you to myself."

He waved to his cousins as they left and in minutes they were in the privacy of their bedroom, where Matt drew her into his embrace. "I love you with all my heart."

She pulled him closer to kiss him, holding him tightly, filled with love and joy for the man she would adore always.

* * * * *

Turn the page for a sneak preview of
The Billionaire's Unexpected Heir
by
Kathie DeNosky

This fantastic new story is available from
Mills & Boon® Desire™ in September 2010.

The Billionaire's Unexpected Heir
by
Kathie DeNosky

"Hi, I'm Jake Garnier, the new owner of Hickory Hills."

From the corner of her eye, Heather McGwire saw the man stick out his hand in greeting, but she chose to ignore the gesture. She knew who he was and she'd just as soon have a snake crawl up beside her. Jake Garnier was the last person she wanted or needed to have to deal with this close to the big race. But now that he was the new owner of the thorough-bred farm she managed, there was no way of getting around it. She either had to get used to working for him or stick it out until after Stormy Dancer won the Southern Oaks Cup Classic, then look for employment elsewhere.

Besides, after what they'd shared, she took exception to the fact that he didn't even have the decency to remember her. The thought hurt more than she would have imagined or was comfortable with.

When she remained silent, he stared at her a moment as if trying to place her. "Heather?"

His smooth baritone caused her nerves to tingle and her heart to speed up, reminding her that a little over a year ago all it had taken was the rich sound of that voice to make her lose every ounce of sense she ever possessed. Now it only made her want to smack him for being the biggest jerk to ever draw a breath.

"Jake." She barely managed a short nod of acknowledgement.

Standing with her forearms resting on the white board rail surrounding the practice track, she concentrated on the stopwatch in her hand as Dancer passed the quarter-mile post and headed down the backstretch. The top contender for the prestigious Southern Oaks Cup Classic, the thoroughbred was on pace to break his own record.

"Come on, Dancer. You can do it." She glanced from the watch to the horse. "Just keep it up."

"I remember you mentioning that you worked at a thoroughbred farm, but I wasn't aware that it was

Hickory Hills," he said, sounding a lot happier to see her than she was to be seeing him.

"For the record, I'm the manager here." As Dancer headed for the home stretch, she added, "The name of the farm and where it was located never came up. Besides, you weren't that interested in hearing personal details, were you?" She glanced his way, and it was apparent her hostility didn't set well with him.

"Heather, I don't know what you think I've done, but—"

"It doesn't matter now," she interrupted. She didn't care to be reminded of how foolish she'd been.

He was silent for a moment. "At the risk of pissing you off further, how have you been?" he asked tightly.

Like you really want to know. If you had, you wouldn't have refused to take my phone calls.

She shrugged. "I've been all right." She didn't bothering asking how he'd been because she had a fair idea of what he'd been doing since they parted ways and didn't particularly care to hear the specifics.

"Is that our contender for the big race?" he asked, pointing toward Dancer.

Doing her best to ignore the man beside her, she urged the jockey, "Let him have his head, Miguel. Turn him loose." She glanced at the silver stopwatch again, and clicked the button on the side as the big bay sprinted past them. "Fantastic."

"I take it that was a good run?"

When Jake leaned close to see the time, his arm brushed hers and a tiny jolt of electricity shot straight through her. "It was excellent," she said, gritting her teeth and backing away. Turning to make her escape, she added, "Now, if you'll excuse me, I have work to do." She barely suppressed the urge to run when he fell into step beside her.

"I'd like for you to give me a tour of the farm if you have the time."

"I'm sure you need to unpack first," she said. Thanks to the mansion's housekeeper, Clara Buchanan, Heather had received a phone call the moment he passed through the security gates at the end of the half-mile-long driveway leading up to the mansion.

She desperately tried not to notice how his outstretched arms caused his snug hunter green T-shirt to outline the muscles of his broad chest and emphasize his well-developed biceps when he stretched. "I've been cooped up in the car for the past four days on the drive from Los Angeles and it feels good to be out in the fresh air again."

"Mornings around here are pretty busy—we have our daily workouts and grooming," she hedged.

When they reached the stables, she grabbed a lead rope by one of the stalls, slid the half-door back, then eased inside to attach it to Silver Bullet's halter in an effort to escape Jake's disturbing presence.

"All right," he said, stepping back as she led the big dappled gray gelding out of the stall and down to the tack room. "This afternoon will be soon enough."

She shook her head as she tied the rope to an eye hook by the tack room door, attached another rope to the halter, then tied it to another hook on the opposite wall of the wide stable aisle. "That won't work. My schedule is pretty full today and to tell you the truth, tomorrow isn't looking all that good."

"Clear it for this afternoon." Jake's no-nonsense tone indicated that he was quickly running out of patience.

For the first time since he walked up beside her at the practice track, Heather met his irritated blue gaze full-on with a heated one of her own. "Will there be anything else, Mr. Garnier?"

Scowling, he stared at her for several long moments before he finally shook his head. "I'll be back after lunch." Turning to leave, he added, "And you might as well plan on working late this evening. After you show me around, I intend to meet with the other employees, then I want to go over the accounting records."

As she watched him walk away, a nudge against her leg had her glancing down at the big Bernese mountain dog that had sidled up beside her. "You could really use some work on your guard dog skills, Nemo. Instead of taking a nap in my office, you're supposed to keep varmints like him away."

The dog didn't act the least bit repentant when he looked up at her adoringly and wagged his thick black tail.

Returning her attention to the matter at hand, she released a frustrated breath as she picked up a brush and began grooming the gray. She had no idea how he'd managed to get his hands on Hickory Hills, but she'd told herself when she learned Jake was the new owner that she'd be able to handle seeing him again. That she could keep what happened between them all those months ago separate from their working relationship.

Unfortunately, that was going to be a whole lot easier said than done. The sound of his voice carried with it the memory of him calling her name as they made love.

Closing her eyes, Heather rested her forehead against the big thoroughbred's shoulder. Over the past year, she'd done everything she could to convince herself that Jake wasn't that good-looking, that her perception of their only night together had been clouded by loneliness and the haze of too much champagne. But she realized now that she'd been in deep denial.

Jake Garnier was well over six feet of pure male sex appeal and it was no wonder that he had an endless stream of women clamoring for his attention. With broad shoulders and narrow hips, he had the lean, muscular body of an athlete. When they'd met at the thoroughbred auction in Los Angeles, he'd been striking in a suit and tie, but today in jeans and a T-shirt, he was raw sensuality from his thick black hair to the soles of his outrageously expensive running shoes.

Sighing heavily, she went into the tack room, retrieved a saddle, then returned to place it on the horse's back. She tightened the saddle's girth, then bridling Silver, led him out of the stable toward the practice track.

As much as she'd like to forget what happened that night in L.A., she couldn't regret it. Jake was arguably the biggest player on the entire West Coast. But there was an earnestness to his charm that she'd found completely irresistible. And she was reminded of how captivating it was each and every time she gazed into her baby daughter's eyes. Eyes that were the same cobalt blue and held the same sparkle of mischief as Jake Garnier's.

© Kathie DeNosky 2009

* * * *

Don't forget to look for
The Billionaire's Unexpected Heir
in September 2010.

2 FREE BOOKS
AND A SURPRISE GIFT

We would like to take this opportunity to thank you for reading this Mills & Boon® book by offering you the chance to take TWO more specially selected books from the Desire™ 2-in-1 series absolutely FREE! We're also making this offer to introduce you to the benefits of the Mills & Boon® Book Club™—

- **FREE home delivery**
- **FREE gifts and competitions**
- **FREE monthly Newsletter**
- **Exclusive Mills & Boon Book Club offers**
- **Books available before they're in the shops**

Accepting these FREE books and gift places you under no obligation to buy, you may cancel at any time, even after receiving your free books. Simply complete your details below and return the entire page to the address below. You don't even need a stamp!

YES Please send me 2 free Desire stories in a 2-in-1 volume and a surprise gift. I understand that unless you hear from me, I will receive 2 superb new 2-in-1 books every month for just £5.25 each, postage and packing free. I am under no obligation to purchase any books and may cancel my subscription at any time. The free books and gift will be mine to keep in any case.

Ms/Mrs/Miss/Mr _____ Initials _____

Surname _____

Address _____

_____ Postcode _____

E-mail_____

Send this whole page to: Mills & Boon Book Club, Free Book Offer, FREEPOST NAT 10298, Richmond, TW9 1BR